To Denise

To Marryat

An Indigo Heartfire Novel

ACKNOWLEDGEMENTS

First and foremost this book is dedicated to my wife, Dee. Her belief in me as a writer invariably exceeds my own, and her encouragement has always revived me when I'm flagging. She gave me the time and space to write, and so many of the best ideas come from her, in brainstorming. Thanking you for seeing things clearly!

To Patrick Rothfuss, who helped me understand what the author needs to give the reader, to engage him in the story. I hope I've succeeded in doing that.

To Jane and Bryan, who helped shape my writing for years with unflinchingly honest advice, critique, friendship and cakes. Your influence is here.

To the many beta readers who read and commented freely, taking so much of their time to help me with my writing.

To Sean and Scott, for being such great kids.

To Gary, for taking the chance and publishing this book. Your enthusiasm and humour means a great deal, long may it continue.

To the Marryats: Frederick and Florence, the writers in the family I've always looked up to.

Copyright © 2014 J Scott-Marryat

Cover Art by Gary Compton

Book Design by Tickety Boo Press Ltd

ISBN 978-0-9929077-4-7

Indigo Heartfire is the first book in theHeartfire Collection.

Check out our other books at www.ticketyboopress.co.uk

Novels

Goblin Moon by Teresa Edgerton
Abendau's Child by Jo Zebedee
Oracle by Susan Boulton
Endeavour by Ralph Kern

Anthologies

Malevolence - Tales From Behind the Veil
After Midnight by Joseph Rubas
Biblia Loncrofta by Simon Marshall-Jones

CHAPTER ONE

Robert had forgotten how much he hated the Underground, but remembered pretty quickly when his face was squashed painfully into the shoulder of the man in front of him, and a strait jacket of passengers surrounding him made breathing difficult. He didn't mind too much at first; inhaling Katy Perry or even Jean Paul Gaultier was just about acceptable, but someone had sprayed Dvb Beckham on with a firehose, and the overwhelming mix of jockstrap and posh spice made his stomach queasy. He'd read once that when the trains stopped running at night, the platforms became dusted with a light coating of human skin particles, that were kept dancing in the air all day by the passing trains. So he breathed David and Victoria through his nose, hoping the nasal hairs would trap it, rather than inhaling DNA of unknown men and women into his lungs.

If he got the job, he'd definitely cycle in. At least that way it was only hydrocarbons to contend with; that and the lorries, hell-bent on solving the world's overpopulation one cyclist at a time. He was convinced that was preferable to the slow suffocation in the toxic incubator he found himself in right now. Only frotteurists and masochists could possibly enjoy rush-hour travel, and he didn't think he fit either category.

At last, the train heaved its way into Hampstead and

Robert fought his way out of the carriage, squeezing past knots of humanity who were determined not to lose the square inches they'd staked their claim to. *No wonder there's so much skin floating around, it gets grated off you.*

He almost wished the lifts were out of order – he'd rather have taken the hundreds of stairs out, but the crush of passengers swept him along and he wondered where they were all going. *Did they all work around here?* Emerging into the fresh air was somewhat ruined by the light rain that fell, and he had no idea which bus he could take. A line of taxis waited over the road, and he diced with death getting to them, reminding himself he could take the exit on that side of the road in future. By the time he got there, only one remained, and he opened the door as the cabbie leaned over to see where he wanted to go. The door was wrenched from his hand and he stepped back, alarmed, as a dark-haired female slid smoothly into the back and slammed it shut. The taxi pulled away before Robert could react, and he slapped his hand on its roof as it went.

"Yeah, you take this one, no problem!" Robert shouted after it. "Cow," he added to himself, wondering for the umpteenth time if he'd done the right thing, coming to London. Five years in Cornwall, too many memories lurked here, waiting to be called forward.

You're thirty-two, he told himself. *Get on with life.*

He checked his mobile for the Google app, to see if he could walk it, but he didn't fancy getting soaked if the rain increased, so he waited for a taxi, looking up and down the road in case one passed. Eventually, one returned to the rank and he kept a firm grip on the door handle as he gave the address, then climbed in, settling back in the seat. He was pretty certain there weren't seat belts the last time he'd travelled in a London cab, and wasn't sure if it was a reflection on the Cabbie's driving or a change in the law. His driver didn't offer his opinion on football, the weather, or the current state of foreign policy in Afghanistan, and Robert gratefully watched the shops and houses slide by in silence.

Some of the houses must be worth mega-millions, the size of them. He'd rented out his own house in Cornwall, and knew it represented an incomplete commitment to moving on, but coming to London had been hard enough, without burning every bridge behind him. Manchester was a lifetime away, and he didn't care for football any more. Not since David Beckham had been forced out, anyway. If he'd stayed, Robert was convinced the perfume would have been much better. More mancunian, at least. 'Trouble at Mill' would have been a great name for aftershave.

He sighed heavily and stared out of the window at the Heath going by, wondering whether he should contact Elaine's parents. He was worried they'd smother him, and decided to leave it a while before he did. Beyond Christmas cards and the very occasional phone call, contact had been sporadic. Going to Cornwall *had* been running away, and whilst he knew nobody blamed him, he could have stayed and toughed it out. He hadn't meant to cut himself off from everyone, but loathed Facebook: its insistence on updating baby Jon's nappy rash as 'news' didn't float his boat. The thought of Twitter made him shudder. People had left him alone in the early stages, something he'd probably encouraged, and as time went on, contact gradually petered out. When his best friends visited him after a year, the awkwardness drove a wedge between them, and he was glad when they left. Kissing and hugging and promising to stay in touch was sincere enough, and Robert had made an effort to do that, but his heart wasn't in it. The best kind of friends were those who sent him a Christmas letter with their card, updating him on what had gone on in their lives. He hadn't told anyone he was moving to London, and the income from his house in Cornwall would cover the rent on the apartment he'd found.

Just get on with life, what have you got to lose?

They arrived outside the clinic and Robert tipped the driver too much, but it seemed like a positive thing to do. Elaine always overtipped.

"Thanks, guv," the cabbie said, reverting to type. "Hope you feel better soon."

For a split-second, Robert thought Derren Brown was moonlighting as a cabbie, but the man grinned and pointed at the sign for the clinic. *Hampstead Natural Health Centre* it proclaimed loudly and largely, with a light above it, to illuminate it at night. It did look professional. An imposing Victorian building, double-fronted, with wide steps up to the entrance, it seemed to tower over him and he felt a moment's vertigo, looking up at it.

"Yeah, me too," Robert said, and turned to mount the steps. A young woman wrestled with a pushchair, pulling it up backwards. Long brown hair, brown eyes, and elfin face, she looked a tad distressed, and the good guy inside Robert pushed him forward.

"Let me help you."

"Oh, thank you," she said, as Robert gripped the base of the pushchair and lifted. The child seated in it looked at him suspiciously, and not wanting to alarm him, Robert looked up at the mother. Leaning forward as she lifted the buggy, he thought her bra was one of those French ones, very pretty, very ornate, and—

Robert looked back at the child, guilty, stumbling slightly on a step. He thought it was a boy, and tried to smile, winking at him. He wouldn't have thought a small child could scream that loudly. They reached the top step and Robert set the buggy down.

"I'm so sorry, he's not well," the woman said.

"No, don't worry, it's a gift I have with children," Robert replied.

She smiled and crouched down to comfort the little mite, leaning forward to stroke his head. Definitely French, Robert thought, and decided to remove himself from the scene before the child expired from air-loss. Or his inadvertent contemplation of French Couture landed him in more trouble. He pulled open the door and entered the health centre.

At first he thought he'd interrupted an audition for X-Factor. People filled the waiting area, and the hubbub they created made rational thought difficult; just like watching it on the television, really. It was a large open space with seats along both walls, and a long wooden counter at the end of the room facing him, with a corridor to the left, leading further into the building. Adults of various shapes and sizes and ages were mostly sitting, talking way too loudly, and without Simon Cowell to slap them down, the noise levels were pretty high. Three children, two boys and a girl, all under ten Robert guesstimated, were throwing magazines and leaflets at each other; and the girl was winning, by the look of things. A copy of Hello hit one of the boys in the eye and his cries drowned out the screams of the French Underwear offspring, who'd followed Robert in.

Behind the reception counter, looking pretty harassed, sat one of the most beautiful women Robert had seen in a very long time. Lustrous black hair hanging to her shoulders, curled under, dark eyes, glossy lipstick, perfectly applied, with a shiny red bindi on her forehead, she was dressed in a white high-collared blouse, and a grey jacket that looked like it might be silk. She was talking to an elderly woman who seemed about to commit actual bodily harm with a solid black handbag.

"Where's my taxi?" the woman demanded loud enough to be heard over the babel. "It should be here. Call them again." She banged the handbag on the counter to emphasise her point.

Probably stolen by the same girl who took mine Robert thought, as he stepped over a child intent on smashing his way into the basement with his fists because his reasonable demands for a sweet had been so cruelly denied. He caught the Sunday Telegraph magazine as it flew past him, depositing it neatly on a low table, and skipped round the little girl as she glared at him for ruining her evil plans to dominate the western world with her ballistic missiles. He smiled sweetly and she poked her tongue out.

"The wind's changed," he told her, and she looked blankly at him. *Ah, the joys of a decent education, what do they teach the kids nowadays?*

He reached the counter, and the beautiful woman flicked a glance at him, and smiled. It was only a quick smile, but Robert thought someone had shone a light in his face. Dimples in her cheeks came and went with the smile.

"Call them now!" insisted the woman. "I've a hair appointment in twenty minutes."

"I'm sure they're on their way, Mrs—" The shrill ring of the phone interrupted her and she grabbed it, tipping her head, sliding the receiver under her hair. "Hampstead Natural Health centre, how may I help you?"

The woman at the counter banged her handbag down, her face livid. Robert reckoned she had all the sartorial elegance of an unmade bed; starting with the hair might not be a bad move, but surely the Oxfam shops in Hampstead did a better line in clothes than that?

From the sounds of things, the beautiful receptionist was booking an appointment for a patient; how she could hear at all was anyone's guess.

"Mrs Johnson?" came a shout over the clamour, and Robert turned, hoping it was the cabbie for the harridan with the handbag. A slim woman, aged in her late twenties, wearing a white clinic coat and black trousers, stood in the corridor entrance. Her dark hair was tied back in a pony tail, which swayed as she looked around the room, searching for her patient. She looked familiar, and Robert wondered if she was an osteopath; perhaps he'd seen her at the compulsory post-graduate courses he'd occasionally come up to London for, to keep his membership to the Register current. She glanced at him, but there was no recognition there.

Mrs Johnson obviously had good hearing, because she got to her feet and made her way towards the girl, completely circumventing the sweetless child who now using his head as well as his fists as battering rams

6

on the wooden floor. Mrs Johnson reached out and shook hands with her.

"Sorry I'm running a bit late," the girl said. "Had a problem getting a cab this morning."

Robert blinked, realising where he'd seen her before. The taxi thief and Mrs Johnson disappeared down the corridor, and Robert jumped as the handbag hit the counter again. The receptionist put the phone down and dazzled Robert completely with her smile.

"I'm sorry," she said. "You are...?"

"Robert—"

"Where's my taxi?" interrupted the woman next to him, just as a child threw a handful of leaflets over the counter, forcing the receptionist to scrabble to catch them. Something hard and plastic bounced off the back of Robert's head and he knew the little girl's arsenal had expanded considerably. He'd had enough. He turned his back to the counter.

"QUIET!" he roared.

The silence that followed was coldly terrifying for the others and immensely satisfying for Robert. The basement digger froze in mid-strike and a second plastic intercontinental ballistic missile slipped from the nerveless fingers of the female launcher. The French Connection baby whimpered, but quietened immediately when Robert switched his implacable gaze to it. A leaflet see-sawed its way to the floor and the motionless tableau that was the reception area for the Hampstead Natural Health Centre waited for someone to wave their wand and release them from their stasis. Robert glanced around the room, and turned back to the receptionist who sat open-mouthed.

"I'm Robert Kirk," he said, and almost had to shield his eyes at the smile this produced, which lit up the whole room. *Photo-voltaic cells, eat your heart out.*

"Oh, you're Robert, we've been expecting you," she said, standing and holding her hand out to him, which he shook. "I'm Payal, I'll tell Ashley you're here."

She pushed her chair back and stood, hurrying to the door behind her. At that moment the front door opened, and a head poked round it.

"Taxi for Mrs Wolverton?"

Every head turned to the deliverer.

"That's me!" gasped the woman alongside Robert, though four mouths had opened to claim it, by the looks of things. The condemned watched enviously as Mrs Wolverton's reprieve set her free, and she hurried out before the cabbie could change his mind. As the door enclosed them once more they all looked away, not wanting to catch Robert's eye. The floor-batterer sucked his thumb, a poor substitute for a sweet, but it would have to do.

"Ashley, Robert Kirk is here," Payal said, smiling widely, stepping aside as a man emerged. Robert put him in his late twenties, the same brown skin as Payal, slim, athletic build, with high cheekbones, and dark eyes. He wore an Armani suit if Robert was any judge, and a broad smile of welcome on his face.

"Robert, so glad you could make it," Ashley said, hurrying to the counter, shaking Robert's hand vigourously. "This is Payal, my wife, the powerhouse around here, runs everything."

Robert thought the smile she gave looked a little brittle, didn't give off nearly as much energy as before. Ashley became aware of the silence, and looked round, puzzled.

"Is everything all right?" he asked Payal.

"Of course," she bristled. "Why wouldn't it be?"

Ashley blinked, uncertain. He shook his head slightly and looked at the waiting area, then at Robert again.

"Come on through," Ashley said, lifting a section of the counter and unbolting the upright, pulling it back. Robert stepped through, and an audible sigh of relief could be heard in the unaccustomed silence. Payal sat back in her chair, and Ashley motioned Robert through. The mute button on the chaos CD popped out and the volume resumed its normal level as Ashley closed the door.

CHAPTER TWO

The office was small, with a wooden desk, computer monitor and keyboard, shelves on the wall behind it, lined with books, and a small two-seater sofa, with a Persian rug covering the floor, two metal filing cabinets on the other wall. In one corner a small table had the elephant God Ganesha, adorned with garlands. Pictures of other Gods were scattered along the walls, staring out benignly, and a gorgeous photo of Ashley and Payal, looking younger, obviously their wedding. A window with slatted wooden blinds looked out at the property next door. Ashley reached over and hoisted his chair up, missing the computer monitor by a whisker, and set it in front of the desk.

"Sit, sit" he urged Robert, pointing to the sofa. Robert sat down and Ashley spun his chair, perching on the edge of it, leaning forward to face Robert, his face intent.

"So, when can you start?" Ashley asked.

"That's it?" Rob asked, surprised. "That's an interview?"

Ashley waved his hand dismissively.

"Ha, what's the point? You've been qualified eight years, normally we only get college leavers who think they know it all, and are wet behind the ears. Your references were great, and you've never been struck off for anything, according to the Register. What more should I know?"

"Well… I don't know, actually."

"Exactly. The sooner you start, the better. I had to let the other osteopath go last week, we've got patients waiting, and I don't want to lose them to other clinics. Bad for business."

"Why?"

Ashley studied Robert for a moment, frowning.

"I mean, why did he go?" Robert asked.

"Oh. He was just too flakey. Off the wall. Joined some institute of classical osteopathy and turned into a fruit-cake overnight."

"Really?"

"Really. You have a sacro-iliac joint out of line, you correct it, right?" He went on before Robert could speak. "Oh no, not Chaffinch – aptly named by the way, he was like a bird fluttering everywhere. Shake all the arms and legs for ten minutes, and it'll correct itself. Institute of classical waggle-opathy, more like. Seventeen complaints in two weeks, he had to go. Can you start on Monday?"

"Well… yes, why not?" Robert said, a tad bemused. "How do you handle the fees?"

"Payal takes all the payments and then I pay you weekly, minus the session rates for the room. I can give you a cheque or do it by bank transfer, if that's easier. You won't have to pay session fees for the first week, just to get you going, but you'll be pretty busy in no time."

"Great, thank you."

"Thank *you*, Robert. I hope you'll be here for a very long time." Ashley stood up. "Come and meet some of the other staff. We've got acupuncture, aromatherapy, kinesiology, herbalism and reflexology, and they're all great people. I'm thinking of getting a chiropodist in, but they need *so* much equipment."

Ashley swung his chair back over the desk and Robert winced, waiting for the crash, but it didn't happen, so he stood up. Had to be the fastest interview ever. But he was drawn to Ashley, his obvious enthusiasm and openness seemed to be matched by his friendliness. This might be the place to start again.

As Ashley opened the door, Phil Spector would have been proud of the wall of sound that hit them. It didn't seem to faze Ashley, but as Robert emerged the volume dial turned down and down to silence. Ashley studied the waiting souls, puzzled by this phenomenon as he lifted the counter top, stepped through, and held it for Robert. Frowning, Ashley indicated with his hand towards the corridor, and Robert followed him.

The first door they arrived at had an ornate sign entitled 'Osteopathy' and Ashley smiled as he opened the door, reached round and turned the light on, motioning Robert in. It was a decent-sized room, very clean; there was a hydraulic treatment table with pale blue towelling cover in the centre, a small changing cubicle, a desk with two chairs, and a wooden cabinet. Anatomical charts were pinned to one wall, and the window had a white blind pulled down and a vase of fresh flowers stood on the windowledge. A small sink was fixed under the windowledge, with a hand-towel hanging from a ring next to it. The whole room looked well-planned, and Robert nodded in approval.

"Nice room," he said

"Couch rolls and spare towels in the cabinet," Ashley said. "Didn't know if you'd want massage oil or cream, we supply it all for you."

"Great. I like arnica oil, if you've got it."

"No problem. Let's see if any of the others are in the staff room."

Ashley led the way and they passed five more doors, either side of the corridor; one was marked as the toilet, and Ashley opened another marked as Private to show the shower and toilet for staff use. The other rooms had their own signs - Acupuncture, Aromatherapy, and the last had Kinesiology and Reflexology together. The door at the end of the corridor opened into a very large room, with a high ceiling, and enormous windows looking onto a cultivated garden, enclosed by green hedges. Two large sofas formed half a square and more armchairs and easy chairs were scattered around the room. Not one cushion matched, but the vibrant colours made it a place of easy comfort, while swirling paintings of dolphins and landscapes adorned the walls. A low cupboard with a sink and a kettle and toaster standing by lined one side. A woman stood with her back to them, waiting for the kettle to boil, by the look of her. Blonde hair tied up and an hour-glass figure, wearing tight slacks and a woollen jumper she hummed to herself, swaying gently.

"Tea, Bren?" asked the blonde.

Another woman lay back on one of the sofas, eyes closed, with a large red crystal resting on her forehead, between her eyes. The thumb and forefinger of each hand formed two circles, which were held in the air. About sixty, Robert reckoned, greying hair tied back and wearing a voluminous kaftan that emphasised her size. She was a big woman.

"Aum," this woman chanted in reply, and Robert felt a twinge of alarm. Ashley cleared his throat and the blonde turned. *'All that meat and no potatoes'* was Robert's first thought, staggered. She had a bust that Katie Price would envy. It strained at the jumper, desperate to leap free, and it was coming towards him. Transfixed in the twin headlights of flesh, Robert couldn't move.

"This is Robert, our new osteopath," Ashley said, as collision was imminent. "Robert this is Pam, she's—"

"I'm single," the blonde announced, taking Robert's hand. He wasn't aware he'd held it out, but he swore he heard hydraulics as her bumpers softly collided with his chest, pushing him back a few inches. She was pretty, with freckles on her nose and blue eyes that should never be allowed in a liars' contest for the sheer unfairness of it.

"Pam's our aromatherapist," Ashley said, as Robert struggled to free his hand

"Any time you need rebalancing, just let me know," Pam breathed, staring into Robert's eyes. "Any time."

Robert took hold of her wrist and pulled his hand from her grasp.

"I'll bear it in mind," Robert said, and found he could breathe more easily as the vertical weight eased from him.

"Your chakras need work, you know that, don't you?" Pam said.

"I had them serviced last week, actually."

Pam thought about this for a second and then laughed. She *was* pretty, and her laugh was genuine, but Robert felt like he was being scrutinised for breakfast, and he'd never liked pushy women, anyway. He caught a hint of movement from the corner of his eye, and almost jumped out of his skin as he turned to find the older woman standing beside him.

"This is Brenda," Ashley said.

Robert held his hand out to her, but she ignored it and folded him in a huge bear-hug.

"It's taken you so long to get here," she said emphatically, over his shoulder.

Robert managed to extricate himself, stepping back from her.

"Well, someone stole my taxi, otherwise I'd—"

"No, no. It's what you've been through to finally arrive," she interrupted. "So many times you've been on this plane."

"Yeah, those EasyJet fares are hard to resist, aren't they?"

She gripped his shoulders and stared deeply into his eyes. "Robert. Robert," she said earnestly.

"Still here," Robert replied. "Both of us."

"You've been given such a wonderful opportunity to..."

She tailed off, and Robert knew his face must have shown what he was thinking, because she took her hands from him, looking a bit flustered. Ashley must have picked up on something between them.

"Let's go back to the office, I'll show you all the

forms we use," he said, and Robert was quite glad to get out of the room, what with soft flesh and soft minds.

"Such a troubled soul," he heard Brenda say.

"Mm," agreed Pam. "Such a nice bum, though."

As Ashley closed the door to the staffroom, he gave Robert a somewhat sickly smile.

"They're wonderful practitioners," Ashley said. "P'raps a bit flakey, but—"

"A bit? A bit?"

"Seriously, their patients love them. They do a lot of good. They're decent people, genuinely."

Robert relented somewhat. It wasn't his place to criticise others, and he knew he was over-sensitive.

"Yeah, you're right. I've worked on my own for so long, I forgot the rich tapestry of life has all sorts of weaves."

"What?"

"It takes all kinds."

"Absolutely," Ashley said, relieved. "You haven't met Ian yet, he's the Kinesiologist. Even I don't understand what he tells me, but he gets people better, that's all that counts. Ah, here he is."

A wandering hippy approached them. His ponytail had obviously wrenched all the hair out from the top of his head, dragging it over the crown to the back, and it looked like the rest of it would fall out any day now. A shirt that had seen life when Jefferson Airplane were still playing live was joined by long khaki shorts and open-toed sandals. He could have been any age from thirty-five to fifty-five, and he muttered to himself as he swung a pendulum from side to side, crossing and re-crossing the corridor.

"Ian, this is—"

Ashley was interrupted by Ian jerking up his left hand violently, a sign that brooked no argument, shaking his head, as he continued on his way, murmuring and swinging the pendulum like a demented altar boy. Robert was reminded of a pinball machine he'd played on the pier as a boy, as he watched Ian bounce off the walls until he finally made it into the staff room. All he needed were Pam's bumpers and some music and it would be just like the real thing. He looked at Ashley.

"He's Grandmaster of the White Lodge," Ashley said, by way of explanation.

"Riiight," Robert said slowly.

"Come on, I'll take your details. Where are you staying?"

"I'm renting an apartment in Camden, thought I'd cycle in."

Ashley stopped, agitated, and gripped Rob's upper arm.

"Don't do that, Robert. Seriously. The lorries in London are lethal, far too many cyclists get knocked off every day."

"I thought I'd come in early, miss the traffic and do some serious fitness work around the Heath."

"Promise me you'll stick to the cycle lanes and the pavement if you do, please."

"Okay."

Robert was touched by his concern, and they walked down the corridor. Word was out by now, and even new arrivals fell silent as Robert entered. 'Avoid eye-contact with the dangerous predator' was probably the advice that had been handed on. Ashley narrowed his eyes, but ushered Robert back into the office, and handed him a pad and pen.

"Write down your full name and address, phone numbers, and your bank details if you want me to pay you directly. I'll have a contract ready for you to sign on Monday. I'll need a copy of your Registration and Professional Insurance, as you'll be self-employed here. We have Liability for the clinic, but not for the practitioners themselves."

"I've got them here," Robert said, reaching into his jacket pocket, and handing them to Ashley. He perused them briefly, and put them on his desk.

"Excellent, I'll get Payal to copy them. What are you doing this weekend?"

"Going to browse the markets, get to know my way around, buy a few things to make it more personal, that kind of thing."

"Go to Camden Lock Market and The Stables, they'll have everything you want. Let me know if you need anything electrical – TV, stereo, X-box – my brother owns a direct-sales outlet. Do you have any family in London?"

"Parents live in Manchester, my sister's in Canada," Robert said, his heart clenching a little. "I've only got a mobile, didn't seem worth putting in a landline just yet."

He handed the pad back, hoping he'd drop the subject and was saved by Ashley's mobile ringtone: Beethoven's 9th, 'Ode to joy'. Ashley jumped visibly, and glanced at the phone.

"I'll have to take this," he said, excitedly. "Would you mind waiting in the staff room, and I'll get all your documents seen to?"

Robert uncharitably wondered what Ashley wanted to hide, as he was given the bum's rush from the office. To his surprise, Pam now sat at the reception counter and Payal was waiting to go into the office, her eyes bright, her face alive. She pushed past him and he could have sworn Ashley was pulling his tie off as the door closed. Pam was delighted at the sudden hush that greeted the entrance of the Terminator.

He wondered what delights awaited him in the staff room, but was pleased to find it empty. He sat in one of the easy chairs and watched swallows... swallowing. Whatever it was they did. Elaine told him they caught flies in the air, and personally he'd have been pecking at the coconut in the neighbour's garden if he had the choice, but was reminded of a Tee-shirt she brought him once – 'Eat Shit! Seven Billion Flies can't all be wrong'. He didn't know if he still had it, but he'd left it in Cornwall if it was anywhere. He wondered what the tenants would make of it, when it turned up behind the washing machine. Still, he'd—

"Excuse me." The voice was icy, and Robert swivelled in the chair. The Taxi Thief stood with one hand on her hip, the other clutching a clipboard. Her lips were compressed into an angry line. "This is the staffroom, it's clearly marked, you need to go back to the waiting room."

At least ten smartarse answers flicked through Robert's mind, but in the end he decided against nine of them, and settled for straight sarcasm.

"Do I look like I'm waiting?"

Her face flushed and she put the clipboard down.

"I'll tell you again, politely: go back to the waiting room."

"Then what? You'll unbalance my chakras?"

Her eyes widened for a moment, and she moved incredibly quickly and grabbed his little finger, twisting it back painfully, forcing him to his feet. He grabbed at her hand, and she clung on, as they struggled for control of his fifth digit. Absurdly, for a second he thought her perfume was really pleasant, and wondered what it was. She tried to twist his finger further.

"Get off!" he shouted, using his strength to pull his hand back.

"I told you to leave," she snarled.

Ashley burst into the room, and rushed to them, making a pat-a-cake pile of hands as he tried to drag them apart.

"Maria, what are you doing? Let go!"

She did so and stepped back, breathing heavily.

"I asked him to leave the staffroom, politely, twice," she said. "And he refused."

"That's because he works here! Robert's the new osteopath."

"What?"

"He's taking over from Chaffinch, starts on Monday." He looked at Robert. "You okay?"

Robert nodded. Maria looked at Ashley, then glared at Robert.

"Well, he should have said!"

She flounced from the room.

"You sure you're okay?" Ashley asked.

"I'm sure. Are you okay?"

Ashley's shirt was crumpled and his tie pulled down. His hair was mussed, and Robert thought his lips looked redder.

"Yeah, sure, sure," Ashley said hurriedly, tucking his shirt in, smoothing this hair. "Quite a struggle wasn't it?"

"What's wrong with her?"

"Just broke up from a long-term relationship – the guy wasn't very nice."

"Oh. I should have told her who I was."

"Ah, don't worry, no harm done. She'll be fine after the weekend. Look, if you're going to cycle in, get the key from Payal for the side gate, put the bike round the back."

"Right."

CHAPTER THREE

Robert spent Saturday in the markets at Camden, and apart from being surprised at how expensive everything was, when they were yelling what a good bargain it all must be, he was pleasantly surprised to find the city-dwellers were generally a friendly bunch. He bought a hand-made rag rug from a Jamaican, who made him laugh with his tale of the rug cuttings shrinking in the rain and two punks buying them all, for their coolness, since they looked: "erratic, man."

"I haven't called anyone 'man' in decades!" the trader laughed, as he rolled up Robert's choice. "Enjoy the rug."

He haggled for two carved wooden cats, and wondered if his lease would allow him the real thing, if he settled here. His house in Cornwall had been a mecca for any stray moggy that came along, and he was mortified when he was told he'd been feeding at least four cats that lived in his road.

He sat outside a cafe and drank cappuccino, single shot, and tried not to remember. He wanted to remember, but somewhere along the way he'd lost the habit of doing it without becoming melancholy. So he kept busy, walked a fair few miles, and went to the cinema in the evening, to see the world saved from Alien invasion by some unshaved teenager. He slept on the right side of the bed, with Elaine's picture on the bedside cabinet, watching him.

Daylight woke him around five, and he remembered he needed curtains. He got up and put his cycling gear on. He was on the empty streets before anyone else was awake. *Whatever happened to the milkman?* He consulted his map and decided to do a run up to Hampstead, to check the best roads and cycle paths, and see how long it took him. A few diversions were needed, but he reckoned he could avoid all the danger spots. The exercise made him energised, and he rode for three hours. The wind in his face and the quiet of the city was calming, though more people were about by the time he got back. He spent five minutes talking to a ginger tabby that complained when he didn't have any food to give him. At least, that's what it sounded like. He bought a Sunday Paper from the newsagent round the corner, and spent a couple of hours reading all the sections from cover to cover, even the adverts. He was sure he'd seen the bra in the M&S advert somewhere...

By three in the afternoon, he'd packed all the clothes he would need the following day in his backpack, and thought he might leave a week's clothes at the clinic, to save him taking it back and forth every day. He was only scheduled to be in four days a week with some Saturdays, and thought he'd maybe get his parents to come down and stay with him for a weekend, he would sleep on the couch. He knew he couldn't visit them yet, and they understood that. So he phoned them, and told them what he'd done. They were pleased, naturally, and making them feel good made him feel good. He promised to look for tickets to Miss Saigon or Les Miserables, and let them know with plenty of warning.

The apartment was quiet when he rang off, and he didn't like the echoes, so he went out and walked the city. His sister phoned within an hour and he sat by the

Thames, telling her everything. Alexa was due to come to London at some point in the next month for business, and demanded to stay with him. By the time they finished speaking, he was looking forward to it. He sauntered back to his apartment and heated some pasta and pesto, and sat on the small balcony, looking out over the street, with a glass of red wine. There was a children's play area a little further down the street and he could hear laughter and delighted screams echoing up to him. *You can do it,* he said to himself. *Just get up every day and see what life brings you.*

He slept well and his idea of making it to the Heath early went out the window, as he didn't wake until seven. He couldn't remember dreaming, which was unusual, but he felt ready for the day. He was outside and on the bike by 7.30 and set off. Robert knew he was unusual because he wasn't colour-blind, unlike all the other cyclists, who didn't seem able to distinguish between a red and green light. He closed his eyes on more than one occasion as he sat at traffic lights, watching some of the idiots literally dicing with death. But his route was incident-free, and he was almost there, pushing fast up a bus and cycle lane, when he had to swerve around a stationary taxi. He checked over his shoulder, saw a gap in the traffic and swung out. Just as the door on the traffic side opened, and a woman stepped out. He locked both wheels, almost went over the handlebars and missed her by the width of a DNA strand, as she shrank back. His foot skidded and he went over onto his thigh. A car swerved around him, horn blaring, and he leapt to his feet.

"Jesus, woman are you blind?" he shouted, fear and adrenaline demanding instant release. "Get out on the pavement, you idiot!"

The woman stood with her mouth open, and Maria and Robert recognised each other. There was a moment's stasis as they stared, then Robert slammed his foot on the pedal and cycled off, seething. Maria watched him go, open-mouthed and jumped out of her skin as a courier motorcycle blasted her with his airhorns as he went by. She jumped back in the taxi and pulled the door closed.

Stupid, stupid woman, Robert fumed. *What the hell was she thinking, getting out there? The clinic's half a mile away.*

He burned up the adrenaline cycling furiously, pushing himself, his anger needing an outlet. He was breathing hard by the time he reached the clinic, and lifted his bike easily as he ran up the steps, leaning it against the wall. His cycling shoes clacked on the wooden floor in reception and the searchlight that was Payal's greeting hit him full force.

"Morning, Robert," she said. "You start at ten, and eight patients booked so far. Your lists are in the room."

"Thanks, Payal. Could I have the key to the side gate?"

"Of course."

She reached under the counter and drew out a large key, handing it to him with another smile. Robert wondered if it affected Ashley the same. He took his bike round and unlocked the big padlock that secured the solid gate. As he wheeled it round the side he saw Ian hugging the big oak tree at the bottom of the garden. *Barking,* Robert thought. *Absolutely barking.*

He chained his bike to a drainpipe, and returned quickly through reception, handing the key back to Payal.

His padded cycling shorts had taken the brunt of the damage, preventing road-rash, and he soaked in the shower for a few minutes, letting the heat relax his muscles, draining the tension from him, and went to his room when he'd dressed. He'd not worn a clinic coat in Cornwall, everyone knew him, so a sports shirt had sufficed, but he'd got the old ones out and they still fit him, which was pleasing. He studied the case-histories for a while, and thought he deciphered the previous guy's writing quite well. With a good thirty minutes before his first appointment he went in search of a coffee in the staffroom. Maria and Brenda sat in one of the sofas, and

Robert fancifully wondered if he'd get an apology, but Maria glanced up at him, then dropped her head to study the magazine she was reading. *Typical.*

"How was your journey?" Brenda asked him.

"This lifetime, or the last?"

Brenda smiled. He walked to the kettle, checked the water level and switched it on.

"Actually," he said, without turning, "someone just tried to push me into the next life on my way in. Opened a Cab door into the road without looking, just as I was passing. God alone knows how I missed them."

"Oh that's terrible," Brenda said, shocked. "Some people have no sense, do they?"

Robert didn't dare turn, but searched for a coffee jar in the cupboard.

"No, not a drop." He thought he heard a snort behind him. "Is there any coffee?"

"There's a jar right at the back, I think," Branda said. "It's pretty old, you might ask Ashley for some fresh."

Robert found it at the very back of the cupboard, behind the green tea, the fruit tea, the herbal tea, the fruit and herb tea, the green fruit and herb tea, and the Earl Grey. It smelled like coffee and it looked like coffee, so he risked it. Skimmed milk was okay by him, and it didn't taste too bad, but Brenda was right – it was pretty old. He decided to get a jar in his lunch break.

He took his cup and sat in a big stuffed armchair. The oak tree looked loved-up enough – Ian wasn't anywhere to be seen. He risked a glance at Maria, and she had her head down, reading. He was about to look away when a lock of her hair fell forward over her ear. For a split-second, unthinking, Robert almost reached out to return the errant strands, the way he'd always done with Elaine; she'd always tip her head into his hand, inviting the caress he'd give. His mind lurched, and he was actually grateful when Pam entered the room.

"Ooh, hello everybody. Good weekends?" Nods and

murmurs of assent followed her as she swayed her way to the kettle and the light from the window was eclipsed by the twin moons passing. "Drink, anyone?"

Robert raised his mug to show he had a drink and the others ignored her. It seemed the normal response as Pam hummed to herself, and brewed herself a tea of some sort. She flopped into the armchair next to Robert. Ian entered the room just then, pendulum in hand.

"Ah, Ian, you've not met—" Brenda began.

"There's a new osteopath, you know," Ian said, as the pendulum lead him towards the fridge.

"Yes, he's—"

"I'm going to let the pendulum lead me to him," Ian interrupted, striding past them.

"Good idea," Robert said, and eased himself out of the chair, leaving the room with his coffee. In truth, he wanted a way out, his heart was still beating too fast from the memory of Elaine, how vivid the picture had been. In his room, he closed the door and sat heavily in his chair. He was glad he'd made the appointment with Dr Eastmann on Wednesday. It had been intended as an introductory meeting, he knew his counsellor in Cornwall had sent up the notes, but it would be good to talk some of his feelings through.

CHAPTER FOUR

ithin two weeks, Robert settled into a routine, and found that hard work *was* helping; his patient lists expanded rapidly, and cycling to and from the clinic raised his fitness levels. Weekends were a bit of a problem, but he'd bought a television from Ashley's brother and found plenty to watch on the freeview channels. He hadn't contacted Elaine's parents yet, but Dr Eastmann had told him to take it at his own pace, not hurry anything.

He'd managed to keep out of Pam's clutches, and began to see she was actually a nice person beneath the lust she continually flaunted. By joking with her about it, she still flirted with him, but he thought she understood it wouldn't go anywhere. He'd even treated her once, when her back really had gone into a spasm. He'd found her in the corridor, leaning against a wall, one hand on her back, in tears.

"What's the matter?" he asked, concerned.

"Put my back out again," she said, tearfully. "It's all this weight I carry around."

She indicated her bust.

"Do you want me to help?"

"What? Carry my boobs for me? Yes, please."

She jerked as a sudden spasm hit her and he helped

her into his treatment room. Just as he closed the door, he heard Ashley's mobile playing Beethoven, and reminded himself to look out for a ticket to the Prom in the Park. Roberts's suspicions that Pam was putting it on were quickly laid to rest when he had to help her take her jumper off, and she got two or three stabs of acute pain. He heard the ode to joy getting louder and it seemed to go into the treatment room next to his.

"Is Ashley looking for you?" Robert asked. "I'd better tell him you're in here."

"No, it's okay," she said. "He's treating Payal, she's not a well woman, you know."

"Really?"

"Has to treat her all the time, a special massage thing he does."

"Oh, right. Show me where it hurts."

Pam indicated a spot in the middle of her spine.

"Okay, can you lie on your side?"

He helped her onto the treatment couch, and started to stretch the muscles of her spine. Noises began to come from the next room - moaning, rhythmical and suggestive. It got faster and faster and Robert knew he'd be struck off if he did that kind of treatment. *What the hell, it's his wife.*

"Roll onto your back, let's see if we can release those joints."

Robert crossed her arms over her chest and had to lower the couch almost to the floor, to get leverage, but managed to manipulate the offending joints. He helped her sit upright, and she shrugged her shoulders up and down, making her chest bounce very pleasantly.

"Oh, that feels wonderful. Thank you."

"You're welcome." He handed Pam her jumper and she slipped it easily over her head. "Have you ever thought of having a breast reduction?"

She tipped her head, a knowing smile on her face.

"Robert, I've got two good things in life going for me,

and these are both of them," she said, squeezing her breasts.

"I think you underestimate yourself, Pam." Robert said. "You're a lovely person."

She smiled at him, emotional, and from that moment their relationship changed. She still flirted with him, only it was like gentle teasing between friends.

But the incident with Maria hadn't helped. Ashley invited him for a drink after work, and since he'd come in on the Underground that morning because of the rain, he thought *why not?* They were into their second pints when Payal walked in with Maria. He hadn't seen Maria with her hair down, and actually, she looked a different person. They still hadn't communicated much, and Robert wasn't bothered. But they sat at a table together and he listened to her talking to Payal, and actually heard her laugh once or twice. But he became aware of the perfume, and thought it was heavenly. But they didn't speak directly to each other, until they were leaving. It was raining again and Ashley called a cab. They saw it arrive and Ashley held his coat over himself and Payal, and hurried out of the pub, dashing over the road.

"Hold on, I've got an umbrella," Robert said, as Maria held the door. He'd forgotten how fiercely it opened when you pressed the button, and in his defence, he *was* aiming the umbrella out of the door. But it opened so quickly and so strongly that it caught Maria on the arm and shoulder and bowled her out of the doorway. She'd probably just have staggered into the rain and run for the cab, but she tripped over a low chain link that had no purpose other than to catch out the unwary, and she sprawled in the road. In a puddle. Robert dashed to her, holding the brolly up, and reached to help her up.

"Shit, I'm sorry about that—"

She smacked his arm away, and got to her feet. Robert could see her tights were torn up her thigh, since her skirt had blown up to her waist, but it didn't look like she'd grazed herself. Unfortunately, just as she got to her feet an incredibly strong gust of wind buffeted Robert and the umbrella, and he staggered into her, barging her over again. Then Payal and Ashley reached them, helping Maria up. The wind battered them all, but the collective clump of bodies stayed upright, and they hurried to the cab. The umbrella was whisked from Robert's hand by a strong gust and he wouldn't have been surprised to see Mary Poppins racing past uncontrollably in the wind.

They fell into the cab, and it pulled away, all of them dripping rain. Robert turned to Maria on the seat next to him.

"I'm so sorry," he said. "The wind took me, I—"

"Shut up," she hissed.

"It was an accident, I didn't mean—"

"Forget it," she said.

He stared at her for a second and then tapped on the glass panel to the driver.

"Pull over here, please, driver," Robert said, and as the cab stopped he looked at Maria. "At least I apologise if I cause an accident."

He opened the door and stepped out, hearing Ashley call to him, and strode away. *Stupid woman.* He turned his phone off, knowing Ashley would call him, and looked for another cab. He couldn't find one, but caught a bus and arrived back at his apartment cold, wet and miserable, wondering if he could change his days to avoid her. He soaked in the bath, and woke up wrinkled in tepid water.

***

He and Maria completely ignored each other after that, which suited Robert just fine. He brushed away Ashley's attempts to play the peacemaker, and got on with his job.

At the end of the next Friday, he was dressed, ready to leave and walked into the Staffroom to get his backpack. He found the other therapists all arranging chairs in a circle. A woman he'd not met before was standing at the sink with all kinds of funnels and rubber tubes, wearing latex gloves, and she turned to him as he reached the coat stand.

"Oh, hello, we've not met yet, you must be Robert," she said, hand outstretched. She was pleasant-looking woman, brown-haired, round-faced, looked about forty, and wearing very sensible clothes. Robert took her hand and she squeezed it firmly. "I'm Christina, Colonic Irrigation."

She released his hand and he tried not to wipe it on his jumper. She burst out laughing at his face.

"Sorry, just teasing. I'm the reflexologist, been away on holiday while you got here. These are for my elderberry wine," she said, indicating the funnels and tubes. "But I could give you an enema if you need one," she added smiling.

"Maybe another time," Robert said. "Or another life."

She smiled, and Robert liked her. He reached over for his pack, and her face fell.

"Where are you going?"

"Home. End of day, start of weekend. Where we should all go."

He turned away from her to see Pam and Brenda staring at him, shocked. He could feel Maria looking at him and didn't bother returning the favour.

"You have to stay for the meditation," Pam said.

"You'll meet the new osteopath," Ian said, pushing an armchair with his thigh.

"We always meditate at the phases of the moon," Brenda said, pleading.

"Tempting," Robert said. "But, no. I'm not into that sort of thing. Thanks anyway."

He walked around Pam, and Brenda stepped into his path.

"Please, Robert, we need you to make up the mystical number." She made two circles with her thumbs and forefinger, and put one on the other to form a figure eight. "Eight of us. Two circles, you see? Caring and sharing."

"You must stay," Christina said.

"No, I mustn't. But you enjoy it."

He walked past Brenda with a sigh of relief. But he hadn't reckoned on Payal. She intercepted him in the corridor, and he tried to look away as she smiled.

"Where are you going?"

"Home. Lots to do. Busy weekend."

He tried to step around her but she turned as he did and placed her hand on his arm, dialling her eyes down low, so they were limpid pools of concern.

"Please don't go. Ashley would like you to come to the meeting. We both would."

Her eyes darkened further, and he swore they glistened, on the point of tears.

"Payal, I'd rather have chiropractic treatment than meditate, honestly. It's just not my thing."

Payal worried her bottom lip with her teeth, and her eyes opened wider.

"Please," she said, and his heartstrings hit a pure chord as she plucked them. There was a movement in the corner of his eyes and as he turned Brenda was there, like a stealth-fitted submarine, smooth and silent in her approach. He turned back and Payal had him hemmed in. He sighed.

"Just this once," he said. "But I'm taking every phase of the moon as holiday from now on."

He allowed himself to be led back to the slaughter, and Ashley caught up with them as they entered the room. A circle of chairs had been arranged and as Robert hesitated, the others sat down. There was only one left, next to Pam and she patted it, smiling. He sat in it, wishing it was over. Payal was to his left and he didn't care to look opposite since Maria sat there.

"Excellent, we're all here, and I'd like to welcome Robert to our circle," Ashley said. Ian looked up, surprised, and Robert shook his head, resigned to his fate. "I'll hand us over to Brenda, who will guide us."

Brenda looked around the circle, smiling benignly.

"I am the earth mother," she said in a mellow voice. "We are complete again. Let us journey to our inner selves"

They all laid their hands in their laps and closed their eyes. Robert saw this and crossed his arms and ankles defiantly.

"The number eight consists of two perfect circles," Brenda continued in a sing-song voice. "We are eight once more. Breathe in the light and breathe out the darkness."

Robert watched as they all filled their lungs and breathed out. How Pam's lungs managed to lift all that weight was beyond him, and he wondered how long he'd have to stay there. He sighed, completely out of synch with everyone.

"Feel the light surrounding you, feel its warmth."

Where's an ecigarette when you need one? Robert mused. *That'll provide more light and warmth than a meditation.*

They continued to breathe slowly and Robert stared at the ceiling, bored. He heard gentle snoring and wasn't surprised to see Ian had fallen asleep. He shifted in the chair, hoping he could do the same, and angled his head back against the cushions, trying to get comfortable.

"We're going to take a journey," Brenda said, and Robert couldn't believe it. As he sat up, exasperated, he saw Maria. Her face was calm, and as he looked, her hair completely unpinned itself and flowed out across both shoulders, like liquid chocolate. She wasn't bad-looking when she wasn't snarling. He rested his head back and closed his eyes, hoping he'd nod off.

"We're standing in a dark cave, with a bright light ahead of us," Brenda intoned

I'll never get any sleep if she doesn't shut up, Robert thought, but he visualised the cave, anyway.

"We walk towards the light."

Oh no! Move towards the light. We're all going to die! Where's Patrick Swayze when we need him?

"We feel the sand beneath our feet, warm and welcoming, as we emerge."

Robert sees a wide sandy beach, blue sky and deep blue sea.

"We see a wide sandy beach and blue sky."

Hah! I'm ahead of you. You forgot the sea.

"The sea is deep blue, and inviting."

A cold beer would be inviting. Wonder if this meditation has them?

Robert moves down the beach, and sees a rocky outcrop ahead of him.

"We see a rocky outcrop ahead."

I'm just too good at this.

He walks up to the rocks.

"There's a figure standing on the rocks."

Nope, sorry. Just rocks. Must be a beer somewhere.

"You know who it is."

Robert looks up and down the beach and is sure he can feel his heart beating in his chest.

Elaine?

He slumps down in the sand, and stares out at the sea.

You're an idiot, he tells himself. *Too much to hope for, especially for a cynic like you.*

He becomes aware of movement in the periphery of his vision, and slowly turns his head. Perching on the rock next to him is a fairy with gossamer wings and long flame-red hair flowing down her back. She's about three and a half inches tall, wearing a clinging dress with a low-cut top and a fully-developed woman's figure. Bare feet, a small snub nose, covered with freckles, and full lips.

Typical. I could have had Halle Berry, or Natalie Portman, or Katherine Jenkins. What do I get? A miniature Lindsay Lohan. Still, she might know where the bar is...

"Spend some time interacting with this figure."

Do I have to? Robert turns to the fairy. "Come here often?"

The fairy screams, her wings beating furiously and leaps into the air, startling him. She whirls round to face Robert, her chest heaving. She hovers in the air, blinking rapidly. Her shoulders suddenly sag and she drops down six inches.

"Oh no, not another loser," the fairy says, exasperated.

Despite himself, Robert looks over his shoulder to see who she's talking about. Nobody's there. The fairy shoots in one direction, then another, furiously zig-zagging as she rants.

"Why me?" she demands, angry. "Why always me? Ariadne's free, why can't she do it? It's not fair, it's not my turn."

She stops in mid-air and looks at Robert again. He feels slightly uncomfortable under this scrutiny.

"I won't do it," she says, and there's a loud crack as she disappears down the beach at impossible speed, gone instantly, trailing vapour. Robert stares after her.

Shit. That's what I call interacting. He looks up and down the beach. *Might as well go for a swim.*

He stands up and reaches to drag off the garish tee-shirt he's wearing.

"Start to come back, now," Brenda's voice interrupted.

Spoilsport.

"Feel the sand beneath your feet, the floor beneath your feet. Breathe deeply and come back into the room. Open your eyes when you're ready."

Robert opened his eyes to find he was standing, dragging his shirt up. He sat down hurriedly, hoping nobody saw him. Luckily, all eyes were closed and the others gradually came back, stretching arms and legs, smiling at each other.

"Welcome back," Brenda said, smiling widely. "Anyone like to share anything?"

"I swam with the dolphins again," Pam said. "It was glorious."

"Wonderfully spiritual creatures, you're so lucky," Brenda said.

There are nods of understanding from the group.

"I saw my Grandmother," Payal said. "She gave me a

beautiful flower."

Ashley took her hand and kissed it.

It's mass delusion, Robert thought. *They really think they've been there.*

"Anyone else?" Brenda asked. "Robert? Anything?"

"Me? No, not a thing."

"It'll come, don't you worry," Brenda said, beaming at him.

I bloody hope not.

He was out of the clinic and on the tube train in record time, courtesy of a taxi pulling up just as he exited the centre.

CHAPTER FIVE

He whistled his way up the stairs to his apartment, ready for the weekend. He had a ticket for the Proms in the Park, and he was going to make the most of it. Pack a picnic tonight, get in the queue early and relax. Perfect.

As he crossed his lounge, heading to the kitchen, his mind refused to take in what his eyes thought they saw. But eventually the message got through and he stopped and turned to face his wall-mounted TV. The shopping bags slipped though his nerveless fingers. Perched on top of the screen was the fairy, legs crossed, swinging her foot back and forth. He stared at her and she stared back at him. He closed his eyes, screwing them tight shut and opened them again.

She was still there, staring calmly at him. He rubbed his eyes, shook his head, and still she sat there, regarding him. He hesitantly walked towards her, screwing his eyes up, tilting his head. He craned forward studying her. When his face was three inches from her, she leaned forward.

"Boo!" she said, and Robert shot backwards in panic, his arms windmilling. His thighs caught the back of the sofa and he hurtled over it, bouncing off to crash onto his rag-rug, his teeth jolting together, seeing stars as his head hit the floor hard.

This isn't happening, this isn't happening. Don't panic, it isn't happening.

He lay there for a couple of minutes, doing the deep breathing exercises he'd learned for the panic attacks.

She's not there, you're imagining it. Get a grip.

He cautiously raised his head, pushing himself up on his arms and craned his neck, peering over the sofa. He could see the top of the television, and there was nothing there. Nothing. He breathed a huge sigh of relief and sank back to the floor.

Just your imagination.

He was certain he screamed as she flew above him, looking down at him, because she winced, clapping her hands over her ears. But she hovered there, like a dragonfly, waiting. When the echoes died away, she took her hands from her ears.

"Nice rug," she said. "Do you want to sit up and we'll talk? I get shagged out with all this hovering."

She isn't there, she isn't there, she isn't there.

The mantra seemed to work, because she flew away. He waited ten minutes at least, and then pushed himself upright. He didn't see her anywhere and let out a cautious sigh of relief.

She wasn't there.

He dragged himself up and flopped back on the sofa. It was the noise that drew his attention. Tiny, quiet scratching, like a mouse in a cupboard. She sat on the edge of his dining table, legs crossed, doing her nails. He heard the nail file going, setting his teeth on edge. She blew on her nails and looked right at him.

"So. Why can't you move on?" she asked in a perfectly reasonable voice.

Except it wasn't perfectly reasonable, and he was losing his mind.

"This isn't happening," he said, just to hear his own voice, to convince himself he wasn't lying on the floor unconscious. He sneaked a peek, just to make sure his body wasn't lying there and this some bizarre out-of-body experience. *Maybe the meditation hasn't finished yet, that could be–*

"Why do I get the difficult ones?" she asked, raising her eyes to heaven. "Look..." she paused, waiting. "What is your name, anyway?"

Someone slipped some acid in my drink, I bet it was Maria. Or some of Brenda's herbs, I'm sure she's growing magic mushrooms.

"Hey! Bozo!"

Robert looked back at the fairy. She looked a bit cross now. She got to her feet and her wings took her up in the air and then down again. Then she flew left and right, before landing on the table again.

"I know you can see me, your eyes are moving. Look, I'm Annabelle, and you are...?"

Robert couldn't move, couldn't speak.

It's definitely Magic Mushrooms, some kind of neurotoxin, wait till I see them.

"Okay," the fairy said, exasperated. "I say 'I'm Annabelle', and you say 'I'm...'" she gestured for him to answer, then gave up. "Gormless." She sighed and shook her head. "Look, dimwit, you called me, I didn't call you. I don't want this job any more than you want me here, but we need to get some communication going between us, all right?"

Robert stared at her for a moment, then sat up, struggling to retrieve his mobile from his pocket as his fingers refused to do what he asked, but at last he got it, and frantically thumbed through his address book. He turned his head away from her and pressed the phone to his ear. She flew into his field of vision, and he jerked his head the other way. She promptly did it again, and this went on again and again, Robert shaking his head like a demented head-banger at an Iron Maiden concert. He heard the ring-tones and prayed someone would answer. His prayers were answered.

"Hello, Dr Eastmann? I have to see you right away, it's an emergency." He listened for a moment, interrupting what was said, frantic. "No it's an emergency. I'm... I'm seeing things."

"Things?" the fairy exclaimed, and flew into his vision again. She had her hands on her hips, an angry expression on her face, and her wings thrummed. "Things? Do I look like a 'thing' to you?"

"No I haven't been drinking," Robert said into the phone.

"Maybe you should, it would lighten you up," the fairy said.

"I'm *not* on medication, you know that," Robert said. "Please, I need to see you right away."

"Please, I need to see you right away," she mimicked, sarcastically.

"Right, thank you," Robert said in relief. "Thank you. I'll be there in no time."

He closed his phone, slid to the side and stood up, avoiding the fairy. Ducking past her, he hurried towards his front door, and grabbed his cycle helmet, quickly strapping it on.

"Bloody hell," she said, admiringly, flying after him. "Are they remaking Rollerball? Some skid-lid."

Robert opened his front door, grabbed the crossbar of his bike and wheeled it quickly through. The fairy started to follow and he slammed the door, trapping her in the apartment. He ran down the stairs, his back wheel scraping the walls on the corners, and almost bowled two elderly people over as he burst onto the pavement.

"Sorry!" he called, jumping on the bike and cycling off, his foot slipping on the pedal without the clipless shoes he always wore. He sped across the road and down the next street, weaving around stationary cars, uncaring, desperate to get to Dr Eastmann's. He increased his speed, going up through the gears, but the lights changed to red ahead of him at a major junction and he slowed down. Something caught his eye: sitting on the pedestrian light indicator was the fairy, legs crossed, filing her nails again. The lights changed and Robert shot through a gap, a motorist honking him for his lack of road manners.

Annabelle finished her nails, blew on them, and threw the nail file in the gutter. She slid forward and took off after Robert, catching him with ease. He became aware of her flying alongside him and almost hit a car, swerving from her. He pumped his legs harder, speeding up. She kept alongside him with ease, her hair flowing out behind her, arms outstretched. He increased his speed and she matched him effortlessly.

"Red light coming up," she said, and Robert ignored her, pumping his legs furiously, gripping the handlebars with white knuckles, head down.

"There's a red light, stop!" she shouted.

Robert raced on. She halted in mid-air, covering her eyes, waiting for the crash. Screeching of tyres sounded as Robert shot across the junction, furious horns and shouts of "wanker!" followed him, but he made it across. Annabelle uncovered her eyes and breathed a huge sigh of relief. She flew on, catching him almost immediately.

"What are you trying to do, kill yourself?" she demanded angrily. "Have you any idea how much trouble I'd be in, if you did? I'm supposed to help you, not kill you. Riding like that is asking for trouble, you never heard of white van man?"

She carried on ranting, and didn't notice as Robert slowed and then pulled into the kerb. She continued flying down the street and he dismounted, hurrying across the pavement to Dr Eastmann's office. Annabelle realised she was alone and stopped, looking back, and caught sight of Robert disappearing into the building. She shook her head.

"Men," she said, exasperated.

But she wasn't bothered. Apart from the fact he'd

almost killed himself, of course. No imagination, these days, she thought. They play the most ridiculous computer games with dragons and monsters and aliens, but bring one little fairy into their real lives and they lose it altogether. She caught sight of herself in a shop window, turning left and right, admiring her shape, pushing up under her bust, checking her bottom. She nodded her head approvingly.

"Not bad," she said. "I like his style."

Annabelle looked around for the man she'd been assigned to, saw the back wheel of his bike disappearing through a door. She flew after him.

Robert hoisted the bike onto his shoulder and ran up the stairs. There was a carpeted landing and he slid the bike down, leaning it against the wall.

"You can't leave it there," came a female voice.

"It's worth over four thousand pounds," Robert said. "I can't leave it outsi..."

His voice tailed off as he realised he was replying to the fairy, who sat on the balustrade.

"Four thousand pounds?" Annabelle said, shocked. "Bloody hell, you could buy a decent car for that much. Four thousand pounds??"

Robert knocked at the door behind him and it buzzed open. He stepped inside, shutting it quickly, but thought he heard a stunned voice repeating 'four thousand pounds?' Robert entered the small waiting room, and Eastmann's receptionist had obviously gone home, as Dr Eastmann himself stood at the door to his office.

"Come through Robert, you only just caught me," he said, beckoning him in. The first time Robert had met him, he thought he looked like John Cleese, only with more hair. White wavy hair, far too long, hung over his collar, and he wore a blue shirt, with a bow tie, waistcoat and matching trousers. A gold watch chain crossed the waistcoat, and Dr Eastmann twiddled at it as he waited for Robert. He hurried into the office and Eastmann closed the door behind him. The room was big, dominated by the large leather-topped desk which sat in front of a whole wall of medical textbooks that filled floor-to-ceiling shelves. Three armchairs took up the rest of the space and Eastmann waved Robert towards them, sitting behind the desk, which was strewn with papers and files.

"Now, what's the emergency?" Eastmann asked.

Robert paced up and down, too twitchy to sit.

"When I got back to my apartment just now a... fairy was waiting for me."

"You mean a gay person? A homosexual?"

"No, a fairy. Wings, tiny wings, like in fairy stories."

Robert heard a faint jingle of bells, and the fairy appeared in mid-air in front of him. Eastmann wrote some notes on a pad.

"There you are," she said. "Now what's going on here?" She looked around the office. "Ooh, a shrink. They're not too hot on fairies unless they're discussing archetypes. Clashes with their understanding of psycho-elemental phenomena and cartesian dualism. Seriously, four thousand pounds?"

Robert started pacing again, back and forth, and the fairy flew with him, trying to see his face. He kept turning, trying not to let her.

"Go on," Dr Eastmann said. "Describe her."

"Well, she—"

"For God's sake, stand still, will you?" the fairy snapped at him. "You're making me dizzy."

Robert stopped pacing. Dr Eastmann waited. Robert looked from Eastmann to the fairy, then back at the doctor.

"She's about three and a half inches tall..."

"Three and three quarters, please," the fairy said.

"... long red hair..."

The fairy tossed her head, throwing her hair over her shoulders with both hands.

"Auburn."

41

"... silver wings..."

"Gossamer, actually. Though I do like silver."

Robert blinked as her wings turned silver.

"Is she pretty?" Dr Eastmann asked.

The fairy perked up at this, and looked at Robert very wide-eyed.

"Well..." Robert began. The fairy turned a shoulder, looked at him, kittenish. She pushed her hair back and pouted. "Erm..." She smoothed her dress down her body, accentuating her figure, coyly peeking at Robert as she pulled the dress up one leg slowly, revealing a shapely thigh.

"Yeah, I suppose so." The fairy beamed at him, and blew a big kiss. "In an ugly sort of way," he added, unable to resist.

The fairy put her hands on her hips and glared at him. He couldn't help smiling and she did, too.

"Thank you," she said to him, smoothing her hands down her thighs, looking down at herself. "I'm not sure what kind of fairy stories you used to read, but you created me, and I like your style. Much better than last time. Let's see what the shrink makes of it so far."

She flew over the desk to see what Dr Eastmann had written.

"Ooh, looks serious," she said, and Robert spoke without thinking.

"What does?"

"What does what?" Dr Eastmann asked, puzzled.

"Oh, sorry... she said—"

"She's here now? You can see her?" Eastmann asked, excitedly.

"Well... yeah... that's what I was trying to tell you."

"What is she doing?"

"Reading your notes, actually."

Dr Eastmann looked at Robert, and lifted the pad, holding it against his chest.

"What have I written?" he asked.

"Psycho-elemental phenomena," Annabelle said, shrugging. "Told you."

"Psycho-elemental phenomena," Robert said.

"Phone restaurant, rebook," she said.

"Phone restaurant, rebook," Robert dutifully repeated.

This did surprise Eastmann and he pulled the pad away and looked at it. He smiled broadly.

"Robert, you have nothing to worry about," he said, reassuringly.

The fairy zipped into Robert's vision.

"Robert, is it?" she said, and he craned to see around her.

"I don't?"

"Not a thing. It's a classic case."

"Here we go," the fairy said, sounding bored. "Cryptomnesia, I bet you."

"It's called cryptomnesia," Dr Eastmann said, smiling broadly. Annabelle licked her index finger and chalked one in the air. "Your subconscious mind has picked up everything. Even though it was upside down and you barely glanced at it, your subconscious mind was able to interpret what I wrote. You've invented this fairy, it's all from your imagination. It's hypersensitive at the moment."

"Why's it happening?" Robert asked.

"You've just come up to London to work, yes? When did your wife die?"

Robert found it hard to speak for a moment, and the fairy looked at him sympathetically. Then faded away.

"Five years ago," Robert finally managed.

"To the day, isn't it?" Eastmann asked gently.

"Is it? I don't remember."

"Come now, Robert. You know very well it is. Your mind is trying to face up to something you've pushed down very deeply into your subconscious. A fairy is always a force for good, as an archetype, and it's your subconscious trying to send you a message that it's okay to open up, and it's selected the most non-threatening persona it could invent. But you have to live in the real world, not the fantasy one your mind's trying to construct, to protect you."

"What do I do?"

"It's very simple."

CHAPTER SIX

The following day, the sunlight finally woke Robert. He'd slept on his side of the bed, and rolled onto his back and stared up at the ceiling, stretching.

"About time, lazybones, it's almost nine in the morning." The fairy sat on the edge of his bedside table, legs crossed, swinging her foot. She indicated the photo standing next to her. "Is this her? What was her name?"

Robert reached over and placed the photo face down.

"Oh, come on. The shrink must have told you to talk about it, bring it out in the open, they always do."

Robert sat up, dropping his legs over the side of the bed, got up and left the room. The fairy flew after him.

In the kitchen Robert headed for the fridge, as she flew up to him.

"Look, Robert— whoa!" Robert swung the fridge door open, forcing her to fly backwards. "Hey, watch it."

Robert took a carton of orange juice from the fridge along with a grapefruit and placed them on the breakfast bar, turning over a glass. He poured juice into the glass as the fairy landed on the tiled surface.

"Ooh, that's cold," she said, hopping from foot to foot.

Robert reached over for a chopping board, took a knife from a wooden block and sliced the grapefruit in half.

"We have to talk," the fairy said.

Robert continued to prepare his grapefruit.

"Robert?" she said. "Robert? ROBERT!" Annabelle finally shouted, as he took no notice.

He reached over and turned the radio on, singing along with 'I'm loving Angels instead' as it played. She glared at him for a moment, then pointed her finger at the radio. It turned off.

"Oh, don't tell me," she said, exasperated. "The shrink convinced you I was a figment of your imagination, made up by your subconscious mind to protect you." She strode up and down and Robert tried not to watch her. "I'm a fantasy construct, and you've got to live in the real world, right? Right?" She didn't get an answer, Robert continued to get his grapefruit ready. "All you have to do is ignore me, and I'll go away, correct? Listen Robert, I *can't* go until you find someone else to fall in love with. We *have* to work together."

Robert turned the radio back on, sat down and started eating the grapefruit. The fairy turned it off again, getting really narked.

"I bet he told you to talk to friends about it, didn't he? Hah! You probably haven't got any."

Robert's spoon paused in mid-air for a moment, then continued its journey to his mouth. The fairy strode up and down, furious; Robert could see her out of the corner of his eye. The fairy stopped suddenly, losing all her anger, and turned to face him. She sat down at the edge of the table and jumped up again, as her butt hit the cold tile. Despite himself, Robert tried to hide the small smile.

"If I'm a figment of your imagination, what harm would it do, to listen to me occasionally?"

The lurking smile disappeared and Robert snapped the radio on again. She pointed at it, and it went off.

"I have to help you find someone you'll be happy with. Someone who'll bring you some joy again, and I'm going to do it, whatever it takes, understand?"

Robert turned the radio on.

"Whether you listen to me or not," the radio announcer said in her voice, and Robert turned it off himself, horrified.

He found his ipod and headphones very useful, because that way he couldn't hear anything his imagination might dream up. He showered, and even his own imagination didn't want to see him naked, apparently, since she disappeared. He found her playing with the ginger tabby when he left the apartment to go to the Prom, and the little traitor was lapping it up. *Just ignore her, she'll go away.*

The Prom was a wonderful day out, but every time he began to think ignoring her was working, she'd re-appear. Just a wave and a smile and she'd be off, playing with any children around. It bothered him that he suspected one or two of the very young ones were involved in his psychosis, because he could see their heads moving as she flew circles in the air, following her every move. *Just my imagination. Keep repeating that.*

He was walking home, humming the Boyz II Men version of 'Just my imagination', when he realised the lyrics were also running through his head, and the gaiety of the day crashed around him, stunning him. He got back to his apartment somehow, and sat on his balcony, watching happy people go by, until it became too much, and he went to bed. The photo of Elaine had been stood upright, though he didn't remember doing it.

***

Next morning, he got up and ignored her. For the main part, she painted her nails, brushed her hair and applied some make-up to her eyes. When Robert packed his gym bag, she perked up.

"Oh, the gym, wonderful. I could sit and watch hunky men work out all day."

She sat on his handlebars as he cycled to the gym, and while he wanted to swipe her off, he thought this was giving in to his wildest imagination, so he ignored her. *She doesn't exist.*

Luckily for him, the fairy seemed interested in watching better chiselled males work out, and he was able to do his weights unmolested, ipod firmly fixed in his ears. In the locker rooms she sat on an open door waiting for him to shower, with her back turned to him. He heard her gasp as a young man walked towards the showers, with just a towel wrapped around his waist. She looked at Robert and then at the back of the man as he padded to the showers. He was an Adonis.

"I'll check the showers," she said, and flew in that direction. Robert followed her, taking the shower nearest to the lockers. Annabelle flew carefully down the central aisle between the two rows of showers. Three of them were in use at the far end, and she flew up to peer over the edge of the first, and looked over. She was about to fly on, but did a double take.

"Wow, the pool must be cold."

She flew to the next and looked over the top. Smiling blissfully, she settled herself on the rail.

"Oh, that is sooo good." She leaned further over, her eyes wide. "Oh my god, you're not going to soap it, are you? This is heaven."

She leaned back, shaking her hair out, and fell off the rail. Her wings fluttered, arresting her fall and she hovered outside the shower cubicle, rubbing her hands. It darkened suddenly, and she turned as she became aware the light was being blocked. The fattest, hairiest, nakedest man advanced towards her, and she was paralysed by the mountain of flesh approaching her. Robert heard her scream and a bang, as she shot into the locker room at supersonic speed. *Explain that one to Dr Eastmann,* he thought. *My imagination's out of control.*

Unfortunately, she'd recovered by the time Robert

left the gym, and the battery on his ipod had died, so he had to listen to her chattering, as she sat on his handlebars on the way back. Robert stopped for a pedestrian light and an attractive blonde crossed, giving him a second glance.

"How about her?" the fairy asked. "She looks good."

Robert stared ahead, and the fairy twisted her head up and saw this, looked back at the girl.

"Not wearing any underwear," she said.

Robert looked before he could stop himself, and the fairy laughed. The lights changed and they pulled away.

"So, what do you want in a woman? Looks? Personality? Good sense of humour? Younger? Older? Come on Robert, give me a clue."

He cycled on. He was almost back in Camden when he pulled into the side, and took out his mobile. 'Be spontaneous,' Dr Eastmann had said. 'That's the imagination in *this* world stimulating you.' He thumbed though his address book, and hovered over the call button, before pressing it. He didn't think they were going to answer, but they did.

"Hi, Paul, it's Rob... I'm fine, how are you both?... Actually, I'm living in London now, moved up a couple of weeks ago, just settled in, really... I know, I'm surprised, myself... Yes, working in a clinic in Hampstead... It has its ups and downs, but it's not bad... Well no, just on my way back from the gym, I wondered if you and Judy would like to... well, yes, I'd like that... I'll be there in an hour... thank you..."

He broke the connection and slipped his mobile back in his pack. The fairy flew up in front of him, and he tried not to look at her.

"I'll leave you until tomorrow," she said gently. "You'll need the time alone with them."

Robert stood for a long time, staring after her as she flew away. *My imagination is being kind to me, things are looking up.* But he didn't understand the why of it. Or the how, come to that. *Split-personality, here I come.*

He got back to the apartment and had another shower and changed. Grabbing a bottle of wine from the rack, he knew he could buy some flowers at the station, and hurried out. He sat on the underground watching the stops go by, thinking how many times he'd made this journey with Elaine asleep on his shoulder, on their way back from a concert or the theatre. Weekends in London were always great, and he knew Elaine used any excuse to book the same shows that came to Manchester, just so she could see her parents. Robert felt a twinge of remorse at how little contact he'd had with them. Maybe it was better that way, without constant reminders. But he knew that was bullshit, a sop to his own guilty conscience for not seeing them more.

He walked from the station, knowing the way by heart. He saw the scullers go by on the river; 'waterboatmen' Elaine always called them, and smiled at the memory. When he reached their house an inevitable cat sat on the front step, and miaowed at Robert as he opened the gate, standing up, waiting to be let in. Long-haired, black and white, his markings gave him a bandit look because of the mask around his eyes, but that hadn't stopped Paul from naming him Fugly, 'because he's so fucking ugly.'

"Hello, Fugly," Robert said, reaching down to fuss his head. The door opened, Fugly dashed in, and Judy stood there. She hesitated a second and then hugged him tight. He returned the hug with one arm, finding to his surprise he was pleased to be here. *Should have come ages ago.*

"It's so good to see you," Judy said as she released him.

"You too, Judy. I see Fugly's still going strong."

"I wouldn't say strong," she said, smiling. "He sleeps eighteen hours a day, and dozes the rest, as far as I can see. Goes out twice a day to check his boundaries and that's it."

She wore a blouse and long skirt, with a cardigan draped around her shoulders. More grey at the temples, he thought, but she looked good.

"How are you?" she asked. "Given up the Cornish sun for London pollution?"

"I'm okay. Frightened by the traffic most days, and the amount of people who live here, but it's been a good move. I brought you these."

He handed her the flowers and the bottle of wine. She smiled and touched his arm

"Thank you. We're out in the garden, please come on through."

He followed her past all the memories that rose up like wildflowers in a meadow, swaying gently; not demanding attention, just showing themselves, pleased to be there.

Paul was tending the barbecue, but his smile was genuine and his handshake firm. Grey hairs creeping onto his head and moustache, well muscled, looking years younger than his age, and Robert bet he still rowed every weeknight.

"So good to see you, Rob," he said. "Take the weight off your feet, and tell us what you've been up to. What do you want to drink? Beer? Wine?"

"Beer sounds good."

"Cold one? I've got some Boddington's inside."

"Cold would be great."

"Grab yourself a glass," Paul opened his icebox and tossed Robert a can of Long Life beer. Robert had to laugh.

"You can still get this?" he said.

"If you know where to look," Paul said, smiling. "Come on, sit down, the potatoes will take at least twenty minutes."

They sat on cushioned seats under a canopy, and Robert found himself talking freely of the decision to come to London, explaining how he'd rented out his house in Cornwall to pay for his apartment. He had them laughing at Ian's antics, and asked them about themselves.

"Firm paid me more money than I thought possible, to retire," Paul said. "Judy and I split our time between here and France." He raised his glass. "Living the middle-class dream."

The barbecue was delicious and the afternoon drifted on. Fugly jumped into Robert's lap, and complained every time he got up to use the toilet.

"How about you, Rob?" Paul asked, when Judy had gone inside to get desserts, and Robert knew exactly what he meant. He shrugged.

"Commitment issues, Paul. Some dalliances, nothing serious."

"She'd hate it if you moped all your life. Another beer?"

That was all they said on the subject, though they talked about Elaine, reminiscing about her childhood. *Waterboatmen*, Robert thought. *She saw them in the pond on the way to school.*

"How's Alexa?" Judy asked.

"Fine. She'll be over from Canada soon, going to stay with me for a few days."

"Bring her over, won't you?"

"Of course. She can't believe I've lived all that time in Cornwall without knowing how to cook fish, so I'm going to have to brush up."

Robert was feeling mellow by the time he left, and glad he'd come. But as he was leaving, Paul glanced at Judy and something in the look warned him.

"You have to give it to him," Paul said, and Judy went into the lounge, and came back with an envelope.

"You have to promise me not to open this until you get home," she said. "Please."

"I promise." Robert said, intrigued and fearful at the same time.

She handed him the envelope. It was faded, but he recognised her handwriting, and his heart tilted as he saw what she'd written: 'To be given to Rob, if he's on his own after five years.'

His mouth dried.

"I didn't want to send it to you," Judy said. "But

then you phoned... Don't open it until you get home, please. You know she'd be upset."

"I won't, I promise."

She hugged him and Robert held her tightly for a second. He shook hands with Paul.

"Take care, Rob. You're welcome here, any time. Come and see us in France if you want a break. Crap beer, but some good wines."

"Thank you both, for a great afternoon. I'll bring Alexa down, rather than subject you to my cooking."

Fugly complained he was going, and he fussed him goodbye. He walked the long way to the tube station, going by the river, the letter in his jacket burning a hole in his heart. He stood and watched the scullers go by, and the sounds of the river softened into melody by the distance he felt from the scene. A tube train arrived as he stepped onto the platform, and whisked him away. But not from the past, he carried that in his pocket, it had caught up with him.

When he got back to his apartment, it was getting dark, and the tabby objected to Fugly on his hands, so he stopped procrastinating and went up. He turned on the light above his armchair and took the letter from his jacket. Sitting back, he turned it over and over in his hands. Elaine was here, right here, telling him something she'd never said before, and he wanted to hear her voice, but was afraid he couldn't take it. But he opened the envelope and slid the two sheets of paper out, unfolding them. She'd written:

Do you know how much I love you? Do you know how much I want to stay with you? That I would give anything for one more year with you, one more month, one more week? The doctors just told us I had ten days, two weeks at most and I saw your anger, and your pain, and I felt the same, that I'd be leaving you. I want to be with you. I want to live my life alongside you, not sharing you with anyone, but having you all to myself, loving you the way you love me. There has been nothing more wonderful in my life than your love, and I want to stay with you, to return that love, to make you as happy as you make me.

But it's five years later, and I'm not with you. You've been on your own, and I hope I've been allowed to watch over you now and then, or there's no heaven at all. You've been given this letter by mum and dad, because you're on your own. Do you remember our first date? We went to the cinema and saw The Kid, with Bruce Willis. It was about time-travel and how he travelled back in time and changed the future. This letter is time-travelling, only it's going forward in time, not back. But it wants to change your future.

Do you know how much I want you to be happy? More than anything. Do you know how unhappy I am writing this, knowing that it might be given to you? That five years from now, you're on your own and unhappy? Did our love mean so much that you thought you'd never find the like again? That you'd never even try? That makes me more than unhappy, it fills me with sorrow. Sorrow that you might not try to be happy, when that is all I want, and it's because I've gone, that you won't try. You gave me so much happiness, and I want to give it back to you.

I hope this letter has been burned, turned to ash, and nobody ever read it but me. But if my words are being read by you, then remember only one thing: I love you. Take my love, share it with someone, and I'll be happy. Elaine. X

He held the letter to his lips, and didn't try to stop the tears. He slept on the left side of the bed.

Annabelle arrived about an hour later, and watched him as he slept, sighing now and then. She knew this was going to be a tough one. Drastic measures might be called for.

CHAPTER SEVEN

He ignored the fairy next morning, went through his usual routine, and she didn't seem that bothered. He thought about the letter so often the fairy had to yell at him for a red light. *Hell, if my imagination is keeping me alive, who am I to argue?* But Elaine's words had wrought a change in him, and he thought about Jackie, back in Cornwall. She'd become a real pal, and they'd walked the beach together, even had the odd meal in the pub, and she was good-looking and funny. But there was no spark, no ignition sequence that lifted his feelings out of the ordinary, and he valued her as a friend, nothing more. He knew he'd have to get out more often, maybe attend some postgraduate courses, get a social life.

I'll start today.

"Oh, this is where you work?" the fairy asked, as he pulled up outside the clinic. "Nice vibes from here."

He had his own key, so he parked the bike and entered the reception area. Payal looked up and smiled.

"Morning Robert," she said. "Good weekend?"

"Different, that's for sure."

The fairy had zoomed down to the counter and was staring at Payal in awe.

"Oh, she is so beautiful, is she available?"

As Robert reached her, Ashley came out of his office.

55

"Robert, how are you?"

"I'm fine. Good weekend?"

Ashley rested his hand on Payal's shoulder and she smiled, reaching up to grip his fingers, lovingly.

"Wonderful. Our sixth wedding anniversary," Ashley said, proudly.

"Boy, are they happy," the fairy said, admiringly. "Wouldn't you want that again, Robert?"

Robert was wrong-footed by this, and cursed himself for not bringing his ipod. He took his patient list from Payal and headed down the corridor. As he passed the shower room, the door opened and Pam stood there, dressed, hair swathed in a towel. She stepped aside, holding the door for him.

"Morning Robert. Want me to scrub your back for you?" she asked.

"I'm sure I'll manage, Pam. Thank you."

"Those can't be real," the fairy said, shocked, staring at Pam, but studied her face, her smile. "She seems nice enough, have you considered her?"

Robert slammed the door to the shower room.

The morning passed quickly, and the fairy didn't bother him too much, just perched on the window ledge and watched him work. She distracted a small baby while he treated the mother, and he tried not to watch her flying around it, seeing the way the baby's eyes followed her, gurgling his delight at her antics.

"You're very good at this, you know," the fairy told him as he wrote up his case-notes. "Are you allowed to date your patients? Sarah, your third patient, was very pretty, wasn't she? Should have seen the look on her face when you massaged her shoulders."

Robert headed to the staffroom for a coffee, and she kept up her inane drivel. *Surely my imagination can find better things to talk about?* As he entered the staffroom Maria was sitting in an armchair and Ian was dowsing tea bags.

"I think maybe you need—" The fairy broke off as

she took in the room. She saw Maria. "Buongiorno, Signorina," she said to her.

Maria frowned and looked up at Robert.

"What did you say?" Maria asked.

"I didn't say anything."

"She heard me!" the fairy said, excited, her wings fluttering so fast they were almost invisible.

"I thought you said..."

Ian turned. His pendulum was going crazy, swinging towards the fairy, jerking on the string.

"This is incredible, I've never seen such energy," he said, his face alight with excitement.

"She heard me!" The fairy said, turning to Robert." She's the one for you, Robert, she's meant for you."

She twirled in the air, joyful. Robert's jaw dropped, despite himself. Ian advanced on them and his pendulum bumped into the Fairy. She was too excited to notice and flew up in front of Robert's face, trying to look him in the eye. Ian's pendulum followed her.

"Robert, this is so important," the fairy pleaded. The pendulum bumped her again, and she shoved at it, irritated. Ian followed the direction it went and ended up against the wall.

"What's her name?" the fairy asked.

Still deeply shocked, Robert answered without thinking. "Maria."

"What?" Maria said.

This snapped him out of his shock and he answered, flustered, as Ian was homing in on him.

"Oh, sorry... erm, do you want a drink?"

"No," Maria said, staring at him suspiciously for a couple of seconds.

The fairy pushed at the pendulum again as Ian got close and he followed it, chortling to himself. Robert strode to the kettle, banging a cup down angrily, grabbing the jar and dashing a spoonful of coffee into it. The fairy followed, hovering alongside him

"Robert look at what's happening. It's no coincidence that... weirdo is picking me up, is it? Please, Robert, listen to me."

Robert filled his cup, spilling water on the work surface in his haste and opened the fridge for the milk.

"Robert, please. I'm begging you."

He splashed milk into his cup, shoved the milk back in the fridge and fell into the armchair furthest away from Maria. Brenda entered the room, and collided with Ian.

"Morning everyone," Brenda said cheerfully. Her face changed when she looked at Robert, turned very quizzical. "Goodness, Robert, there's something in your aura today."

"Not you as well," Robert said quietly, dejected.

"I've never seen so much energy," Brenda said brightly, coming closer. Maria glanced at him scornfully.

"I know, it's incredible, isn't it?" Ian said.

"Do you feel it, Robert?" Brenda asked, her face as lit up as Ian's.

"Feel it?" Robert burst out. "I can't shut the bloody thing up, won't leave me alone."

Brenda nodded, knowingly.

"It's trying to tell you something."

"Oh really?" Robert said. "And what if I don't want to hear it?"

"Why wouldn't you?" Brenda asked, puzzled.

"Because..." He glanced at Maria, struggled for the right words. "Just because, that's why."

The fairy settled on the arm of Robert's chair and he turned away from her.

"Robert, you have to listen to me," she said.

If he could, he'd have stuck his fingers in his ears and gone 'la, la, la,' but settled for humming loudly, trying to drown her out.

"For God's sake Robert, this is your future," she said firmly. "Listen to me."

Robert hummed a bit louder. Brenda sat down next

to Maria and started talking. Robert stopped humming only to sip his coffee.

"Please, Robert, I'm begging you. Again."

Robert closed his eyes and hummed.

"Right. That's it," she said. "I'm taking all my clothes off." Robert stopped humming, froze with his cup half way to his mouth. "You won't listen to me, I'm going to fly around butt-naked from now on. You gave them to me, let's show them off. See how you explain *that* to the shrink," she said.

Robert opened one eye, horrified. The fairy stared at him, determined.

"How did you get on with Mr Short?" Brenda asked.

"Fine," Maria replied. "Gall bladder meridian, some moxibustion."

The fairy slipped one strap of her dress down her arm, then the other. Robert opened both eyes wide, on the verge of panic.

"Did you use many needles?" Brenda asked.

The fairy pulled her dress down to her waist. She was wearing a very sexy bra, lacy material, vivid colours. She started to push the dress down further.

"Stop!" Robert called.

Silence filled the room and they all stared at him.

"Are you all right?" Brenda said, concerned.

Robert looked at Brenda, back at the fairy.

"What? Oh."

The fairy moved to push the dress down further.

"No!" Robert said, then looked at Brenda. "I mean yes... I'm okay."

Ian gave Robert a pitying look and sloped out of the room. Robert looked back at the fairy.

"Okay, I'll do it."

"Do what?" Maria asked.

"Promise?" asked the fairy.

"Yes."

Maria and Brenda exchanged looks. The fairy pulled

the dress up, slipped her arms into the straps, and adjusted them.

"Are you hearing voices?" Maria asked him, scornfully.

He stared at her, speechless.

"Tell her you had an experience with a needle when you were small," the fairy said.

"No... It's just I had an experience with a needle when I was small, had my lip sewn up. Thought I was over it, but listening to you made me remember."

"There's no problem with acupuncture needles," Maria said, bristling.

"No, I know... just reminded me, that's all."

"It's understandable," Brenda said. "And the energy in your aura has calmed a lot."

"Let's hope it stays that way," Robert said, forcing a small smile.

The rest of the day passed without any major incidents, or fairies stripping off and Robert was just opening the main door to leave when he sensed something alongside him. He jumped as he turned. Brenda stood there, and he held the door for her, following her through. The fairy hovered, obviously impatient to get going.

"I'm glad I caught you," Brenda said. "My son is getting married on Saturday, and I'd be delighted if you could come. Everyone from the centre is going, do say you will."

Robert had met Jason, Brenda's son on two occasions, and he was a good guy, with a great laugh, and seemed incredibly normal.

"I'd like that, thank you."

"I'm so pleased, I'll bring an invitation tomorrow. Goodnight."

"Bren, can I ask you something?" Robert said, as she turned to leave. "Is it possible I did something so dreadful in a previous life that I'd end up with a partner I couldn't stand, as punishment?"

"Good lord, no," Brenda said, laughing. "Free will. Nothing can be forced on you, the choices you make in life are yours and yours alone."

"That's what I thought," Robert said, glancing at the fairy, who looked bored. "Thanks Bren, have a wonderful evening."

Just as he reached the gate with his bike, he heard the main door being locked and hung back as Maria and Payal went down the steps.

"Any luck with...?" Maria asked.

"Not this month," Payal said, and she sounded despondent. "It's not for lack of trying, either."

"It'll happen soon, don't worry."

Robert waited until they were out of sight before emerging. He climbed onto the bike and the fairy sat on the handlebars, as usual, as he cycled home.

"Free will, she said, did you hear that?" Robert said. "My choice."

"I heard it, and of course it's your choice," the fairy said. "It's just that you have to choose Maria."

"I can't stand the woman and she can't stand me," Robert snorted. "She's rude aggressive, sarcastic—"

"Beautiful, sexy, sensitive—"

"Sensitive? Hah! I've seen wooden blocks that had more sensitivity. Why her?"

"I can't explain, but she heard me when I spoke Italian to her."

"Yeah, why did you?"

"Her grandmother is Italian, had a lot to do with raising her."

"Didn't do a very good job. Probably where she gets her temper from."

"She's passionate about things."

"That's one way of looking at it."

They cycled on, and Robert was amused to see her hold out her left arm as they approached a T-junction he was turning at.

"So I do exist, then?" she said.

"I bloody hope not." But he couldn't help smiling. "What was your name again?"

"Annabelle. Like Tinkerbelle, only better."

They cycled on in silence for a while.

"You said one thing about me that was true," Robert said. "When you first saw me, you said I was a loser."

"Well, you are."

"Thanks."

"You lost someone who was your whole world." Annabelle shrugged, as though the explanation was simple. "A loser."

Robert was taken aback a little, but content when he thought about it.

"How could you tell?"

"Your Heartfire was indigo."

"My what?"

"Heartfire. It reflects your soul. The flames burn brightest when you're in love and when you're with the one you love. Look at Ashley and Payal. It should be richly orange and yellow, not a dull, dark colour."

"Mine must be out."

"No, the pilot light's still on. You just need igniting, that's all."

They pulled up at a pedestrian light and watched as the blonde crossed over in front of them. She looked great.

"Won't work out, believe me," Annabelle said.

Robert smiled at the blonde and winked. She sauntered over.

"How about a ride, mister? Got a helmet I can pull on?"

Annabelle buried her face in her hands, shaking her head. Robert took a hand off, and she glided her pert bottom onto the crossbar.

"I'm not wearing underwear," she breathed in his ear.

"I know."

She jumped off and slapped his face hard.

"How dare you!" she snarled, and stalked off.

"Told you," Annabelle said. "But do keep trying."

They made it back to the apartment and Robert showered. When he walked into the living room, Annabelle was playing with Tabby.

"How did he get in here?" Roberts asked.

"I showed him how to climb up the balconies. He's very lonely, his owners are out all the time."

Robert opened a tin of tuna at Annabelle's insistence, and the cat curled up on the rag rug, purring, after it polished off half of it. Robert used the other half to make a sandwich.

"How did it go, yesterday?" Annabelle asked. "They must have been pleased to see you."

"Yeah, it was a good day..." his voice tailed off.

"What? What is it?"

Robert considered Annabelle, thinking hard.

What the hell? he thought, and retrieved Elaine's letter from the jacket he'd hung on the hook in the toilet. He spread both sheets on the breakfast bar. Annabelle studied his face for a moment, and then flew over, landing next to them. She walked on the pages as she read the letter, and tears were rolling down her face by the time she got to the end.

"Oh, that is beautiful," she said, sniffing, dabbing at her eyes with the hem of her skirt, showing a lot of leg. "I wish I'd known her." She glanced at Robert. "I have to go out for while, I'll see you tomorrow."

"Okay."

She took off and then flew back, grabbing Robert's cheek and kissing him noisily. Then she shot out of the window and the tabby raised his head, alarmed.

"It's okay," Robert reassured him. "She'll be back."

He was surprised to find he was happy about that.

CHAPTER EIGHT

Saturday dawned bright, and the forecast was good, so Robert wore a light suit for the wedding. Annabelle chose his tie for him, insisting the blue one didn't go with the colour of his jacket. She'd not been pushy all that week, and even suggested he might meet someone at the wedding, which made him very suspicious. He was beginning to enjoy her company, strangely, wondering if enjoyable delusions were as bad as scary ones. Annabelle wore a white crinoline for the wedding, with tiny white shoes, the first he'd seen her in, and tied miniature daisies in her hair. .

"Where do you get those from?" he asked her.

"Not this world. How do I look?"

She pirouetted in the air, and her skirts billowed.

"Terrific. Shame you're not my size."

Annabelle grinned, and he had to smile.

"You look so much better when you smile," she said. "I'm glad you're doing it more often."

He pulled a mock long face.

"Let's go. There's an open-topped bus we can get, I hate the tube in the summer."

The bells were ringing as they approached the church, and they just beat the bride in as she arrived in a horse-drawn carriage. Robert hurried in and took a service leaflet from the usher. The church was quite a small one, with stained-glass windows throwing multi-coloured light across the congregation. Robert's tiny, lingering, so unfair doubt that Annabelle had really been sent by the devil to plague him disappeared as she flew into the church happily without bursting into flames. Both sides were packed with guests and he couldn't spot a free seat. He walked slowly up the aisle, hoping the wedding march wouldn't start before he found one.

Annabelle stopped at one bench and he heard her speak over the organ music.

"Mi scusi, per favore."

The woman on the end shifted up the bench and Robert gratefully dropped into the space created, just as the organ began to blast out the wedding march. Robert turned to thank the woman, and saw it was Maria. She wore a powder-blue dress, with a pattern of swirls, deeper blues and greys that showed her figure off, and she had on that perfume again, They stared open-mouthed at each other for a second, and then stood with the rest of the congregation. Annabelle wasn't anywhere to be seen.

The service was bright and the sermon mercifully short. As the vicar gave his final blessing to the couple and they kissed, Annabelle flew above them sprinkling them with what looked like stardust. *Let's hope none of them have allergic asthma.* After the bridal party passed down the church Robert stepped into the aisle to let Maria out. She actually smiled at him, and then Payal followed her, looking stunningly gorgeous in the most colourful sari. Ashley followed her, smiling, and Robert walked out with him.

Photos were taken, people milled around, the official bossy photographer did a good job, and confetti and stardust was thrown all around. Robert stuck with Ashley, Payal and Maria, though Pam and Christina joined them briefly before circulating. Robert was listening to Payal at one point and Maria was standing next to her. She wore a minimal amount of make-up, and he became acutely aware of the hair over her ear. As he watched, a lock of it escaped, and flowed down the side of her face. His hand was reaching out to replace it when he realised with horror what he was about to do, and made a poor job of coughing into his hand instead.

Maria's face suddenly lit up, and Robert almost had to take a step back. A bridesmaid, aged about five, pretty as a picture, rushed towards Maria and she bent down and scooped her up.

"Rosie, you were wonderful!" Maria cried, and Robert couldn't believe the vibrancy in Maria's eyes, the change in her. Maria kissed the bridesmaid, and whirled her round, before settling her on her hip.

"Rosie is Brenda's niece," Payal said. "Rosie, this is Robert."

"Hello Rosie," Robert said, and she buried her head in Maria's neck, shy. A sudden movement of atoms told Robert that Brenda had arrived, and sure enough, there she was, beside him.

"And she's wanted for the photos," Brenda said.

She reached out and Rosie went to her happily.

"Ooh, you're much too heavy, young lady. No wedding cake for you!"

"It was a lovely service," Maria said, but Brenda pulled a slight face and walked away. Rosie looked back at them over Brenda's shoulder and Robert waved his fingers at her and winked. She smiled.

"Can that woman fold time and space?" Robert said.

"Who?" Ashley asked.

"Brenda. She appears out of thin air all the time, it's very unnerving."

"She's quite upset about the wedding," Maria said. "She was hoping for a New Age ceremony in the forest, but the bride's father put his foot down."

"They look so happy," Payal said.

They all looked at the bride and groom, who did

appear loved-up and genuinely happy. Robert saw Annabelle from time to time, usually zooming around the children. After all the photos had been taken, the bride and groom left in the horse-drawn carriage and Robert had to smile at Annabelle perched on the top of one of the horse's heads, waving to the crowds. Ashley drove the four of them to the reception, and Robert was pleased Payal got in the back with Maria, though he kept seeing the errant strands of hair, and his hand kept twitching.

The reception was held at a grand hotel surrounded by lawns which swept down to a small river. Ashley and Payal had taken a room, and disappeared with their bags, leaving Robert with Maria. They followed other guests into the hotel and were directed through to the back. An enormous Marquee had been attached to a large conservatory, which had a bar along one side, with staff waiting to dispense drinks. Ornate chandeliers hung from the roof of the marquee, and white carpeting was laid with the wedding tables all adorned with fantastic roses and lilies.

"Wow," Robert said. "Beats a New Age forest ceremony, I'd say."

He saw Maria tried to hide the smile and thought she should smile more often. Just like Annabelle had told him to. A scrum developed around the table plan as people checked where they were sitting. All the clinic staff were on one table, bar Brenda, who sat on the top table, and Robert was disconcerted to find he was between Maria and Pam. Champagne was served, and the noise levels grew. At one point Maria turned to him, and he was surprised when she spoke.

"Great wedding, isn't it?"

"Perfect. Doesn't get any better than this."

There was a slightly awkward silence, and she leaned a little closer to him. How he stopped his hand replacing the hair was a testament to iron will and the desire not to be slapped, really.

"Robert... do you speak Italian?"

"No," Robert replied, too quickly. "No, I don't. Why?"

"In the church, I thought you spoke Italian, asked me to move..."

Robert looked around for Annabelle. Nowhere to be seen. Typical.

"No, I don't, did some French at school, but no Italian."

"Oh... that's very weird..."

"You speak Italian, then?" he asked, seeking a way out. *Wait till I see that fairy...*

"Yes, I learnt it as a little girl."

"Your grandmother, wasn't it?"

He could have kicked himself when she looked at him in astonishment.

"How do you know that?" she asked, her eyes wide, more hair falling over her ear.

"Oh... er... I think someone mentioned something..."

"I've never told anyone about my childhood," she said, and he thought she was getting angry. "How did you know?"

"It was... I think I—"

"Tell her you got it in the meditation!" came Annabelle's shout.

"In the meditation, that was it," he said hurriedly. "There was an older woman you spoke to in what sounded like Italian... Looked a bit like you..."

"You said you didn't get anything from the meditation," she said, and the suspicious look was back. He tried not to look at the hair.

"Yeah, I was a bit embarrassed, I thought it was just my mind making things up, never done mediation before..."

Robert was saved by the Master of Ceremonies announcing a ten minute break before the speeches, and hastily excused himself. He stretched his legs outside, watching the children playing with a football. Rosie wasn't allowing her bridesmaid's dress to hamper her, she had a mean left foot. Annabelle flew up to him.

"Isn't it beautiful?" she gushed. "I love weddings."

He glanced around to make sure nobody was nearby, before speaking.

"What did you say to Maria to make her move?"

"'Excuse me, please' in Italian. Worked well, didn't it? She looks lovely, doesn't she?"

"No, she looks... all right. She thinks I spoke to her in Italian, you landed me right in it."

"I didn't mention her grandmother, that was you. Got you out of it, though, didn't I?"

"Why don't you tell her in Italian that I'm meant for her, and see what that does? She'd run a mile, break the world record."

"She doesn't hear me in the same way you do, it's more like a tiny quiet voice inside her head."

"Lucky her, she can probably ignore it more easily," he said, but he smiled.

The call to return for the speeches came and Robert wasn't sure if he was pleased that Maria had re-captured the errant hair, but she didn't look at him as he sat down, which was a relief.

"Going to dance with me later?" Pam asked him, nudging. She looked great in a flared skirt and bolero jacket and blouse.

"Of course, wouldn't miss it. I think I have a waltz on my card."

"Sod the waltz, can you jive?"

A twinge wracked Robert for a moment, as he remembered. "Actually, I can, though I haven't done it for a few years."

"I'll lead," Pam said. "Just hold on to me."

"That'll be easy," he said and she laughed. Her nose wrinkled when she laughed, and he liked her a lot.

The speeches were relatively brief, and Robert looked forward to the Best Man's effort - a good Best Man's speech was invariably funny, and often embarrassing for the bride and groom. He recalled his own, briefly, and wondered what Chris was doing these days, making a mental note to try and get in touch again. The MC announced the Best Man and moved the microphone down to a good-looking guy aged in his mid-thirties.

"I'm not crazy about making speeches," he began. "But I've been married for ten years myself, and this is the one chance I'll have, to see if my mouth still works."

"Works for me, baby!" came a shout, obviously his wife, which brought laughter.

"Thank you for that reference, darling," The Best Man said. "You always told me I was bad-mouthing you." There was more laughter. "You know, it's not that difficult to find Miss Right. Although her first name usually turns out to be 'always.'"

There was more laughter, especially from the men, and Robert thought he heard the sonic boom Annabelle always made when she was in a hurry. She shot into the marquee, swerved around a pillar and headed straight at him, frantic.

"But can any man tell me what's the only way to have the last word in an argument?" the Best Man asked.

Robert barely heard what Annabelle said, but was galvanised into instant action.

"No!" he shouted, jumping to his feet, his chair tipping over. He raced across the dance floor as the guests stared at him. "Get out of the way!"

He leaped the top table, scattering glasses and cutlery. The Best Man staggered back, shocked, and knocked the wedding cake over. Robert pushed the MC out of his way, vaulted another table, and dashed out of the marquee. There was angry shouting and chaos as other guests streamed out after him.

Robert sprinted down the slope, his heart pounding, racing past children heading up towards the marquee. His shoes shot off his feet with his speed and he tugged his jacket off frenziedly, throwing it from him, desperate to get to the river. He scarcely heard the shouts behind him, concentrating on Annabelle, who zoomed in front of him, over the river surface, hovering a few inches above the water, moving sideways with the current. He didn't slow, launched into a racing dive over the reeds and the cold of the water almost made him gasp. He could barely see in the green murk, but kicked strongly, pulling hard with his arms, drawing himself down as the water darkened, searching. His diaphragm spasmed, desperate to breathe, and he ignored it, kicking stronger. His hand collided with something, and he felt cloth under his hands. He kicked forward, got both hands around her and pulled up, scissoring his legs frantically.

He broke the surface, gasping in air, and turned Rosie, bringing her head out of the water, shifting onto his side to hold her clear. He heard the screams, saw the shocked faces, pulled with his free arm and side-kicked towards the bank.

"Get a doctor!" someone shouted. Guests splashed into the reeds and took Rosie's limp body from him, hauling her up onto the bank. The Best Man offered his hand and Robert took it, helped out by Ashley and another guest. Robert stood, slumped forward, hands on his knees, trying to recover.

"Call an Ambulance!" Maria screamed and a dozen people hauled their mobiles out. She reached Rosie and skidded to her knees. Maria checked Rosie's mouth, tipped her head and began CPR. Annabelle hovered anxiously in the air. Maria pressed rhythmically on Rosie's chest, over and over and she coughed, bringing up water. Maria quickly turned her on her side, and she choked up more as Maria pushed on her back, holding her head. Rosie coughed and choked, and began jerking as she brought up more water. She took in great gasps of air, trying to cry, but spluttering and coughing shook her.

"Oh my god!" came a scream and a woman looking a lot like Brenda pushed through the onlookers. "Rosie!"

"She's all right," Maria called, as the woman scrambled to her. "She's all right."

Rosie began to cry in earnest and Maria lifted her to

her mother, who clasped her in her arms weeping. Maria looked at Robert, and nodded. He slumped forward to his knees, relief taking the last of his strength from him. A siren sounded in the distance, and Maria stood, helping Rosie and her mother up, with others aiding.

"Get her to the ambulance," Maria said. "She's going to be all right."

A crowd of people surrounded Rosie and her mother, helping her as they hurried up the slope towards the building.

"I'm going to stay with Rosie," Annabelle said. "Are you okay?"

Robert managed to nod. She gave him a big smacking kiss on his cheek and shot off after the departing crowd. Robert was helped to his feet by the Best Man and Ashley. The Best Man held his hand out and shook Robert's.

"I don't know how you did that, and I don't care," he said. "Fucking ace. You try and buy any drinks for the rest of the day, and I'll throw you back in, okay?"

He clapped Robert on the arm, and walked away.

"Are you okay?" Maria asked.

"Yeah, I think so."

"I've got spare clothes in our room you can have," Ashley said. "I was going to change for the evening, but you take them. You can use our shower." He hesitated, examining Robert's face. "How did you know?"

Maria looked at him, waiting for the answer. He shrugged.

"I... just knew. I think I heard the children shouting... but I just knew..."

They both studied him, and he shrugged again. *Maybe I should tell them.*

"No other explanation, is there?" Ashley said, smiling. "Who cares? Without you two, I'd hate to think what would have happened."

Robert looked at Maria, and they both blinked.

"Come on, you'll catch cold," Ashley said.

A small boy brought Robert his jacket and shoes as they walked up to the hotel, and his wallet and mobile phone were intact. Wedding guests kept shaking his hand. He was intensely aware of Maria alongside him, that perfume again. Brenda almost suffocated him, hugging him so tight he swore his clothes were dry when she let go, crying tears of relief. Eventually he managed to extricate himself and Ashley led him up to his room. It was expensively luxurious and Robert hurried into the bathroom, trying not to drip on the thick carpet.

"Here," Ashley said, laying clothes on top of a marble-topped washstand. "The trousers have an adjustable waistband, should fit you okay. I'll get yours cleaned, they do a two-hour service here."

"Thanks Ashley, I appreciate it."

"No problem. I'll leave you to it, see you downstairs."

"Great."

It took him a while to work out the shower, but he turned it up and luxuriated in the heat. The shower gel promised to be lime, basil and mandarin, which Robert thought probably belonged in a fruit salad, but he used it anyway, and a shampoo that contained magnolia. He hoped there weren't too many bumble bees on the prowl when he went out, or he'd be engulfed.

The towel was Egyptian cotton, the thickest and softest he'd ever laid hands on, and it seemed a shame to get it wet, but he rubbed himself dry and tied it round his waist as he used the hair-dryer. He turned it off and had just put it back in the receptacle when the door opened and he heard Payal's voice, speaking with a lazy drawl.

"Well, what do you think?"

She stood with one arm leaning up the doorjamb, the other hand on her hip and her hair was loose, tumbling over her shoulders. The white stockings gave a contrast with her brown skin that was electrifying, and the suspender belts had red flowers. Her bra was white gossamer and see-through. The red shoes with high heels stretched her legs perfectly.

They both froze, and stared into each other's eyes for what seemed like minutes. Robert gave the only answer he could.

"Absolutely breathtaking," he said slowly.

He saw her mouth twitch.

"Probably best not to mention this to Ashley," she said, still not moving.

"Agreed. Would it be okay if I dreamed about it now and then?"

"That would be perfectly acceptable," she said and then her smile almost knocked him over. She put both hands over her mouth and giggled, making him grin so wide it hurt his mouth. He closed the door and heard her giggling for ages, as he got dressed. When he came out, the bedroom was empty except for her perfume. *Helluva woman.*

CHAPTER NINE

By the time he got downstairs, his pulse was almost normal. Brenda met him as he walked through the hotel and hugged him again.

"They're keeping her in tonight for observation," she said, "but she's fine, bouncing round like a button, demanding to be allowed to come back."

"If it was me, I'd let her," Robert said. "Keep her away from the river, obviously."

"I'm so glad you were there, Robert. Bless you."

She hugged him again and as he made his way through the hotel, everyone seemed determined to shake his hand. A four-piece band was playing and people were dancing when he reached the Marquee, but as he headed towards his table people got to their feet and applauded him. The music died away, and everyone in the marquee joined in. He could feel his face burning, and it crept up to his ears. The clinic staff all stood, clapping, and he shook his head, mortified, more embarrassed than he thought possible at the fuss.

It can't get any worse than this.

He turned and bowed to four directions, hoping they'd all stop. Eventually they did, and he sat down. Payal wore a pleated skirt, almost a kilt in its patterning, and a stunning light blue woollen top, with a string of pearls. And white tights. Or stockings. He daren't look at her face.

"Ladies and gentlemen, we've had a request from Pam Mackintosh for a particular piece of music, and she's asked that you clear the floor for her and our hero, Rob."

It just got worse.

Pam put on that high-stepping walk that professional dancers always did, swaying her hips, and lifted him out of his chair by his tie. She gripped the lapels of his jacket and flipped it off his shoulders, pulling it down to raucous cheers from the guests, as she let it fall to the floor.

Pam led him by the tie to the dancefloor. She turned, and when he looked into her blue eyes, he saw how nervous she was, how badly she wanted it, so he gave in, relaxed his shoulders, rolling his neck. She slid her feet apart and held out her left hand. He took it, matching her stance. She raised her right hand and clicked her fingers. The band swung into 'Stuck on you' and they danced.

Pam did lead him at times, but he was amazed how much came back once he started, losing himself in the movements, seeing only her, the steps coming without conscious thought. They jived their way through the whole thing, covering the entire floor, and he enjoyed it more than he thought possible. As they did their final crossover, he lifted her arm, pirouetted her twice and clasped her to him in perfect time as the music died. She almost bounced from him, but he managed to hold on to her.

He saw glitter falling around them, and glanced up to see Annabelle flying a circle above them, raining fairy dust, grinning like a Cheshire cat. He unwound Pam to arm's length and bowed to the applause as she curtsied. She pivoted across him and they repeated this in the other direction. Robert clapped his hands to the band and the leader gave him a big thumbs-up as he took Pam's hand and led her back to the table.

"That was fantastic!" Maria said, surprising him, as they crowded round.

"Pam led, I followed," Robert said, and the smile Pam gave him made it worthwhile. Her eyes positively shone with happiness, and he felt good.

"Thank you, Robert," she said.

A Jeraboam of champagne arrived at their table in an enormous ice-bucket, and the wine waiter said it was courtesy of the Best Man. Robert saw him across the room and raised a glass in salute, receiving one in return.

"I didn't know you could dance like that," Ashley said. "It was amazing."

"Neither did I," Robert said. "It's years since I learned jive, but Pam is fantastic."

She tipped her head slightly and winked at him.

I'm enjoying myself. When was the last time that happened?

The band started playing, Ashley took Payal onto the dance floor and Pam was surprised when a good-looking guy asked her to dance, but leapt to her feet immediately.

"Care to dance?" Robert asked Maria, carried away with the feelings inside him.

"I'd like that," she said, and he led her to the dancefloor.

She moved really well, and Robert was almost sorry when the music stopped. They applauded the band and there was that awkward moment before the next music started. It was slow and Robert held out his arm to indicate the table, about to ask if she'd like another drink when she stepped forward, and his arm slotted around her waist. She took his other hand, and rested her free hand on his shoulder. He held her loosely, and they moved slowly in circles. He heard her sigh, and she pulled herself to him, their bodies touching, and laid her head on his left shoulder, turning their hands in, resting them on his chest. Her perfume was wonderful and her hair against his cheek was soft. His breath caught.

Can she hear my heart beating? Feel it racing?

He wanted the music to go on and on, but it

stopped. Maria lifted her head and kissed his cheek.

"Thank you," she said, and stepped away from him. He followed her from the floor in a daze. He didn't know if she was thanking him for the dance, or for saving Rosie, but he felt light-headed with emotion, suddenly uncertain.

"Look whose Heartfire has ignited!" called Annabelle, swirling in happy circles above him.

He danced with Christina, and then Brenda, and helped Pam drag Ian onto the floor, and laughed. A lot. When Ashley asked Maria to dance he glanced across at Payal, who looked back mischievously at him.

"Stop thinking about it," she said, trying not to smile

"Only if you'll dance with me."

She felt warm in his arms and they laughed for no good reason other than their shared secret. He was certain he could feel a suspender belt pressing into his thigh at one point, and her giggle told him it was true.

I thought this lot were the flakiest chocolates in the box, and now I love them all.

The band took a break and the disco was a bit loud, so he left the marquee for some fresh air. It was a balmy evening, and he wandered down to the river. Annabelle caught up with him and he saw she'd changed back into her clinging dress, though the daisies were still in her hair. He checked to make sure nobody was near him.

"Everyone's thanking me, but I didn't say thank you to you," he said. "Without you..."

"But I couldn't do anything," she said, smiling. "Needed you to believe in me, and you did. You think I *do* exist."

"You know... against Dr Eastmann's advice, against my better judgement, against all rational explanations, I actually hope that you do."

She kissed his cheek, and he tried to ignore the triumphant look on her face.

"You and Pam looked great on that dancefloor."

Robert laughed.

"Pam's like my best pal. She's a little girl looking for acceptance from everyone around her, and I hope she finds someone who appreciates her."

"So, Maria then...?"

"Robert?"

Ashley caught up with him just as he reached the stone bridge that crossed the river.

"Oh, hi Ashley. Great evening isn't it?" Robert said, a little guilty, half-expecting Ashley to demand to know what happened between him and Payal in the bathroom.

"Yeah. You escaping the disco, too?"

"God, yes. You know, I can't even remember enjoying music that loud when I was young."

"Yeah, you're such an old man," Ashley said.

"You know what I mean."

They leaned against the bridge. Annabelle flew loops under the arch and over their heads, and Robert enjoyed the relative tranquillity.

"We've been trying for a baby, you know," Ashley suddenly said.

"I heard," Robert said. "Through the walls mostly."

Ashley laughed, embarrassed.

"Yeah, well... Payal has this temperature thing, shows ovulation, and when it goes off, we... you know. Can happen any time."

Robert stared at Ashley open-mouthed for a moment.

"Wait, let me get this straight. Any time, day or night, the temperature hits the jackpot, your wife drags your clothes off and you two get it on?" Robert shook his head, admiringly. "You're living the dream, Ashley, you really are."

And boy, are you in for a great night.

"Yeah, I know. But..."

"But what?"

Robert saw Ashley struggle to find the words.

"It's just... we've tried everything... I'm not sure it's ever going to happen."

"It'll happen, Ashley," Robert said emphatically.

"Well..."

"Well, what?"

"Well... what if it's not supposed to happen?"

"What? Give over, of course it'll happen."

"Is this the sort of world we should bring kids into? Look what happened today."

"Ash, that was an accident."

"Yeah, and what would have happened if you weren't here?" Ashley paused, and Robert couldn't think of what to say. Annabelle had stopped her flying antics and stood on the bridge, hands folded in front of her. "Just not sure I'm cut out for that sort of responsibility. Not everyone is a good father... or..."

Robert gripped Ashley's shoulder for a moment.

"Worrying about it won't help. I'm sure every couple goes through this."

"You're probably right," Ashley sighed. "Oh, by the way," he added, perking up. "There's a weekend break booked for the team, we're going up to the Lake District, do it every year. It's in three weeks, I forgot to tell you."

"Right. Sounds good."

"Reduces the tax bill, good team building, that kind of thing."

"Great."

Ashley looked up and saw Payal waving for him to come back. "I'd better go, looks like Payal needs me."

Robert watched him walk away, and hoisted himself up to sit on the stonework of the bridge.

"Poor guy," Annabelle said.

"Yeah."

Ashley passed Maria heading towards the bridge, she held two bottles of beer.

"I'm going to keep an eye on the children," Annabelle said. "Can I trust you on your own?"

"Managed before you arrived, didn't I?"

"Duh." They both smiled. "Just enjoy yourself, will you?"

"Yes, dear."

"If you want to ask Maria how her grandmother is, say this: 'comé sta tua nonna? Okay?"

"What does it mean?" Robert asked, suspicious, and Annabelle laughed.

"How is your grandmother. Trust me. 'comé sta tua nonna?' Got it?"

She flew off in the direction of the children, and Maria reached him. She handed him a bottle.

"Thank you."

"Going in again?" Maria said, indicating the river.

"No but Brenda is, if she thanks me one more time."

She smiled, and they clinked bottles. She slipped off her shoes, and sat beside him.

"I thought you'd lost your head," she said.

"Oh, thank you very much," Robert said, with as much indignation as he could muster, and liked her laugh. "The Best Man was about to give away our only secret weapon in an argument, I had to stop him, somehow."

Maria looked at him quizzically.

"A man should always have the last words in an argument." Robert quoted, pausing theatrically. "Even if they are 'yes dear'".

Maria laughed and Robert couldn't help smiling. A moment passed between them as they glanced at each other, both looked away at the same time.

"I'm so glad you were here,"

"Do you want a swim?" Robert said sternly.

He nudged her shoulder, she pushed back at him.

"How did you know?" she asked. "Really?"

"I'm honestly not sure... just knew, somehow... something told me."

"I'm not a thing!" he heard Annabelle shout.

"Hey, I don't care. I just thought... it's just that I keep hearing things myself... in Italian..."

She looked at him, obviously expecting a reaction, but he nodded, then smiled.

"What? Things like: comé sta tua nonna?"

Maria dropped her bottle in astonishment and it hit the bridge and fell in the river. She nearly followed it and Robert grabbed her shoulder, as she clutched at his arm.

"How do you know that?" Maria asked, astonished. "You *do* speak Italian!"

"No, I promise you, it's a phrase someone taught me."

"Do you know what it means?"

"How's your grandmother," Robert said, and had a sudden terrible suspicion. "Doesn't it?"

"Si, é vero. It was the traditional way of courtship in my grandmother's times."

"What?"

"The man always asked the woman about her family, starting with her grandmother, then her grandfather, then her mother, her father, and so on. After half an hour or so, when he's covered all the relatives, he'd ask her to walk with him. With chaperones, of course, very old-fashioned."

"I'll say. Wait till I find her."

"Who?"

"The person who taught me it."

Maria laughed and Robert had to smile. They looked at each other, and the lock of hair escaped from behind her ear. He reached out and smoothed it back into place, leaving his hand touching her head. They stared into each other's eyes and he slowly leaned in and their lips met tentatively. It deepened into a passionate kiss and Maria's arm came up around his neck, pulling him close. His arm snaked around her waist and the kiss went on and on.

Maria suddenly jerked back, pushed his arm away and jumped down.

"I'm sorry," she said, not looking at him as she slid her feet into her shoes. "I can't... I mean... I've just broken up from a relationship... I'm not ready..."

"It's all right," Robert said. "I'm coming out of a long-term relationship, myself."

"I'm sorry," she said, and hurried away, head down.

See what happens when you let your guard down?

It was two in the morning when Christina's husband dropped him within walking distance of his apartment, and he strolled back along the streets, quite saddened by the turn of events. Tabby waited for him, following him up the stairs, and he didn't have the heart to reject him. The cat made a beeline for the rug; Robert thought he could leave the window open for him to get out, if he wanted to. He made a coffee and sat in his chair on the balcony.

He'd danced with all of them, but there was only one perfume that lingered on him.

Don't fall in love with her.

He fell asleep with that thought in his head.

Robert walks along the sandy beach. He's wearing swimming shorts, and the sun's warmth is comforting. The sea and the sky are impossibly blue, and there's a figure sitting on the outcrop of rock. It's Annabelle, only she's full-sized, no wings, just a stunning halter-neck red bikini, and she looks sensational. She smiles as he approaches.

"Hello, Robert."

"How did I get here?" Robert asks, confused.

"It's just a dream, don't worry about it." She stands up and dusts sand off her legs. "Let's walk."

They stroll down to the edge of the sea, along the lapping water and she takes his hand.

"What are you afraid of?" she asks, gently.

"I don't know," he says. "Finding someone and losing them again. Being on my own."

"You've been on your own for five years," she said, quietly. "You know what Elaine thinks of that."

"I know," he said, sighing. "You push it down so deep, you think it's gone forever, but it surfaces, the hurt."

"I know. But you have to face it, to move on."

He looks along the beach.

"I'd like to stay here, it's so... safe, I guess."

"Life isn't safe, there are always risks to be taken. It's

when they pay off that the rewards are worth it, and the risk-taking becomes growth."

He pulls a face, wondering if he should tell her.

"It'll happen," she says, interrupting his train of thought. "Promise me you'll try."

"I promise."

She stops him, stands in front of him and slips both arms around his neck, pressing against him, and kisses him sensuously.

"I'll help you," she says.

He's suddenly alone.

"Stay here as long as you like." Her voice comes from nowhere. "Your heart's desire is here, if you know where to look."

He turns and looks along the beach behind him, then back the way he was facing. In the far distance he sees a figure, hair flowing out behind her, but can't make out who it is. He starts to run along the sand and hears a siren in the distance.

Robert woke on his balcony as a police car wailed its angry cry in the street below. He wanted to join in, but remembered to drink some water and hauled himself into bed.

CHAPTER TEN

He'd woken and drank more water during the night, and hadn't felt that bad when he finally dragged himself up midmorning. He punished himself by stepping into the shower before it had warmed up, and briefly considered the gym, but discarded it in favour of fresh croissants and a Sunday paper. Hangovers always felt worse in warm weather. He was reading the sports pages when Annabelle arrived.

"Oh, you're up," she said. "Didn't think we'd see you until mid day, at least. How do you feel?"

He knew she didn't mean physically.

"Confused," he said. "Annabelle, can I ask you something? Did you see the moment my... heartfire ignited?"

She thought about it for a second.

"No. When I returned you were dancing with Pam – Rosie's fine, by the way, they discharged her this morning – and I didn't taken any notice, to be honest. I was dazzled by your footwork."

"Ha ha."

"It was after you stopped dancing with Maria, as you walked back to the table I really saw it."

Robert was lost for a moment, reminiscing.

"I think her perfume must have been exothermic," he said. "But she can't—"

"Yes, she can," Annabelle interrupted. "She's hurt and trying to get over someone, but you both took such a massive step last night. Don't lose it now."

Robert stared at her, trying to take in what she was saying.

"Speak to Ashley about it," she said.

"Ashley?" Robert asked, shocked.

"Maria and Payal are really good friends. He'll know what happened with Maria and the last boyfriend. Maybe you should tell her about Elaine."

"When I'm ready," he said, his heart beating a little too fast. "I don't want the sympathy vote to sway emotions, I hate people feeling sorry for me."

"I know. But look how much you've changed in the last few weeks."

"Thanks to you."

She huffed on her nails and polished them on her chest, smiling.

"Did you send that dream last night?" he asked.

"What dream? I wish I *could* send dreams, would make my job a lot easier, putting ideas straight into your subconscious mind, even if Freud would disapprove. What was it about?"

Oh... nothing really."

"So, what are you up to today?"

"Recovering mostly. Alexa's arriving on Wednesday, I promised her I'd take her out to a show, thought I'd check those agencies that sell last-minute tickets."

"Who's Alexa?"

"My sister. She lives in Canada, one of those incredibly successful bankers on obscene salaries you read about all the time. She was Elaine's best friend."

"What's she like?"

"Wonderful. Bossy. Pushy. Loving. Reminds me of someone I know, funnily enough."

He swore Annabelle blushed.

"I'm meeting her at Gatwick Airport, she'll stay one

night, go up and see mum and dad, then come back down for the weekend." He hesitated for a second. "I was thinking of asking the others over on Sunday, to meet her. She suggested it."

"I like her already!" Annabelle exclaimed.

Robert grinned.

"You coming with me, then?" he said, folding up the paper. "Might need you to tell me where the best seats are, they always try and sell you the crap ones first."

"Let's go," she said, smiling.

Robert got up and she flew through as he held the door for her.

"Thank you, kind sir."

"Nice bikini, by the way," he said conversationally.

"Oh, thank you, I..."

She hovered and tried to look cross and stamp her foot, but only bobbed up and down in the air.

"That was sneaky," she said, wagging a finger.

"And what you did, wasn't?"

She smiled, knowingly, and he had to smile back.

"Where was I? In the dream? It was the same place as the meditation."

"It's an inner world," she said. "Half way between yours and mine. You know I'd been sitting on that rock for days before you first came?"

"Seriously? Why?"

"Your heart was calling. You were resisting, but I figured you'd be along soon, and didn't want to miss you. I acted really bad-tempered, said all that stuff so you'd remember me when the meditation finished."

"It worked very well, thank you. I think. You know, in the dream, there was someone else there, when you'd gone."

"Really?" Annabelle looked at him intently. "Who was it?"

"I don't know, she was too far off. I started running towards her and a bleeding police siren woke me."

"Who do you think it was?"

"I don't know... she had long hair, that's all I saw."

"I told you your heart's desire was there, didn't I?" Annabelle said, knowingly.

"You did... and that's the last time I support my local bobby."

In truth, part of Robert was glad the siren had woken him. His heart's desire was still Elaine, and it would have been too cruel to see her and then be wrenched away.

Annabelle stayed close to Robert for the day - she got him the best seats in the theatre by looking over the shoulder of the girl selling them, and distracted him when he came to pay, so he didn't see how much they were. She was a little embarrassed about the dream, but Robert was such a lovely guy, and he deserved her best possible effort.

***

Monday found Robert approaching the clinic nervously. He'd noticed Annabelle hadn't brought the subject up, and was quite grateful. She'd be around most of the times, but he'd see her flying with butterflies outside, or settling on big flowers, inhaling the scent. He thought of speaking with her about what bothered him most, but decided against it. He parked his bike and his heart quickened a little as he ran up the steps.

I hope she's not wearing that perfume. I hope she is wearing that perfume. I hope she's not... should I ask her what it is, and buy some?

Payal's smile made him less anxious, and by the way her eyes danced impishly, he thought her weekend had been good. He didn't see Maria until the mid-morning break. She was sitting in her room with the door open as he passed, and she looked up briefly, flushing slightly as she saw him.

"Hi," he said. He didn't want to crowd her, so he

stood in the open door. "Listen, about Saturday, I'm sorry I was a bit forward."

"It's okay." Her eyes half-met his and flicked away.

"Look, would it be okay if I asked you out for a drink one evening? Crowded pub, loads of people. No rain, obviously," he added as an afterthought.

She hid the smile. He took a deep breath.

"I know we got off on the wrong foot, and we're both pretty raw, but I really like you, and I'd like to spend some time with you. But say no, please, and I'll leave you alone."

"I'd like that," she said and his heart lurched.

"Great. How about tomorrow, weather permitting? I'll take the train in, we could even share a cab to the station."

She did smile at this.

"All right. The Green Man does good food, we could eat there."

"Great," he said, cursing himself for the inane repetition. He turned to go, turned back again. "Listen, my sister's over from Canada later this week, and I'm thinking of having everyone over to my apartment on Sunday. I am reputed to be the world's worst cook, so I'll get a local restaurant to cater, obviously, but she'd really like to meet you all."

Maria's eyes sparkled.

"Okay. Should I bring anything?"

"A bottle, if you want to. Any dietary requirements I should watch out for?"

"I'm pretty omnivorous. Brenda's the vegan."

"Right, thanks for that. I'll... er... see you later."

He tried not to run down the corridor.

"That was really good," Annabelle said. "The diffident young man wins through."

An enormous 'thank you' card from Rosie with a huge box of chocolates waited for him in the staffroom, along with the inevitable lung-busting hug from Brenda. Pam was humming 'stuck on you' and a smile lit up her face when she saw him. He told them about Sunday and both agreed readily to come. He thought Brenda looked a bit careworn, some of her vitality was missing. But it had been her son's wedding, she was probably recovering from the stress of it all. Ian seemed surprised to be asked, but declined the invitation as he was away on a lodge weekend. While he waited for the kettle to boil, Robert thought he'd pop down and ask Ashley, but stopped at the counter as Payal wasn't there. The door to Ashley's room was open and while the voices weren't raised, there was a definite edge to them.

"We can't afford a receptionist," he heard Ashley say. "Not just yet."

"Please, Ashley," Payal pleaded. "When I get pregnant, you'll have to replace me."

"Of course, but we—"

"I'll have to train her," Payal interrupted. "That'll take time."

"I know, but we're not making enough just yet."

"You could put the fees up, they've been static for three years," Payal said, and Robert thought she was close to tears. He turned and walked back down the corridor.

"I'll think about it," he heard Ashley say.

He ducked into his room, picked up the case notes he'd written, and strolled back to reception. She smiled, but it was an energy-saving smile, not the full wattage. Robert put the notes in the box for filing.

"Listen I'm inviting everyone to my place next Sunday, could you and Ashley make it? My sister's over from Canada, she's desperate to find out if everything I've told her about you lot is true."

Payal raised one eyebrow quizzically, and the playful look was back on her face.

"Everything?" she asked, and he couldn't think of a snappy reply. "We'd love to," she added, letting him off the hook. "What time?"

"Two o'clock. Is there anything you don't eat?"

"We're not that strict, but no pork or beef. What should I wear?"

She looked at him with such wide-eyed innocence he was sure he was blushing.

"Casual wear. A suit of armour."

She laughed aloud, and he walked away, trying not to smile. But Maria came out of her room just at that point, so he let the smile out, and was rewarded with one in return. He held the door open for her and they went into the staffroom and chatted with the others about the wedding over coffee, while Annabelle filed her nails, watching benevolently.

They were on their way home when Annabelle said she was going to leave him alone for a while.

"It's going really well," she said. "I'll pop over next Sunday, I'd love to meet your sister. Will you tell her about me?"

"Probably. She'll think I'm joking, she's very pragmatic. Why am I the only one who can see you?"

"You're the one who needs me. But it's getting less all the time."

"What will you do after I'm cured?"

"You know that beach? I'm going to lie on it and get an all-over tan. What will you do?"

"Live my life," he said. "Try and be happy."

She craned her neck to look up at him.

"If you have to *try* to be happy, you're with the wrong person. There is no try, only do."

"Yes, Master Yoda."

***

Robert didn't get a chance to talk to Ashley about Maria, and he wasn't sure if that was a good thing or not, but Payal winked at him as he left with Maria after work, which he took as a good sign. It was a warm evening and they strolled the mile to the pub. It wasn't crowded and they took a table in the garden. Robert hid the ashtrays on the two tables closest, to try and discourage smokers and they decided on a bottle of wine between them. It was well-chilled, and just what the palate ordered.

"Cheers," they both said, and clinked glasses.

"So what made you come to London?" Maria said. "Payal said you lived in Cornwall before."

"That's right. When I first qualified I had a practice in Manchester, but a relationship broke up, and I felt the need to get away." He was surprised his voice didn't tremble as he spoke. *I'm not exactly lying, just being selective with the truth.* "Had five years down there, and it began to get a bit quiet. I love it, though, I'd like to retire down there."

"What made you want to be an osteopath?"

Slowly, the paper barriers between them folded up and were put away, and Robert relaxed. They ordered food and agreed it was excellent. He even managed to keep his hand still when the inevitable hair escaped from behind her ear. She didn't talk about her relationships and he didn't ask.

"Is your sister married? Any nephews and nieces?"

"Civil partnership," he said. "She's gay. Very happy with her partner."

"So your parents look to you for grandchildren?" Maria said smiling, and the knife stabbed his heart. In and out, rapier fast, and just as deadly.

"Going to be a long wait," Robert said, and tried to smile. "I need the loo, can I get you another drink while I'm up?"

"A coffee would be good," she said, and he escaped quickly. He damned the mirror for the face that stared at him, and splashed water over it, to see if it would melt into someone else. Just a wet version of him, unfortunately. He ordered two coffees, and went back into the garden.

He managed to keep her talking about herself, and

they decided to walk to Hampstead Heath mainline station, rather than hail a taxi. She tucked her arm into his, and he liked the touch. He had to buy another ticket, but they travelled together as far as West Hampstead, and then changed. They took opposite directions on the Jubilee line, and she stepped quickly to him and kissed his cheek.

"Thank you, Robert, I enjoyed this evening."

"Me too. See you on Thursday."

He almost missed his stop, lost in his reverie, and found himself wishing Annabelle was there.

CHAPTER ELEVEN

Alexa hit him harder than a linebacker, and he barely caught her. She tried to compete with Brenda as a life-squeezer as he lifted her from the ground and whirled her round and round. He thought she was happy, but couldn't be altogether sure, the amount of tears she was shedding. Eventually he put her down and she released him, scrabbling for a tissue to wipe her eyes.

"How are you, Alexa? How was the flight?"

"Slept the whole way, told the stewardess if anyone disturbed me I'd have them fired."

"Really?"

"Absolutely. They tend to believe you in first class, so I've had seven hours sleep and I'm having you all to myself for the rest of the day." She stared into his eyes and more tears glistened. "Oh Rob, I'm so glad to see you."

She hugged him tight again, and then let go. She had a trolley with two suitcases on it, and he pushed it towards the train station.

"I couldn't believe it when mum told me you'd moved to London," she said. "Had to stop myself flying over, there and then. When are you going to come and visit us? And don't say 'next year', that's what you always say!"

"Okay, the year after." She punched his arm. "How's Carrie?"

"She's beautiful and gorgeous and wonderful, and I adore her more each day. You *must* come over, you'll love it."

He waited until they were ensconced in the First Class carriage before he had the chance to look at her properly. She looked amazing; short brown hair with blonde streaks framing an elfin face, with his brown eyes and lips. He never knew a girl who wore no makeup and looked as good as his sister. Even if he was a little biased. He doubted her matching top and skirt cost under a thousand dollars, and it looked great on her.

"How are you, Rob?"

"Not bad, honestly. The apartment's paid for by the rent from my house. I like work, and the people I work with, and I'm trying to get on with life."

Her eyes softened, and she reached for his hand.

"Is there anyone special? Any good friendships that might go somewhere?"

"There is one," he said slowly, and her eyes widened. "She's called Annabelle, and she is gorgeous. She has long red hair and freckles across her nose, hardly ever wears shoes, a figure the word 'hour-glass' was invented for, and legs up to here." Alexa stared at him. "She's three and a half inches tall with wings and she's a bossy madam."

She slapped his hand.

"Don't be mean!" she laughed. "For a second I thought you were serious."

She looked at him reproachfully, half-smiling. *Do I tell her the truth? Will she believe it?*

"Okay, there is someone else, and we've just stopped fighting, so there may be, and I emphasise may be, something going on between us. It's such early days, and if you say the slightest word to anyone, especially the gang I work with, I'll go back to Cornwall the next day, and never speak to you again."

Her eyes widened and she leaned towards him. He took a deep breath but hesitated for a moment.

"She's called Maria. She's almost as tall as me, has long

brown hair that can never stay behind her ears, a great figure, and the most kissable mouth I've ever seen. And yes, I did, once, but she's just getting over a nasty relationship and we've sort-of agreed to take it a step at a time."

"Oh my god." Alexa's eyes filled with tears, and she threw her arms around his neck. He patted her shoulder, patronisingly.

"You'll meet her on Sunday, I work with her."

She sniffed and pulled back, and he had a tissue ready for her. "Sorry," she said, dabbing her eyes. "I thought you'd never..."

"Move on? It's damn difficult, Sis, but if you want a good blub, read this. Paul and Judy gave it to me."

He handed her Elaine's letter and she cried all the way to East Croydon.

"Shit, she was the best of us, wasn't she?" Alexa said, when she'd finally got control. "So unfair."

"Nobody knows about Elaine, I've not said anything, so please don't breathe a word about her. When I'm ready, I'll face that."

"Of course. I'm so pleased, Rob. Do mum and dad know?"

"I don't want to tell them unless it looks like it's going somewhere, they'll get over-excited."

"I will sacrifice to all the gods, and cross everything I've got, Rob. You deserve it, you really do."

Alexa insisted on getting a taxi to his apartment from Victoria Station.

"The Bank's paying it, and I'm saving them the hotel bill, which would cost thousands. I hate the underground, it's so sweaty in the summer."

"Have you got to do any work in London?"

"One meeting tomorrow morning, one on Monday morning, fly back in the afternoon. I've booked the train to Macclesfield, only takes two hours, now."

Robert felt a twinge of guilt for not having been, but he knew he wasn't ready to face it.

"I told Paul and Judy I'd take you over, we can go for lunch on Saturday."

"Fine."

Alexa inspected his apartment, and then made him walk her around the local sights, her arm tucked firmly into his. They ate Italian, drank French and never stopped talking.

"I've missed you," Robert said, as they clambered up the stairs to his apartment.

"Not as much as I've missed you," she said. "I'm so glad you're here."

She turned to kiss his cheek, and nearly fell over the cat. "Who's this?" she said, bending to fuss him.

"No idea, but he sleeps here most nights. Fugly's still going strong."

"No! God, he must be... what? Sixteen? Seventeen?"

"At least. It'll be hard for them when he goes, their last link to Elaine."

"There's still us," she said gently.

Tabby made a beeline for the rug and started pudging it furiously.

"I have to Skype Carrie, she'll wonder what's happened to me," Alexa said, bringing her mobile out of her bag, hitting a speed dial button. Robert went into the kitchen and filled the kettle, took down the cafetiere from the cupboard. He heard the ringtones, and the crackle.

"Hi baby," Alexa said, walking into the kitchen, holding the phone at arm's length. "Guess where I am?"

She turned the phone round and Robert saw Carrie sitting at a desk, obviously in front of her computer. Robert always thought Carrie was a handsome woman and he could see her First Nation heritage, even though she only quarter Native American. A tranquil face, round, with a constant smile in her eyes. Her hair was tied up in a towel, and she wore a bathrobe.

"Hi Carrie," he said, waving. "How are you?"

"Better now I know your sister's arrived safely," she

said, but there was laughter in her voice. "How are you?"

"I'm good. Or getting there, at least."

Alexa turned the phone to herself.

"I'm fine, too. Doesn't he look great?"

She turned the phone back and Robert saw her peer at the screen, so he struck a Napoleon pose, chin up.

"Don't do that, you look like Alexa when she's in a huff," he said.

"I do not look like that!" Alexa said indignantly, turning the phone back to herself. "Let me show you his apartment."

She walked round, giving a running commentary on everything, and Tabby miaowed hello to Carrie when Alexa shoved the phone at him.

"Did you give Rob the present?" Carrie asked, as Alexa finished her tour.

"Haven't unpacked yet," Alexa said. "We've been seeing the delights of Camden and eating and drinking too much. I'll do it as soon as I'm off the phone. What are you doing today?"

Robert made the coffee while Alexa talked with Carrie, letting them have some privacy to make verbal love to each other. When they'd finished, Alexa brought the phone into the kitchen and held it out to Robert.

"Bye, Rob," Carrie said. "You're coming out next year, yes?"

"Looking forward to it," he said, smiling. "Take care of yourself, Carrie."

Alexa kissed the phone a few times and rang off.

"I'll get the present," she said. Rob poured coffee and took them through into the sitting room, setting them down on the low table. He sat back in the sofa, feeling very mellow.

"It's in two parts," Alexa said. "Here's the first."

She handed him a small package, neatly wrapped, and he knew it was an item of clothing. She plonked down next to him, watching him with a smile. He tore off the paper to reveal a Tee-shirt with the wording: 'Don't worry. Be Hopi.'

which made him grin, and he knew he'd be humming Bob Marley every time he wore it.

"Now this," she said, handing him an ornately carved wooden box, "is what brought Carrie and I together. I saw it at her craft shop and something about it pulled me in, I had to have it. Carrie says I bought it without asking the price, left my purse on the counter, and she had to chase after me. We both want you to have it."

"Wow. Thank you."

"Open it, open it," she said, and he saw the small excited child who'd always got as much pleasure from other people's presents as her own. He opened the lid. Inside, a carved wooden heart was mounted on what looked like stony ground, growing out of it, with leaves enfolding the sides, curling around. A small indentation in front of the heart had a gold-coloured candle mounting. The hues of polished wood caught the light, and it was masterful work.

"This is beautiful," Robert said.

"Isn't it? May I show you?"

"Of course."

Alexa took the box from him and carefully lifted the carving out. She set it on the table and took a white candle from the box and inserted it into the holder. The candle was flecked with tiny blue and yellow pieces. In a small receptacle inside the box lay some red-tipped matches, and Alexa took one out, struck it on a roughened area and lit the candle.

"Only someone who truly loves you must be allowed to use these matches on the candle," she said. "They light your Heartfire."

How Robert didn't spurt the mouthful of coffee all over the cat, he'd never understand, and swallowing it made him choke, since most of it went down the wrong way. She pounded his back and tears ran down his face, as he tried to recover.

"It's wonderful," he croaked, when he could speak."I love it."

She threw her arms around his neck, and he hugged her tight.

"I know it will bring you someone you love," she said.

She decided it should sit on the mantelpiece above the fireplace, and moved Robert's wooden cats to either end, to guard it. She stood the carving on top of the box, and it made for a very artistic display. She snuffed the wick with wettened fingers.

"What happens if I get to the end of the candle and I haven't found the girl for me?"

"You put another candle in, dummy."

"Oh."

***

Alexa was up before him next day, brought him coffee at six thirty, then proceeded to bash the hell out of her laptop, frowning and chewing her lip.

"Problems?" Robert asked.

"What? Oh. No, just going over what I want to do at the meeting. Way too much testosterone in board rooms, still. Bunch of weary bankers, the lot of them."

Robert recalled the spoonerism and smiled.

"Why do you do it?" he asked.

"Because it pays me enough that I'll retire at thirty five and then spend all my time with Carrie."

"Five years, wow. Good plan. Are you thinking of adopting, still?"

"Not sure. We've discussed it, but not made any firm decisions."

"You'd be a great mum. Or dad."

"Let me do my work, idiot."

Robert showered and fetched fresh croissants for breakfast. He was ready to go when she left, and hailed a passing cab for her.

"Give my love to mum and dad, I'll see you on Saturday," he said, hugging her. "I'll come up to Euston and meet you, text me with your arrival time."

Feeling good put power in his muscles and he reached the clinic in record time, to see Payal struggling up the steps, carrying a big cardboard box. He shoved a pedal down, parking the bike at the kerb and ran up to her.

"Here, give me that," he said, and took it from her.

"Thank you," Payal said. "It is heavy. Did your sister arrive okay?"

"She did, we had a really good day. Where's Ashley?"

"Seeing the accountant, he'll be in later."

She unlocked the door and hurried to decode the burglar alarm.

"Where do you want this?" Robert asked, following her in.

"Oh, could you put it in Ashley's office, please?"

She lifted the counter top for him, and he squeezed past her, waiting as she unlocked the door. She touched the Ganesha statue as she entered, smiling a little shyly as she waited for him.

"On the desk will do, thank you," she said, and Robert put it carefully in the centre.

"I'd better get the bike before it goes walkabout," he said, and hurried out of the office. Luckily, the bike was where he left it, and he quickly locked it round the side of the building. Payal was checking the answerphone, so he hurried to the shower. He'd taken his shoes off before he noticed there were no towels, and padded down the corridor in his socks to Payal. She was humming to herself, and twiddling her finger in her hair.

"Payal, could–?"

He could have sworn there was daylight under her, as she jumped and let out a squeal.

"Don't do that!" she scolded, her hand on her chest, shock on her face. "Scared the shit out of me."

"Sorry. I hate being a laxative, but there are no towels in the shower room."

She tried not to smile, and he knew she was going to tease him.

"You shower, and I'll bring one to you," she said, raising one eyebrow.

"That isn't fair," he said. "Stop teasing me."

"But you're so easy to tease," she said, grinning. "Maria said... well, I won't tell you what Maria said, but she really likes you." His pulse pounded a little faster. "Don't hurt her, will you?"

"I'd sooner hurt myself, honestly."

And I will, rather than tell her the truth...

"Good."

Payal got up and opened a cupboard, bringing out four towels, neatly folded. He took them from her and walked back to the shower with as much dignity as he could muster.

Hell, Maria really likes me.

Robert waltzed through the day, and even found time to talk to Ian about Kinesiology. Some of it even made sense. He was acutely aware of Maria, and they skittered around each other, joking now and then, looking at each other in sidelong glances. He wanted to take it further and was afraid of taking it further, so he was happy she needed to take it so slowly. The alternative was too painful to think about, but he realised he was looking forward to Sunday immensely. *See what Alexa thinks, she'll know what to do.*

CHAPTER TWELVE

Saturday was a whirlwind: Alexa reached Euston at eleven in the morning, and they took Paul and Judy out for lunch by the river, going back to their house for coffee and Fugly, and Robert envied Alexa's ability to be so tactile. She hugged them both as they left, and there were tears all round. But good tears, mixed with laughter, and with promises of contact which sounded genuine.

"Rob is definitely coming out next year," Alexa told them, "so you have to. Vancouver is wonderful any time of year, and you don't have to speak French. Not that the Canadians do, it sounds like a bastardised version of Franglais to me. I can only ever understand every third word. I always shrug and say I'm Scottish, rather than English. Get away with murder."

"I'm Scottish on my father's side," Paul said.

"See? You'll fit right in."

Alexa refused to travel on the Underground, and she held Rob's hand in the taxi.

"I'm so glad she was married to you," she said. "The best friend I ever had, and my brother made her really happy. God, I miss her. Sorry."

"It's okay. I've spent the last five years not talking about her, and she'd hate that."

"Yeah, she would. Did you fancy her straight away?"

"From the moment I first saw her, even though I didn't understand what I was feeling. She had something, I had no idea what it was, but..."

"You were thirteen. She was eleven, had no boobs, a really scrawny arse and spots. What boy wouldn't be attracted to her?"

Robert laughed.

"That's the first time you've laughed when you were talking about her," Alexa said, squeezing his hand.

"I smile a lot, to myself," he said. "And I try not to wish I was thirteen again."

"Just as well, you were an ugly sod back then."

The theatre was fabulous and Robert made a mental note to thank Annabelle for booking the box. She'd distracted him at the booking agency, making him agree with whatever she said and his credit card statement hadn't come through yet, but he really didn't care how much he'd spent – they had a great evening.

Sunday dawned, bright with promise, and Robert tingled with anticipation. He let Alexa re-arrange all the furniture, pushing the table back against the wall and scattering the chairs around the L-shaped space the dining area and sitting room created. She was cleaning the bathroom when Annabelle arrived.

"Ooh, this looks good," she said. "There's room for dancing later."

"There won't be any," Robert said. "Have to consider the neighbours."

"They're out. Did you tell Alexa about me?"

"Yes, she didn't believe me."

"Oh well. Where is she?"

At that point Alexa came out of the bathroom, wearing rubber gloves and an apron.

"Who were you talking to?" she asked.

"Annabelle."

"Ha ha. Have you got any bleach for the loo?"

"There's some in the cupboard under the sink."

"I'll get it, you start stacking the glasses on the table."

"She looks like you," Annabelle said, as Alexa disappeared into the kitchen. "Oh my goodness!"

"What?"

He swore Annabelle glowed brightly as she flew up to the carving.

"Do you know what this is?" she asked excitedly, her eyes wide.

"It's a present from Alexa and Carrie," Robert said, opening a box of glasses. "Only someone who loves you is allowed to light the candle."

Annabelle stared at him in shocked silence, mouth open.

"How do you know that?" she finally said.

"Carrie made it, it's what got her and Alexa together."

"She made it? Oh my god, I wish I could meet her. It's so beautiful."

"Is it true?"

"Of course it is. It was made with love, and it's been used with love, over and over."

"Alexa said it lights your Heartfire."

"Almost," Annabelle said. "It actually ignites the Heartfire of the person who lights it, because they're declaring their love, bringing it out in the open."

"Stop talking to yourself, or we'll never be ready," Alexa called.

Robert raised an eyebrow to Annabelle.

"Wonderful. Bossy. Pushy. Loving," he said quietly.

Christina and her husband Terry arrived first, closely followed by Brenda and Pam. Terry had a roundness to him that suggested he'd been a fit man at some time, and Robert guessed he must have played Rugby, judging by the flattened ears. Sandy-coloured hair that was thinning, but an open face and an easy smile. Robert did the introductions and got the drinks. Alexa turned on the charm and chatted with them, handing round nibbles. Pam seemed unusually shy with Alexa, but became her vibrant self within a few minutes.

Tabby seemed determined not to miss the party, arriving over the balcony, though he seemed put out his rug wasn't where he'd left it yesterday, so he jumped on Pam's lap and tried to suffocate himself, nudging her chest for attention. Laughter echoed and it sounded good.

Alexa was standing next to him, helping him with more drinks when the doorbell rang.

"I'll get it," Christina called, and opened the door. Maria entered, closely followed by Payal and Ashley.

"That's her, isn't it?" Alexa said quietly. "I can tell by your face."

She strode over to meet them. Robert's mouth was dry and he took a gulp of his wine.

"She's good, isn't she, your sister?" Annabelle said, admiringly. "Knows you so well."

He took another gulp and gathered up the drinks, listening as Alexa introduced herself. He gave the drinks to Terry and Christina and, trying to control the fluttering in his stomach, he walked over to them

"Hi," he said. "You found it okay?"

"Ashley's satnav did it," Maria said. "Where shall I put this?"

She held out a bottle of white wine.

"Take this too," Ashley said, giving him a bag with bottles that clinked.

"Thank you. Let me just put these in the chiller, then I'll get you drinks," he said.

He took the wine from Maria, trying to ignore the perfume, knowing she'd be wearing it, and escaped into the kitchen, checking Ashley's bag, putting the white wine in the sink he'd filled with crushed ice. He stood for a moment, took a deep breath, and walked out again.

"What can I get you?" he asked, looking at the three of them in turn.

Within an hour he'd relaxed a fair amount. He'd drunk a bit, circulated, trying to be the perfect host, keeping everyone's glasses topped up.

"Was I sober enough to thank you for running me back after the wedding?" Robert asked Terry. "I hope I did."

"You did," Terry said. He was a likeable guy, an Inspector on the Underground and Robert was tempted to ask about the human skin particles, but thought it might lower the tone.

"He what?" Alexa said in a loud voice, and they all looked at her.

"Didn't he tell you?" Pam said, glancing at Robert for a moment. "Dived right in, saved her life."

Alexa looked at him quizzically, half-amused, and he shrugged.

"I don't suppose he mentioned his dancing skills either, did he?" Payal asked innocently.

You wait till tomorrow, I'll sneak around in my socks all day.

"This is news to me," Alexa said, and he thought she put the wide-eyes on a bit much. "Tell me everything."

"I'm going to check the food," Robert said.

He went into the kitchen, and was peering into the oven when he heard the door open behind him. His heart stuttered a little, but it was Brenda, who seemed to have lost her stealth capability altogether.

"Can I help?" she said.

"Thanks, I think it's all about ready. The microwave has the vegan food, and this one is for carnivores, so I thought I'd keep them apart in case they attacked each other. Could you put the vegan on the far end of the breakfast bar, we'll separate them with the salads?"

"Right." He handed her the only pair of oven gloves, and used a hand-towel to protect himself, as they got the food out. It smelled fabulous, and Robert saluted Toni from the Greek Restaurant on the corner.

"Bill couldn't make it, then?" he asked as they arranged the dishes.

"He's at The Oval, had tickets for the Ashes series back in February. Cricket is his passion, and I'm afraid he wouldn't miss it for anything."

"Wouldn't want to come between a man and his cricket," Robert said. "I can think of better places to be, though. Like here."

Brenda's face fell a little.

"You okay, Bren?"

She shrugged, he could see unhappiness lurked there.

"Jason told me he's been offered a job in New Zealand," she said, and her face crumpled. He knew he couldn't do as good a job as her in the hugging department, but he put an arm around her. "They want to emigrate."

He reached over and pulled a roll of kitchen towel with his free hand, snatched two pieces off and gave them to her. She dabbed her eyes and blew her nose noisily.

"What am I going to do?" she sniffed. He took her shoulders and turned her gently to face him.

"I'll tell you what you're going to do: a bit later on, you'll sit and talk with Alexa, who went to Canada for a three-month placement six years ago and never came back, because of the fantastic opportunity she was given. And she has no intention of ever coming back. But she skypes mum and dad three times a week because it's free, and they actually talk more than when she lived in England. Alexa comes to London occasionally, like this visit, and pops up to see them. They've had fabulous holidays in Canada, and I'm pretty sure that if you and Bill start saving now, you can be in New Zealand for the next England cricket tour. The Maoris have an incredible healing tradition, and they're going to love you. You will wish Jason and his wife every success in the world, because their happiness is your happiness." He took a breath. "Lecture over."

Brenda laughed through her snivels and showed how hugging should be done. "I'm so glad you came to London," she said over his shoulder.

"Me too," he just about managed, with the little breath that remained in his lungs. "Me too."

They started stacking plates and cutlery.

"You can't help it, can you?" Annabelle said. "It's natural for you to help others. It's about time I did something more for you"

"Bogoff," he said pleasantly, without thinking.

"What?"Brenda asked.

"Oh, sorry, the napkins I bought – buy one get one free. Bogof."

"I think you ought to get back in there," Annabelle said. "Alexa's telling them about the guide hut and the airbombs."

Robert pushed the door open.

"Grub up," he called. "Stop listening to the lies my sister is telling you, and get it while it's hot!"

There was genial chaos in the kitchen, as everyone served themselves, and Maria's eyes twinkled at him as he helped load her plate.

"Airbombs, eh?" she said, smiling.

"It was my best mate Chris's idea," Robert said blandly. "But it did work well. You've never heard adolescent girls scream that loud since Take That reformed."

"Kay Bish wet herself," Alexa said, "and half the troupe didn't come for weeks afterwards. You scared the hell out of us."

"We nearly wet ourselves laughing so much," Robert said, grinning at the memory.

"How old were you?" Maria asked.

"Fourteen. Ah, happy days."

Alexa winked at him, and he felt good. Really good. The food was a minor sensation, and the lounge and dining area filled with noises more suited to a humming convention. Everyone was tucking in, and Robert was trying to explain how to gauge the best angle for an airbomb to explode directly over a guide hut to Terry, when Annabelle sat herself on the carving, and winked at Robert.

"Attento!" she called, and Maria looked immediately. Robert turned his head away, fearing she'd look at him, and he'd appear guilty.

"What's the carving?" Maria asked, frowning, pointing her fork, and everyone turned to see.

"What? Oh, it's a present from my little sister," he said, hoping Alexa would explain it.

"My partner carved it," she said, and Robert sighed inwardly in relief. "If you truly love someone, you can show it by lighting the candle to their heart."

A collective "aaah" came from all the women, and Annabelle grinned and crossed her legs, bouncing her foot the way she did when he first met her here. Terry raised his eyebrows. Robert copied him, not daring to look across the room.

I wish you would light the candle he thought, terrified by the possibility, but wanting it so much, knowing she wouldn't. *Maybe in time. A lot of time.*

The afternoon passed in a haze of laughter and silly games that Alexa instigated. Sticking a name to everyone's forehead, and only giving yes/no answers to questions as to the identity of the person was well-received, but Robert was convinced she'd written the name on Maria's paper much smaller, so he had to lean towards her to read it. *She and Annabelle are working together, I'm sure of it.*

He couldn't stop the women washing all the plates and tidying up, but spent at least five seconds trying, and when the place was spick and span, they all gathered to leave. A lot of hugging and kissing went on, and he wished he had Alexa's lack of inhibition, as she hugged everyone tightly, kissing them all on both cheeks. So he took the chance and kissed Maria twice, then had to do the same with Payal and Pam, who followed her in the lineup.

The goodbyes finished, and he and Alexa stood at the door calling more, hoping nobody would trip going down. Robert closed the door, and looked at Alexa.

"They are *lovely*," she said. "What a great bunch of people."

"Yeah. I almost walked out the first day," he said, leading her back to the sitting room. "But I'm really glad I stayed."

"They all adore you," Alexa said, folding her legs under her on the sofa, as she sat.

"Robert?" Annabelle called, and something in her voice made him turn his head. She stood on the mantelpiece next to the carved heart and the candle was burning.

"What is it?" Alexa said, picking up on his surprise. She turned and saw the candle. "Oh my god!"

She leapt up and was at the mantelpiece in four strides. She turned and looked at Robert. She picked up the burnt match, showing it to him.

"She even used the match," Alexa said. "How did she know about that?"

"Who?"

"Who do you think? Maria, of course! She couldn't keep her eyes off you the whole time she was here."

"But when? I mean, how? Everyone was milling around, she'd have been seen."

So?" Alexa shrugged. "They know something's going on between you two, probably distracted you while she did it." She flopped back into the sofa, happy. "Either that, or that Annabelle did it," she added, grinning at him.

"Wasn't me," Annabelle said, smiling. "I would if I could handle the match, but I promise you it wasn't me."

Robert smiled at what she'd said, but his mind was whirling.

"Maria's lovely," Alexa said. "And I'd agree with your description of her, but for one tiny insignificant detail."

"What?"

"Kissable mouth, yes, but not the most kissable mouth I've ever seen. And I think I should know, I've kissed more women than you have."

"Did I say that? Must be a man-woman thing, then."

"Did I miss something?"Annabelle asked, flying to sit on Alexa's shoulder, looking gloatingly pleased with

111

herself. "You said Maria has the most kissable mouth you'd ever seen?"

They are definitely working together.

"So, what are you going to do next?" Alexa asked.

"She said she wants to take it slowly, so I guess I'll go at her pace and see what happens."

"Good plan, women hate to be rushed, sometimes."

"Did Brenda speak to you about her son?"

"Yes, I think she was a bit happier when we'd finished, she said you'd given her really good advice. Payal's a little dynamo, isn't she? She has a cousin in Vancouver, I told her to contact me if they visited, and I'd show them the town. I think Ashley would love to come out, but he's worried about leaving his businesses."

"Businesses?"

"Didn't you know? He's set both his brothers up, has a fifty percent share in each of them. Sounds like they're doing all right."

"Pam seemed very shy with you to start with, not like her."

"She's in love with you, just like all of them, only she knows she's not good enough for you."

"That's bollocks."

"That's what I thought. She's way too good for you. Maybe it was her who lit the candle."

"I don't think she could reach the mantelpiece," Robert said. "God knows what I'm going to say to Maria tomorrow."

"Ask her out again. Go to a proper restaurant or a show. For god's sake, you live in London, there's millions of things to do." She looked into his eyes. "I'm so glad the bank sent me over here now. I wish I could stay longer."

"Yeah right. Carrie would kill me."

"I'm going to skype her," Alexa said, excitedly. "She'll be so pleased."

Carrie was delighted, and Robert promised three times to go and visit them next year.

"I'm holding you to that, Rob," Carrie said. "If you

don't come, we'll be over and kidnap you."

"I promise," Rob said, for the fourth time. He saw Carrie look at Alexa, whose face was right next to him, and she nodded to Alexa.

"Bye, Carrie," Annabelle called.

"Bye," Carrie said, and she did a double-take. She opened her mouth to speak and Annabelle pointed at the phone, and the call cut off instantly.

"Oops," Annabelle said. "She heard me."

She flew onto the table, and sat on the edge.

"I've got just the thing to celebrate," Alexa said, putting her phone down. "One of the clients gave it to me, and I was going to leave it with you, since I can't take it through customs."

She jumped up, went into the kitchen and returned with a bottle of Louis Roederer Crystal champagne and two glasses.

"Impressive," Robert said.

She pulled a face. "I made him two hundred million in three years, so a thousand pound bottle of bubbly is a drop in the ocean. The Bank isn't keen on us taking gifts, but this isn't going to corrupt me any time soon."

Alexa opened the bottle with ease, and poured two glasses, giving him one.

"Here's to you," she said, holding her glass up, touching the rim to his. "I'm so happy for you."

"Thanks, kid."

They sipped the champagne. Robert swallowed fifty pounds in a gulp, and burped at least two quid's worth of bubbles back up.

"It's very fizzy," Alexa laughed.

They drank more, and Robert thought it was okay, but not worth a thousand pounds. *That's three hundred pints! In Cornwall, anyway.*

Alexa took his glass from him, and placed it on the table alongside hers. She took both his hands, and looked inexplicably nervous.

"What is it?" Robert asked.

"I need to ask you something. It's mega-weird, and you don't have to answer now, and I promise you I'll accept whatever you say, and never mention it again, ever, if you don't want to do it."

"Do what?"

She took a deep breath and it came out shaky. Her hands were trembling, and he was suddenly scared for her.

"You asked me about adopting, and Carrie and I... we've discussed it, we do want to have children... but..."

"What?"

She bit at her lower lip, and he thought she would start crying any moment.

"Alexa, what is it?"

"We wanted to know if... if you'll be a sperm donor for Carrie. I said it's weird."

There was no warning, the cry just burst from him, and she jumped, startled. He couldn't stop the volcano once it erupted and floods of tears followed. He found himself hunched over, crying; great racking sobs that tore up from the depths of him, and part of his mind recognised Alexa had her arms around him, was crying too, saying she was sorry, over and over, but he couldn't stop, and he clutched at her, weeping into her lap as she held him, rocking him.

It took an age for him to regain control, and the back of his shirt was soaked with Alexa's tears. Tabby was standing on his back legs, patting at his face with a gentle paw, and absurdly, this helped. He stroked the cat's head and pushed himself upright. Alexa's face was stark, white as snow, and she looked as frightened as he'd ever seen her.

"Come here," he said, holding out his arms, and crushed her to him as she cried against his chest. "It's not your fault."

He stroked her hair and she slowly stopped, so he told her.

"Elaine was pregnant when she got ill. We didn't

114

know, but an arrogant prick of a doctor hooked her to an IV drip of chemotherapy before all the tests were in. It killed the baby and Elaine miscarried. They held an internal inquiry, and said on the balance of probabilities the baby would have miscarried anyway, so they did nothing. Nothing." He fought for control for long moments. "The miscarriage weakened her terribly, and they didn't say anything, but she knew, we both knew. The cause of death was leukaemia, but she couldn't fight any more after the miscarriage, it took all her strength."

"I'm so sorry, Rob."

"I didn't want anyone else to know, I was frightened of what I might do if I told those who loved her, and they couldn't handle it. I would have killed the stupid quack."

"Me too."

They sat holding each other for ages, and it comforted them both.

Annabelle watched them from her position outside the balcony, hovering upside down, just one eye peering in. She wished she'd seen Maria lighting the candle, she'd have made sure Robert saw it as well. She could barely see Robert and Alexa, anyway, as her eyes kept filling with tears. But it made her more determined to help Robert, and she knew she'd be complaining to head office about poor subject information. Might take her a day or two, but she didn't think he'd get in any more trouble while she was gone.

CHAPTER THIRTEEN

Telling Alexa should have helped, but it didn't. They didn't mention it again, and he couldn't get his mind around being his nephew or niece's father either, so he didn't bring that subject up until she was leaving.

"Give me a bit of time to think about you and Carrie," he said as she held him.

"I shouldn't have asked." She kissed his cheek. "Love you, Rob."

"Love you too, Sis. Have a safe journey back."

He tried to burn the residual feelings up on the bike, but it burst into life when the inevitable Volvo cut into the bus and cycle lane to jump a queue of traffic. It clipped the front wheel of a cyclist in front of him and she went over her handlebars, spilling heavily onto the pavement. The car drove on.

"Oi!" Robert shouted and took off after it. Traffic stopped it about a hundred yards later, and Robert skidded alongside the driver's door. The driver was a man in his late twenties, smartly dressed, and Robert saw his hands drumming on the wheel, obviously impatient.

"Hey!" Robert called, knocking on the window. "You just knocked a cyclist off her bike. Pull over."

Another cyclist pulled up beside Robert.

The driver's window rolled down about half way, and he looked up at Robert with bored arrogance.

"You hit a cyclist," Robert said, seething. "Pull over."

"Fuck off, you peasants," the man said. "I don't have time for this."

The lights changed and he pulled forward, winding his window up.

"Bastard!" Robert yelled, and chased him. There was a bus in the lane ahead, and it didn't make it through the lights, forcing the car to stop. The Volvo's indicator came on, and he tried to edge into traffic. Robert slid on his inside and jumped off the bike, letting it fall. He tried the passenger door, but it was locked. He ran around the front of the car, and hammered three times on the back of the bus with his fist, hard. The hazard lights came on immediately. Robert tried the driver's door, but that was locked.

"Get out of the car!" Robert shouted.

He received two fingers and the driver tried to edge further out. Robert's clip-on cycle shoes were made of a very hard polymer plastic, and when he thought back to the incident, he realised how good they were. It was frustration and anger, but the dent it caused in the driver's door showed Volvo's assertion of crumple protection zones to be a fallacy. He didn't kick with the toe of the shoe, but the sole. The raised moulded shapes responded really well to the rage Robert used to drive them into the metallic paintwork. It might have been the third kick that caused most of the damage, or possibly the fourth, but then someone grabbed him from behind and lifted him off his feet, pulling him away.

"S'okay, he's not going anywhere," came a rough voice, as he was set back on his feet.

Seeing Robert held, the driver surged out of his car and swung at him. Robert ducked and his own fist connected with the man's chest, and then they were grappling with each other. Robert's helper stepped between, them pushing them apart. He was a big man, dressed in blue motorcycle leathers, the face of his helmet pushed up. Stubble beard and moustache and a wide grin showed themselves.

"Stop it, you two, you might actually harm your hands."

The driver glared at the man, red-faced, eyes livid, then slid back into his car and slammed the door. The effect was rather ruined as it didn't close properly.

"Always wanted to do that to a Volvo," the motorcyclist said cheerfully to Robert. "You okay?"

Robert's heart was racing with adrenaline, and the urge to do more damage still surged inside him, but he had it under control now. A crowd had gathered on the pavement, and the bus driver was arguing with passengers. Mobile phones recording the scene were everywhere, and the driver of the Volvo had his mobile pressed to his ear..

"Yeah, just about," Robert said. He held out his hand and the guy shook it in his leather gauntlet. "Thanks."

A siren sounded, and a police motorcycle pulled up behind them.

***

It seemed Monday morning was popular for misdemeanours, as Holborn Police Station was crowded when they eventually got there, and Robert had to wait over an hour before being processed. A police sergeant told him he was being charged with assault and causing criminal damage to a vehicle, and did he understand that? He did. They took his shoes from him for forensic testing; fingerprinting and DNA swabbing took even more time. Robert sat in a cell while they checked he wasn't wanted for any terrorist offences or other crimes, and they took him to the interview room with two officers to make his statement. He waived his right to have a solicitor present, and the two officers seemed quite relieved, admitting the duty solicitor was up to his eyes at the moment. They were quite friendly, and even provided a sausage sandwich and tea at one point. He told the truth about what had happened, and they took him over it a few times. He commiserated with them about the weight of their utility belts, pointing out they probably had a lot to do with the backaches they both suffered.

"Anyone you want me to call?" Police Officer Lloyd asked. She was cheery and bright, said she wanted to move up to detective eventually. Robert thought, uncharitably, that she should dye her hair from the natural blonde she was, to increase her chances of being taken seriously. She was far too pretty to be a detective. "Lawyer, relative, work? I can get your mobile for you, if you want to do it."

"Oh." Robert honestly hadn't thought about this. "I suppose I should."

It was almost two in the afternoon, and Alexa would be in the air by now. He didn't fancy calling his parents, but felt guilty about not telling the clinic. They'd have had to cancel all his patients.

"Erm... what will happen? Do I have to be bailed?"

"Depends on the magistrate. You've no previous, but the intent to assault can be taken seriously. I imagine they'll release you on your own cognisance."

"Could you phone work for me? Tell them I'm sorry I'm not in, but—"

The door to the interview room opened.

"Your lawyer's here," the sergeant said, surprising Robert enormously.

His lawyer was late thirties, dressed very smartly, slicked back hair and a pencil-thin moustache, carrying a laptop bag and a briefcase. He followed the sergeant into the room, and placed them on the table.

"I'm John Crowther, I've been appointed by your sister to represent you," he said to Robert. "What is the charge?" he asked the sergeant.

"Assault and causing criminal damage to a vehicle."

"I see. Statement prepared?"

Police Officer Lloyd handed it to him and he read it through. "Right. What charges are you bringing against the driver?"

This surprised the Sergeant.

"None. Your client admits chasing the witness, and kicking the door of his car, causing considerable damage, and being involved in affray."

"My client was trying to make a citizen's arrest, after the witness, as you call him, caused actual bodily harm to a cyclist, knocking her from her bicycle and wilfully left the scene. Mr Kirk's statement clearly states he saw the driver swerve unlawfully into the bus lane, hit the front wheel of the cyclist, and drive away. My client told the arresting officers all this at the scene, but they chose not to believe him."

"The driver stated the woman fell from her bike after he passed her, he was adamant he was nowhere near, at least twenty metres in front of her when he pulled into the bus lane," Officer Lloyd said. "He did not hit her, and we saw no damage to the vehicle. He said he spoke politely to Mr Kirk, telling him this and then his car was attacked."

"Did you write all that down?"

"Yes I did, before we left the scene, within fifteen minutes of our arrival."

"Good. A bicycle tyre would hardly cause a dent to a Volvo, would it?"

"He was a doctor on call, responding to an urgent request for medical intervention."

"Did you check he *was* actually called at that time?" Crowther said. "Do you have his statement to hand? I'd like to see it."

Officer Lloyd flushed, and Robert thought her chances of making detective had gone down a little.

"We took all his details, ensured there were no warrants outstanding, and asked him to come in later to make a statement. As I said, he had to leave urgently."

"How convenient. Did you take statements from other witnesses? Did they corroborate what my client said?"

"One gentleman said he thought the Volvo may have hit the cycle wheel, but couldn't be sure. He was cycling behind her, as well."

"And the lady cyclist herself?"

"An ambulance was called to the scene, my colleague informed me she appeared to have a bad fracture to one wrist, and contusions to her thigh, but I haven't—"

"Actual bodily harm, then," Crowther said. "Do you have the registration of the Volvo, Constable?"

"Yes." She flipped her notebook open "Gulf Uniform twelve, Whisky Bravo Whisky."

"Excellent. Please watch this."

He unzipped the bag and took out a slim laptop and opened it.

"This was taken by the helmet camera of a cyclist at the time." He pressed a button and the screen lit up. A picture of cyclists in a bus lane was shown. Crowther pointed at one of them. "You'll see this is my client, I'm sure you recognise the marmite jersey he's still wearing, and the black and yellow shorts. Watch carefully."

He pressed a button and the video played. It was a little jerky, but very clear. The Volvo swerved into the bus lane, hit the cyclist and drove on. The camera swung to the woman and Robert winced as she went over the handlebars. He heard himself shout, and the camera swung back to the road, moved up and down a little as the view chased Robert. It caught up with him and he heard himself call as he knocked on the window, telling the man to pull over. Crowther pressed a button and the video paused.

"I think we can all agree this was the Volvo in question, GU12WBW. What you'll hear now is a Doctor's polite response to my client's request."

'Fuck off, you peasants. I don't have time for this.'

They watched the rest of the film in silence and Robert winced as he saw the ferocity he used to kick at the door. The courier lifted him off his feet, and the driver came after Robert. The courier pushed them apart and the video stopped.

"What a bloody wanker," Officer Lloyd said, which Robert thought was good detective work, if a little late in the day. He smiled as he realised the WBW registration fit the driver by her description.

"Your witness drove into a bus lane illegally, used his vehicle to assault a cyclist, caused actual bodily harm, left the scene, and lied wilfully to police officers about his actions. I have no doubt he had *not* received a call requesting urgent medical intervention, but I'm sure you can find that out. I don't wish to tell you your job, but I assume you will arrest him and charge him accordingly. My client attempted to make a citizen's arrest to prevent this criminal from leaving the scene. I'm certain you're dropping the charges and he's free to go?"

"We'll need the video," the sergeant said.

"You'll find it on YouTube, but I can give you the name and address of the man who filmed it, since you may need the original."

He handed a slip of paper to the Sergeant, closed his laptop and slipped it back in the bag.

"Let's go, Mr Kirk."

"I'll get your things," Officer Lloyd said.

There were a ton of missed calls on his mobile, mostly from the clinic, but one or two from numbers he didn't recognize. Alexa was waiting for him, and she hugged him tight for a second, then let go and turned to Crowther.

"Thank you, John," she said, shaking his hand.

"My pleasure, Miss Kirk," he said. "Can I drop you anywhere? My car's around the corner."

"I'll walk with Robert," she said. "He's got his bike here, somewhere."

Crowther smiled, shook hands with Robert and left. It turned out his bike hadn't reached the Police Station yet, so they hailed a cab.

"You've missed your flight," Robert said. "How did you know?"

"Payal phoned me, I'd given her my number in case they visit Vancouver. When you didn't make it in, they got quite worried and since you didn't answer your mobile she rang me. I got John on it straight away. They'd been ringing the hospitals, scared you'd been in an accident."

"Shit. I should have used my one phone call to let them know."

"I've told them. John found you pretty quickly, I think he has teams listening in to police wavebands, to be honest."

"He's damn good."

"The Bank uses all kinds of Barristers and Solicitors, and he's the best at investigation work. By the time I got out of the meeting he knew where you were, and someone delivered the laptop to him as we reached the police station." She smiled. "We watched it before he took it in, I hope you didn't damage your foot."

"No. What are you going to do? Is there a later flight?"

"I've transferred to tomorrow's, and we're going out for dinner tonight, just you and me."

"I'd better phone the clinic. God, I hope mum and dad don't watch YouTube."

"I doubt it. It's titled 'cyclepathic rage', I don't think that's the kind of thing they'd watch."

Robert dialled the clinic.

"Hi Payal, it's Robert... No, I'm fine honestly... I'm sorry I frightened you all... No, she's here with me. Getting a flight tomorrow, thank you for calling her... No, there were no charges... I lost it with an idiot who knocked a cyclist down, that's all... Thank you, and please thank the others, I'm sorry I didn't call sooner... No, that's fine, I'll do the extra day to catch up... thank you... No, I haven't had a shower yet, stop it... I've got to go, I'll see you tomorrow... I'll tell her... Bye."

"Tell me what?"

"She said you were incredibly calm, said you'd find out what had happened, and they all felt a lot better because of that."

"I was bricking it, inside, but that's the beauty of my job – I know someone who knows someone who'll know how to fix it."

"Thanks, kid."

"Listen, Robert, I want you to forget what I asked you. I had no right putting that sort of pressure on you, I'm really sorry."

"It's okay. I should have told you about Elaine years ago. I'm kind of touched you asked me, but still getting over the weirdness of it."

"I'm sorry."

"I'm sorry I frightened you. Both times. Where we going to eat?"

"I've booked a table at Carluccio's in Leicester Square, and I'm paying."

The closeness that had been lost between them returned as they dined and wined and walked, and got wet in a sudden shower, sheltering in a doorway, laughing.

"I'm going to come out to Canada next year," Robert said, as they strolled along Tottenham Court Road. "I'd like to meet Carrie properly, and see some of the country."

"We'll take you on the grand tour," Alexa said, squeezing his arm. "You'll love it so much, I promise."

Robert wondered where Annabelle had got to, hoping he hadn't frightened her away altogether.

CHAPTER FIFTEEN

Since he didn't have the bike, he wasn't rushed the next morning, and Alexa was up before him, fetching croissants and Danish pastries, with cappuccinos and fresh orange juice. She walked him to the Underground station and he was very sorry she was going.

"Going to miss you," he said and her eyes glistened as she hugged him.

"Don't miss me too much, come out and see me."

"I will, I promise."

A woman on the train had a perfume that was so similar, and he almost asked what it was, but was worried she'd think he was trying to chat her up. Being pressed up against her for two stops wasn't that bad, and she was about his age, as well. But she didn't have the long hair, or the soft skin at the nape of the neck, and he was quite glad when he reached his stop. He looked out for Maria in the taxi queue, but she didn't leap out at the last second and steal his cab, so he travelled in alone.

When he got to the clinic Pam was behind the reception counter and squealed, running out to hug him tightly. She almost took his tie with her as she pulled back since it was caught in the cleft of her bosom, and she flicked it up, catching him on the chin.

"We were so worried about you," she said, her eyes dancing. "Don't do that again."

"I'll try not to."

"Has Alexa gone now? She's lovely, isn't she?"

"My favourite sister, to be honest. She's flying out this afternoon. Where's Payal?"

"Hospital appointment," Pam said. "Ashley's gone with her, nothing serious, just women's things. I'm covering till lunchtime."

She hugged him again. Robert retrieved his lists and saw he was fully booked for the day, thinking there was time for a coffee before he started. Maria was in the staffroom with a laptop open on a low table, and she jumped up as he entered. They almost collided, and she put her hand on his chest, to steady herself. It felt warm, and he liked it there, but she took it back.

"Rob, how are you? What happened?"

"Erm... had an altercation with a Volvo in a bus lane."

"Oh my goodness," Maria said, concern in her eyes and her voice. "Are you okay?"

"Yeah, but you should see the Volvo."

"Were you hurt?"

Her eyes were very round and very dark, and he took a deep breath.

"No, not at all."

"Thank god for that. What happened?"

"Erm... can you get the internet on that?" he asked, pointing at the laptop.

"Yes, we've got wifi in here."

"Well... I'm not *totally* proud of what I did, but if you go to YouTube and search for cyclepathic rage, you should be able to see the whole sordid affair. Another cyclist posted it an hour after it happened, apparently."

"Really?" she said, frowning. "Psycho what?"

"Cyclepathic," he enunciated carefully. "As in bike, a bad pun."

"Oh."

She sat down and turned the laptop round, her fingers flying over the keys, working the touchpad.

"Is this it?"

He looked at the screen and saw the picture.

"Yes. That's me in the marmite jersey."

She pressed play, and he saw the shock on her face, she raised both hands to her mouth as the cyclist went down. He didn't want to watch, but heard the drama play itself out as he filled the kettle and switched it on.

"Oh my god," he heard her say, shocked, but when he looked at her she was trying not to smile.

"Yeah. Alexa's solicitor convinced the police I was trying to make a citizen's arrest, and they dropped all the charges."

She leaned back in the chair, one hand over her mouth, and he could see she was struggling not to laugh.

"It's not funny," she said.

"No."

She burst out laughing, and played it again.

"Could he use the door after you'd finished?"

"Erm, I think they had to tape it shut, so he could drive."

"Will you have to pay for the damage?"

"You know, I haven't got a clue. Probably."

"Serves him right, you should have legged it. Or biked it." She held her hands up to indicate a headline. "Marmite Soldier flees road rage scene."

She looked at him for a moment and her eyes flicked away shyly, making his heart slow, his mouth dry.

Ask her about the candle.

He didn't, he knew it might embarrass her.

"I'm so glad you were okay," she said. "We had a palpitating few hours here."

"Sorry about that."

Brenda arrived and fussed round him, trying to get him to promise to take the tube in future, and he promised to think about it. He wanted to talk with Maria on her own, but then Ian came in, and had to be told the whole story.

"Doctors and Volvos, bad combination," he said, shaking his head, after he watched the video.

Robert hoped he'd catch Maria in the morning break, but ran late when one of his elderly patients arrived with his daughter, and Robert had to explain what osteoarthritis was, and how best to manage it. He thought one of the missed calls on his mobile might have been her, so when he finally got to the staffroom, he produced his phone.

"Did any of you call me yesterday?" he asked them. "I've got a load of missed calls, they can't all be about mis-sold insurance."

It turned out Pam and Christina had been free the most, and they'd tried to call him repeatedly, so he listed them in his address book.

Maybe Payal will give me her number.

He didn't see Payal until the afternoon break, walking to reception to return cases, and she sat behind the counter looking miserable. Ashley stood alongside her, and she rested her head against his side, as he stroked her hair.

"Robert!" Ashley exclaimed. "Thank goodness you're all right."

Payal straightened up and smiled, seeing him, and he was saddened to see it lacked its usual brightness.

"Yeah, sorry about all the stress." He looked at Payal. "Thanks for calling Alexa, her solicitor got me out pretty sharpish."

"What happened?" Ashley asked.

He explained, and they tutted and winced in all the right places.

"Sorry to have messed things up," he finished with.

"Don't worry," Ashley said. "The important thing is you're okay."

Robert went back to his room, and perused the next case, looking up as his door opened to Maria.

"Do you fancy a drink with Ashley and Payal, later?"

she said. "They need cheering up, by the look of them."

"I'd love to. Not going to rain later, is it?"

She poked her tongue out at him. The last session dragged horribly, but finally he stood outside with Ashley as he locked the outer doors. Maria and Payal had walked on, arms linked, and Ashley checked the gate was secure before walking after them.

"Bad day?" Robert asked.

"No, far from it. We went to the fertility clinic, and we're both fine, no reason at all we can't conceive."

"So...?"

"We've been trying for two years. If they'd found any problems with either of us we could understand it. But they say we can't have fertility treatment, because there's nothing wrong with us. Just have to be patient."

"What about private clinics?"

"Cost thousands we haven't got," Ashley said.

"Sorry, Ash."

"It's what Payal wants," he said, shrugging. "I hate to see her so unhappy."

It seemed he and Maria were on the same wavelength in trying to cheer them up, and it mostly worked, so they stayed in the pub and had a meal and more drinks. It wasn't raining when they left, and Maria took his arm as they walked. It felt good. They said goodbye to Ashley and Payal, and caught the tube together. As they reached the top of the steps at West Hampstead station she stepped in front of him, standing one step higher, putting her head on the same level as his.

She slipped her arms around his neck, and kissed him. Really kissed him, raising the hairs on the back of his neck, making his thymus gland work overtime as a tingle ran through him. He wrapped his arms around her and tried to compete. Someone passing gave a wolf-whistle followed by a shout and a raucous laugh.

"Get a room!"

Maria eventually pulled back from him, and looked deep into his eyes.

"Don't frighten me like that again," she said.

"Well, I don't know. I kinda like the response it gets."

She kissed him again.

"See?" he said. "Well worth it."

"That's the last one you get if you do it again, and that's a promise."

"I believe you."

They kissed again.

"Listen, there's a theatre group I help out with, they've got a dress-rehearsal tomorrow," she said. "I wondered if you'd like to come, help make up the audience. We could go out for supper, after."

"I'd love to. Police haven't returned my bike yet, so I'll get the tube in to work, anyway."

"Good."

They kissed once more, and caught their separate trains.

What a day.

When he got back to his apartment, Tabby was nowhere to be seen, and Robert let himself in quietly, not wanting to disturb the neighbours below him. He heard her before he saw her, as she was cursing loudly.

"Come on, you bloody thing, lift!"

Annabelle was struggling to lift a match to the striking pad. For her, it was like hauling a massive piece of timber and she held it with both arms, leaning back to raise the head of it.

"Want me to help with that?" Robert asked, amused

"No, I have to do it myself, or it won't mean the same."

"Okay. I'll make myself a coffee."

He went into the kitchen and brewed himself a cup of instant, and when he returned she looked very pleased with herself as the candle was lit. She also looked sweaty and her hair was mussed up.

"Did it," she said, pointing to it.

"I see that. Thank you, it means a lot to me."

She waited until he sat down and then perched on the arm of his chair, her hands folded in her lap.

"I've been to head office, to complain," she said. "Normally, when we get the assignments, we're told everything, so we know what to speak about and what *not* to speak about. That didn't happen, and I'm really sorry."

"It's okay. I'd hidden it so deep, I'm not surprised head office didn't know."

"I understand why it took you so long to move on," she said, quietly, pulling at the material of her dress. "I'm sorry I called you a loser, that must have hurt."

"I only thought about Elaine when you said it, Annabelle, honestly. The other bit only surfaces now and then, when something unexpected happens. Like Alexa asking me to be the father of Carrie's child. It is weird, and I'm not even trying to get my head around it at the moment."

"She loves you so much, Alexa. Did she get back okay?"

"Well, sort of... she was delayed a day."

"Why?"

"Well, I was arrested and charged with assault and causing criminal damage to a vehicle, namely a Volvo estate, and she had to come and rescue me."

"See, this is what happens when I leave you on your own," she said, scolding, but he could see the smile lurking, and thought she knew very well what had happened.

"How did you know?" he asked, smiling.

"You think we don't have access to the internet? YouTube tells us so much about how foolish you all can be. So, anything else?"

"Well, Maria and I spent a very nice five minutes on the steps of West Hampstead station, kissing." Annabelle's eyes opened impossibly wide. "I'm seeing her tomorrow, we're going to a theatre group she helps out with, and then dinner afterwards."

Annabelle clapped her hands in excitement and Tabby looked up at her.

"That's wonderful! Shall I teach you some more Italian? Ti amo molto!"

"I've learned a few words of my own. I don't think telling her I love her very much would be correct, at the moment."

"Very good," she said patronisingly, and he raised an eyebrow at her. "Do you want me along, just in case?"

"I think I'm grown up enough to handle a date, thanks."

"The weekend in the Lake District is coming up soon, isn't it?" Annabelle said, knowingly.

"Yes it is," Robert said, suddenly frowning. "Annabelle, how is it Carrie heard you speak? You told me Maria heard you because she was the one for me, and Carrie is most definitely spoken for."

"She still believes. Probably she'd see me, if she were here."

"What do you mean?"

"Oh come on, the whole Tinkerbell syndrome, you know? If you believe in fairies you can see them. Why do you think all the babies can see me? They haven't had time for this cynical world to get its grips into them, they're much more in touch with the inner worlds. Carrie's upbringing must have instilled a belief in that world, and she's kept it to this day. She carved the heart, and understands instinctively how it works. I shouldn't have been surprised she did hear me, really."

"But I didn't believe in fairies."

"You saw me in the meditation, your subconscious mind believed. It re-awoke the magic that was your childhood imagination, and once you'd seen me, part of your conscious mind believed, as well. You *wanted* to believe, you'd been lost for so long."

"Oh. So I did deserve you, then?"

Annabelle smiled and the candle burned even more brightly.

"Absolutely."

Annabelle basked in Robert's smile, and the mutual feelings they were sharing. Things were shaping up, and with a little influencing, two people could become very happy together. *I love my job*, she thought.

CHAPTER SIXTEEN

aria asked him. "Will you be okay here?"

"Of course. Should I applaud at the end?"

"Definitely. It'll help the actors, try and keep it going, so they can do the encores. I've got to go."

"Wait." Robert caught her arm and pulled her down, kissing her. "Break a leg."

"I'm lighting, not acting," she said, kissing him in return.

"Oh. Break a lightbulb, then."

"Maria!"

"I've gotta go."

She turned, and he patted her bottom as she went. She tried to glare through her smile, but didn't manage it as she hurried up the stairs. Her bottom looked great in blue jeans, made her legs seem longer, and showed how good they were.

The theatre was tiny, just a hundred seats, with hardly any legroom. It had a tradition for quality, and according to some of the photos in the entrance, some pretty famous people had started out here. Maria had explained she'd never had the confidence to do any acting, but had done theatre technician work at school and loved it, keeping it going with amateur groups ever since.

"Places, everybody!" came a shout from the man Robert assumed was the director. He stood at the front of the stage with a clipboard and an assistant in tow. Two actors wearing orange boiler suits came onto the stage, a good-looking man and a stunning blonde woman, and stood opposite one another. The stage was bare apart from a wooden table and one chair.

"Lights down, please," called the director.

Robert thought Maria did a sensational job, he'd never seen lights go down that well. All he could see in the dark was the torchlight on the director's clipboard.

"Dress rehearsal for 'End of the Beginning'," came the shout. "Curtain up, lights up, action!"

There weren't any curtains to go up, but the lights came slowly on and the actors fell into each other's arms.

Robert thought he understood most of it, but was full of admiration for both actors, who didn't leave the stage for almost two hours. Admittedly, they took turns in curling into foetal shapes under the table while the remaining actor told their story, but it was still a fantastic achievement. There were six people watching, and Robert took his cue from the others when they started clapping. The actors got to their feet and bowed. The Director kept clapping.

"Step back," he called to the actors, who did just that. "Curtains close, audience applauds, curtains open, step forward, bow."

He made them repeat this three times and Robert's hands started to hurt, but he figured he'd had the free show, so he kept on applauding.

"Curtains close. House lights, please." All the lights came on, and the Director was standing looking up at the actors "Well done, everyone. George, you need to roll out from the table in act two, not crawl. Julia, remember to turn away from him *before* he sits in the chair, but well done, both of you, well done."

A discussion started between the actors and the director and Robert looked round for Maria. She emerged from a tiny door at the back row, and danced lightly down the steps.

"And the Bafta for best lighting goes to…"

Robert didn't realise he'd spoken so loudly, but all conversation stopped.

"… mio buon amico, Maria."

She grinned at him, waltzed along his row and sat next to him. The others resumed their conversation.

"What did you think?" she asked.

"I think the lighting was the best bit," he said, quietly, and she punched his arm. "Fantastic actors, aren't they? I *think* it took place in a maximum security prison during a breakout, or did I get that wrong?"

"They're both dead, didn't you get that?" she said. "They're in Bardo, the place between life and death, where you stay for three days before moving on."

"Seriously? Why the boiler suits?"

"That's just for the dress rehearsal. They do the play completely naked."

"You're kidding," Robert said, astonished. "Where can I get tickets?"

"I'm kidding," she said, and he saw her eyes sparkle as she smiled. She leaned over and kissed him on the mouth. "I'll check with David about the lighting, and we'll get out of here."

He followed her down the stairs, and waited while she spoke with the director. Robert became aware of the way her hair settled on her shoulders every time she nodded, lifting and settling. She smoothed one side behind her ear, and he almost groaned. Maria touched the director on the arm, saying goodbye, and turned to Robert. The smile disappeared from her face and she looked stricken. He started towards her when the voice came from just behind him.

"Maria, I have to speak with you."

A man overtook Robert and reached Maria first. Sandy-coloured hair, tied back in a pony-tail, slim, wearing smart shirt and skinny jeans, oozing class. Maria took a step back.

"Please, I must speak to you. You must let me explain."

Maria looked from him to Robert and back, and then Robert was alongside them both, his heart fearful. The man glanced at Robert, then at Maria.

"This is... Robert," Maria said, and her voice trembled. "We... work together."

"Hi." The man didn't even glance at Robert. "Maria, please. I have to talk with you." He reached out and took her upper arm, and she flinched. "Please. Things have changed."

She tried to pull back but he held her firmly.

"Hey," Robert said. "Let her go, you're hurting her."

The man turned to Robert and a sneer spread across his face.

"Sir Galahad, is it?"

"No, it's someone who doesn't like to see bullies at work," he said firmly.

"It's all right," Maria said, her eyes beseeching Robert not to get involved.

"See?" the man said, sarcastically. "It's all right."

"No, it isn't." Robert reached out fast and grabbed the man's little finger where it was gripping Maria's arm. The flesh had gone white underneath and Robert twisted the finger up. "You're hurting her."

The man gasped in pain and let go of Maria's arm. Robert released the finger, glaring at the man, who stared hatefully at him.

"Please, Robert," Maria said. "Don't."

Robert glanced at her and almost sagged to his knees. She looked frightened, but stepped towards the idiot, concern on her face.

"Are you all right?" she asked.

"Sure. Now that Mister Macho has asserted himself, can I talk to you? Please?"

The look Maria gave Robert sealed it for him – it was a mix of dislike and annoyance, and he turned and walked away from them. He half-expected, and hoped she'd call out to stop him, but he found himself out in the street with the urge to smash something raging inside him. No Volvo estates went by, so he settled with striding out fast, back towards the Heath. Everyone got out of his way.

***

"I knew I should have come with you," Annabelle said, when he told her what had happened. "That must be the guy she broke up with recently."

"I think we may have to restart the search," Robert said. "It ain't going nowhere with Maria."

Annabelle didn't say anything. But a ring at his doorbell made his heart surge, and they looked at each other.

"Is it her?" Robert asked, his scalp tingling at the thought. Annabelle disappeared, and reappeared almost immediately.

"It's a policewoman," she said. "With four thousand pounds worth of bike. Four thousand pounds, how's that possible?"

He opened the door. Woman Police Officer Lloyd stood there, holding the handlebars of his bike. She wore her uniform, but not her utility belt or shoulder radio.

"Hello," she said. "It's amazingly light, isn't it? I thought I'd return it to you, save you coming to collect it."

"Well... thank you," Robert said. His legs felt rubbery from the hope that had coursed through him when the doorbell rang, but he reached out and took it from her, wheeling it in and leaning it against the wall.

"If you can sign here," she said, holding a pad out to him. "Says it's been returned to you in good order. You might want to check it over. Do you have a pen?"

Robert leaned the bike both ways, checked the chains and the gear cogs.

"Looks okay," Robert said. "I'm sure I can trust the Met. Did you ride it here?"

"In this skirt? I'm just going off duty, got one of the carriers to drop us off round the corner."

"Oh. Do you want to come in? I'll find a pen."

"She's got one in her blouse pocket," Annabelle said, sounding very amused, as the policewoman followed him into his apartment. "She's quite cute, isn't she? See if she wants coffee."

"Do you want a coffee?" Robert asked. "I've just brewed some."

"Thank you."

Annabelle flew ahead of them into the kitchen, and sat on the bread bin.

"I thought you'd like to know that Doctor Sanderson was arrested yesterday, and charged with assault, causing actual bodily harm, failing to stop after an accident, and making false statements. They'll drop the last one, because it'll be his word against ours, but the rest will stick. Tosser."

Robert grinned. She was cute, he had to agree.

"Did you arrest him?"

"Damn right. I was hoping he'd resist arrest, but he went white, started crying and I had to keep handing him tissues."

She chuckled, and Robert thought she'd have a really dirty laugh if she got going.

"I'll see you in the morning," Annabelle said. "I'd hate to cramp her style. Don't do anything I wouldn't."

She wanted to do a little checking on WPO Lloyd, just in case head office decided that Maria wasn't the right one for Robert. She'd never had a failure before, but this case was become more vexing as it went on.

***

"So?" Annabelle asked, sitting on his handlebars as they travelled to work next morning. The streets were almost deserted, it was barely five-thirty.

"She left after an hour, we chatted about loads of things, nothing more. She's a fun person."

"Not going to be a fun morning," Annabelle said,

and Robert stood up in the pedals working himself hard.

"No, it's not."

He got to the Heath and did some serious fitness work. When the rest of the population began to emerge, he stretched down, coasted to the clinic, and was still early. He unlocked the gate and sat in the back garden, waiting for Ashley and Payal to arrive and open up. Fat pigeons obviously expected him to feed them, since they collected in the garden, strutting up and down, orchestrated by Annabelle who made them march comically in line, trying to keep Robert's mind occupied, he thought. They took off with a clatter of wings when Ashley opened the window in the staffroom.

"What are you doing there?" he called.

"Beating the Volvos in," he said, standing up and stretching.

"Front door's open, I'll put the kettle on."

Payal's smile failed to lift him as much as it usually did.

"Well?" she said, innocently. "How was the show?"

"The show was good," he said, and he couldn't be bothered to joke with her. "Maria took off with some prat with a pony tail straight after it, and I went home."

He walked down the corridor, leaving her open-mouthed. By the time he'd had his shower and got to the staffroom, Ashley had obviously been told.

"Was this a slim guy, sandy hair?" he asked.

"Yes it was, and I'd really rather not discuss it, Ash."

"Ah. Sorry."

"I assume that was her ex?" Robert said, feeling stupid for asking, especially after what he'd just said.

"Yes."

Robert shook his head, sighing.

"Fresh coffee on the top," Ashley said, pointing, obviously a little embarrassed, and sloped out of the room.

"Annabelle, I'd rather not bump into her today, could you keep an eye out, so we don't meet?"

"I'll try," she said.

It worked pretty well. Annabelle informed him when it was safe to take his patients back to reception, and Robert had to keep one talking for a couple of minutes at one point, to avoid Maria. He stayed in his room during the morning break, knowing he was being immature, but simply couldn't summon up the energy to face her. He had a free appointment later, and got himself a drink, chatting with Pam, who was as effervescent as always. Annabelle stayed in the background, being his spy, and he seriously considered a new career in industrial espionage until she told him she wouldn't do it, that was the imps' job.

"Seriously?" he'd asked.

"No, they work with the pixies on gold smuggling, idiot."

He smiled.

"What are we going to do?" he asked her. "I'm seriously thinking of phoning WPO Lloyd. How does Maria seem?"

"Out of sorts. She looks quite cross, to be honest. Payal tried to ask her, and she refused to talk about it."

"Is that good or bad?"

"I'm not sure. They're really good friends, and I have a feeling Maria's not too happy with herself right now."

"I don't want to get into a relationship that hasn't got a chance because—"

There was a tap on his door. Annabelle's eyes widened.

"It's Maria."

"Shit," he whispered.

They stared at each other for a moment and he shrugged, resigned.

"Come in," he called, and Maria opened the door, stepping inside quickly, and closing it. She wore her clinic tunic and black trousers, hair tied back.

"About last night," she said, and he could tell nothing from the tone of her voice or her face. "You really hurt his hand, you know."

"Show me your arm," Robert said, stung by the

apparent criticism. "Let's see the bruises."

She flushed and her hand went to her upper arm, but she didn't pull her sleeve up.

"You shouldn't have done it," she said.

"Oh, sorry for trying to stop a bully from hurting a person I care a great deal about," he said, sarcastically. "I'll know better next time."

"It was none of your business," she said forcefully.

Robert almost retorted angrily, but held his hand up in surrender.

"You're right, and I apologise" he said, without rancour. "It's none of my business. It was none of my business yesterday, it's none of my business today, and it'll be none of my business tomorrow. Let's just forget it, shall we?"

He thought he glimpsed something in her eyes for a split-second, but then she nodded, a short, hard nod.

"Right."

Robert turned to the case in front of him, and started reading it. After a moment's hesitation Maria turned and left the room. Robert buried his head in his hands.

"She can't be the one for me," Robert said, and half of him wanted to accept that, the other half argued. "Maybe it's in the next lifetime."

"There've only ever been three wrong assignments in a hundred years," Annabelle said. "And they were triplets, Ariadne got them horribly confused. Still, you know the best thing to do when this happens? Nothing. Wait for the ripples to settle and see what's reflected in the water."

"Can I sleep with WPO Lloyd in the meantime?" Robert asked, sitting up.

"If you want," she replied, which shocked him enormously. "She is gorgeous."

"I was joking," Robert said.

"I know. You disapprove of casual sex, always said you had to be *in* love to *make* love. You're almost unique in the male of your species, you know."

"How do you know that?"

"It's in your file."

"Oh."

"You need to do something to take your mind off things. Pam's going dancing tonight."

Annabelle had to remind him he had her mobile number on his phone, and she cajoled, and pushed, and bossed him into calling Pam, inventing the pretext for him that his phone had dialled her number by mistake. She could hear Pam's excitement when Robert said he'd go dancing with her, and he had to hold the phone away from his ear. But she could see Robert actually looked forward to it, as he left, and that made her feel good.

Chapter Seventeen

They won 2nd prize in the open jive section, and Pam almost burst into flames in excitement. Seeing her vibrancy, the sheer delight in their success, Robert envied her – he wanted to feel that alive again. When enough of the flames were extinguished, he took her to an Italian restaurant nearby, and enjoyed himself being with a good friend, and wondered again about contacting Chris and the others in Manchester. It would be great to see them.

"Penny for them," Pam said, smiling.

"Sorry, I was miles away, thinking about some old friends I've lost touch with."

"Any single ones?"

"I've no idea, actually. Been a while."

"You should contact them," she said. "They'll have missed you, if you've missed them."

Robert assumed it was everything he'd been through recently that made him almost well up, and he wanted to kiss her, out of sheer affection. He lifted her hand and kissed that, instead.

"You're a terrific person, Pam. Thank you."

She smiled and opened her mouth to reply.

"Pam? Pam Mackintosh?"

They looked up to see a young guy staring at Pam,

his eyes round, his mouth open. He was good-looking, dark curly hair, a Mediterranean look about him. She stared, blinking for a second, and then her face cleared as she recognised him.

"Carlo? Oh my god, Carlo!"

She jumped out of her seat and threw her arms around his neck, squealing delightedly. He had long arms, luckily, and they reached all the way around her. He lifted Pam off the floor a few inches and put her down, his face as alight as hers, as he held her at arms' length. Robert watched the blush spread up Pam's face.

"God, Pam, you look terrific, how are you?"

"Fantastic. Oh, it's so good to see you, how are you?"

"Cannot complain, business is great, thanks to people like you," he said, indicating the restaurant.

"This is yours?" Pam asked, amazed. "I thought you'd gone back to Italy."

"I did, the restaurant was Poppa's. He's retired and I'm running it now."

"That's wonderful," she gushed, "How long have you been back?"

"About two years." He looked at Robert. "Is this your husband?"

"Much better than that," Pam said, looking at Robert, smiling broadly. "He's my best mate. This is Robert. Rob, this is Carlo, the worst tease you could ever have the misfortune of sitting in front of, at school." Robert saw the way they looked at each other, the affection spilling out of both of them. "He's the one who got me into dancing."

"Are you still doing any?" He turned to Robert. "She was amazing."

"Still is," Robert said, as Pam bent to her handbag and showed the 2nd place rosette they'd won. She held it, waggling it in her fingers.

"That's fantastic," he said, excitedly. "Where are you working these days?"

"Listen, I'm really sorry," Robert said before Pam could answer, "but I have to phone Alexa. My sister's in Canada, the time change," he added to Carlo, by way of explanation. "Will you excuse me a minute?"

"Sure," Carlo said, stepping aside, so Robert could stand. Pam smiled over Carlo's shoulder and tipped her head a little, nodding her understanding. He went outside the restaurant, pretended to dial, and stood on the pavement with his phone to his ear, watching them.

"That's what I want," he said. "Look at them. Nobody else exists but them, right now."

Carlo had taken his chair, and he and Pam leaned towards each other, straining almost, the electric tension of two people focused entirely on the person opposite. Their faces were alive, their eyes wide, and they looked exultant as they talked.

"They could live happily ever after."

"They might," Annabelle said. "They're both Catholic, and the Italians prefer a womanly figure, think it's a sign of good child-bearing pedigree. Leave them to it."

"I haven't paid the bill."

"Carlo owns the place, doesn't he? I'm pretty certain he'd insist, anyway."

For the second night in a row, Robert walked home without his date, but this time he was humming.

***

The following morning he stopped at reception, trying to avoid Payal's eyes, knowing she'd ask him about Maria.

"Payal, can you look at the Monday and Tuesday after the Lake District weekend, see how busy I am, please?"

Payal called it up on the computer in front of her.

"Three booked for the Monday, one on the Tuesday."

"Would it be possible to shift them? I'm thinking about hiring a car, going back to Manchester to see my parents on the way down. I'll do the Thursday, extra."

"That's no problem, I'll move them today," she said. "We always hire a minibus to go to the Lake District."

"Yeah, Ashley told me. I'll come up with you guys, and arrange for a hire car on the Sunday at the hotel. What's the name of it?"

"I'll bring the number down to you."

"Thanks."

He showered, and when he got to his room, an envelope with his name printed on it lay on his desk. Payal had written the number of the hotel in pen, alongside it. He opened the envelope, and unfolded a sheet of clinic-headed notepaper. It informed him, regrettably, that the room session rates were going up, and also the fees to patients at the same time, which would result in a small increase payable by him. He looked at the maths of it, and it seemed to make sense, so he put it back, and didn't think about it again.

"Look out," Annabelle warned him as he sat in the staffroom, later. "There's an aura approaching like I've never seen before, and it's headed this way."

"Who is it?"

"Pam."

He'd never actually seen anyone levitate, but Pam almost managed it, when she arrived. She pirouetted in, floating lazily into the chair next to him, a look of ecstasy plastered across her face. She looked at him.

"Oh. My. God." she said.

"Good evening, then?" Robert asked, so pleased for her.

"Un. Be. Lieveable. We were still talking at three in the morning, people going by thought the restaurant was still open, we had to turn all the lights off. Carlo drove me home, and I wanted every light to be red, all the way. It broke my heart when he went back to Italy, and I believed that stupid cow Suzie Wellington when she told me it was to marry his childhood sweetheart, so I tore up the letters he sent, never replied to them. He thought I'd found someone else, that was why he didn't try and contact me when he came back. All those years..."

"How old were you when he left?"

"Sixteen. Is it possible to find the love of your life at that age?"

"God, yes, definitely. So...?"

"We're going out this weekend," she said, drumming her heels in a flurry into the carpet. "His cousin's getting engaged, there's a big party, and he told me to bring my dancing shoes. I can't wait."

"I'm so pleased for you, Pam."

She grabbed his face and kissed him hard on the lips. He couldn't lift his arm to push her away as it was trapped by her chest, but she broke away, and stared deeply into his eyes.

"Hadn't been for you, I don't think I'd have met him again," she said.

"I don't know, seems like you were meant to meet. I'm sure it would have happened, somehow. I envy you."

She leapt to her feet, bouncing, and spun a complete circle. "I envy me," she said. "I've never felt this good, and it's incredible."

She shimmied to the cupboard, humming.

"Do you want a drink?" she said.

"I'll have a coffee to celebrate," he said. "There's some good stuff in the cupboard behind the jars."

Pam crouched down and opened the cupboard.

"Yuck," she said, disgustedly.

"What is it?" Robert asked, getting to his feet.

Christina's brewing concoction had pushed the stopper out of the jar in its efforts to escape and a frothy trail of red ooze covered with white mould, inside and outside the jar, marched all along the shelf.

"Out of the way, I'll lift that into the sink."

"Wait, I'll get kitchen towel, it'll stain the carpet."

They manoeuvred the large jar into the sink.

"What do we do with it?" Pam asked.

"It's mouldy, we get rid of it."

"I don't know if we should," Pam said. "Tina's very particular about her home brew."

"It's stinking the place out," Robert said. "Stand back."

He carefully tilted the jar and a gallon of red sludge lolloped its way down the drain, helped along by three kettles of boiling water.

"That's disgusting," Robert said.

"It's the elderberries from the garden," Pam said. "Tina makes it every year."

She cleaned out the cupboard, using a whole kitchen roll to mop up the mess, and the room smelled of alcoholic sweetness when they'd finished.

"Phew, open a window," Annabelle said, wafting a hand in front of her face. "I'm off, this is too intoxicating. No naked lights, please."

***

When Robert went to the staffroom at the end of the day there was chaos. All the therapists were there. All the therapists were arguing.

"—just not right—"

"—it's above inflation—"

"—shabby way to treat—"

"—threw it away? How dare you?"

This last outburst was addressed to Pam by Christina, who was red-faced, standing over her. Pam looked on the verge of tears. Robert only just heard them over the hubbub.

"It had mould—"

"It couldn't have, it's only been in there a week."

Robert slid onto the arm of Pam's armchair and looked up at Christina.

"*I* threw it away, Tina," he said. "It had fermented its way out of the jar, and was all over the cupboard. The smell was disgusting, and it was covered in white mould. Granted, it could have been penicillin growing, but it wasn't fit for human consumption, I promise you. Pam didn't want to throw it away, I insisted, okay?"

Tina stared at him, two white patches appearing on her cheeks.

"You should have asked me, first!" she said, vehemently. She stalked off, flung herself onto the sofa on the far side of Maria, who was talking loudly over Brenda and Ian. Robert squeezed Pam's shoulder, and her hand came up and gripped his for a moment. He stood up.

"Tea, anyone?" he said in a very loud voice, and the hubbub died immediately, as they all looked at him. "There's some green tea, it's very calming."

"It's not right," Ian grumbled.

"What isn't?" Robert said.

"This increase," Ian said, waving the paper. "Twice the rate of inflation. Not right."

"But the fees the patients pay have gone up, as well. I worked it out to be about a five per cent increase, overall."

"Which is way above the current rate," Maria said caustically, to nods of agreement from the others.

"When was the last increase?" Robert asked.

"Three years ago," Brenda said, after a short silence.

"Three years? So it's actually about one point seven per cent per annum, isn't it?"

"It's all right for you, you're really busy," Ian said, and this time Maria and Christina nodded their assent.

"Ian, you do four sessions here, if I recall correctly, and I'm pretty certain you don't have many free slots," Robert said, a little irritated by their attitudes. "I *am* busy, and I'm very grateful for it. I don't have to do any promotional work at all, I don't have to worry about advertising. I just turn up, see my patients and go home. That's a pretty good number, if you ask me. Every morning I'm in, Ashley is here, working on the website, pushing the clinic, doing editorial for the local papers, mailshots to local businesses. Payal runs herself ragged for us, handling all the bookings, making sure our rooms are laundered, our case notes are out, and the clinic is neat and tidy and professional, so we can saunter in and treat patients, without worrying, without any responsibility, other than what goes on in the treatment room. I've run my own practice in the past, and let me tell you, they're doing a damn good job. Try doing it yourselves and you'll find out how hard it is."

There was a silence after he finished speaking, and nobody moved.

"And they're standing behind me, aren't they?" Robert said, cringing inside. *Where's Annabelle to warn me when I need her?*

"I'm happy to discuss any concerns you all have," Ashley said. "Anything."

He and Payal walked past Robert, and sat down. The silence was embarrassing and mercifully brief.

"Perhaps if we didn't do the weekend, you'd have more to spend on advertising," Christina said. "Despite what Robert said, we could all be busier."

"It's a waste of money," Ian muttered, and Maria nodded in agreement.

"I increased advertising at the beginning of the year," Ashley said. "The new website is up and running, and there's been an eleven per cent increase in new patients since May, which has benefitted you all, not me. I'm happy to cancel the weekend, if that's what you all want."

"Won't you lose the deposit?" Payal said, and Ashley shrugged, clearly unhappy. The silence dragged on a bit, until Brenda spoke.

"Money and healing have always been uneasy bedfellows," she said. "Nothing in this life is free, but we all do the best we can, don't we? Shall we put it aside for a short time? Give thanks for what we do have?"

Reluctantly, they dragged all the chairs into a circle, and this time Robert chose to sit next to Pam, making sure Maria wasn't opposite him. The body language of the whole group wasn't terribly good, Robert thought, but he had little choice but to join in.

"Right," Brenda said, trying to sound positive. "Everyone breathe deeply. Breathe in the light. Breathe out the darkness. Feel the light surrounding you, feel its warmth as it enfolds you. You're standing in a cave."

Robert visualised the cave.

"Walk towards the light, feel the warmth of the sun on your face."

Robert walks out of the cave, and there's a howling gale, black thunderclouds approaching, the sky dark. The seas crash onto the beach in enormous waves. His tee-shirt and shorts are whipped around his body.

"We feel the sand beneath our feet."

Robert feels sand stinging his legs, driven by the force of the wind.

Bloody hell, I'm in the wrong meditation!

"We see a wide sandy beach, the sea lapping gently."

You must be joking.

Robert pulls the neck of the tee-shirt up over his mouth and leans forward, trying to make progress.

"We see a small rock formation ahead of us."

Robert struggles towards it. A flash of lightning and instantaneous crack of thunder make him jump, and he struggles on, to reach the rock.

"There's a figure standing on the rock."

No way.

"Annabelle?" he calls.

"You know who it is. Spend some time interacting with this figure."

"Annabelle?" Robert shouts.

"Robert?"

She's clinging to the rock, the wind whipping her almost horizontal. Robert drops down, shielding her from the wind, and they scramble into the lee of the rock, where there's some respite. She spits sand out, shaking her dress.

"What's going on?" Robert shouts. "This is chaos!"

"This is your inner mind," Annabelle calls. "It's in turmoil, but it's also picking up the group feelings. What's happened?"

"Just about everything that could go wrong, has gone wrong. We're all at each other's throats."

"Can you fix it?"

"I doubt it," he shouted. "Pam and I are the only ones talking, they're all against Ashley for increasing the prices."

"He's doing it so he can get the money for the fertility clinic," Annabelle shouted back. "But if they stay stressed out it won't make any difference."

"Shit. I'll give it a go."

"You'd better go back, they're worried about you."

Robert gets to his feet, leans into the wind and staggers off to find the cave entrance. He can't see it anywhere, but hears a voice in the distance.

"Robert, come back... come on... Robert... come back..."

Robert opened his eyes to see them all staring at him. He was hunched up in the chair, clutching his shirt. He straightened up, very self-conscious, smoothed his shirt down with his hands. Brenda smiled at him, and looked around the group.

"Does anyone want to share anything?"

A very awkward silence followed and they all avoided looking at each other.

"Well then, we'll—"

"I'd like to say something," Robert interrupted. "I think it's really important we do the weekend away together."

They all looked at him with varying elements of surprise or suspicion.

"Look, we've all been out of sorts with each other for one reason or another, and I'm sure some of it is my fault. When I first got here, I thought meditation was for the fairies...

"Oh, very good," Annabelle said from somewhere in the room.

"... but I've learned a good lesson being here, sitting

with you guys. You can't keep running away as soon as things get tough, can you? We all work together here, and we do it to help others, so maybe we could use this opportunity Ashley's giving us, to work things through."

He looked round at the group, and everyone except Maria looked back at him.

"As cynical as I am about most things, I really believe it will do us all good to go – most of you have told me how great they were in the past, let's all work to make this a good team bonding event. Ashley's paying for it all, we just have to turn up. I'll even arrange an event or two, myself. The worst that can happen is we have a weekend in one of the most beautiful parts of England and get pissed every night."

There were one or two smiles at this, and Brenda winked at him.

"I think we'd be foolish to throw this opportunity away, that's all."

"I'm going," Pam said.

"Me too," Brenda said.

"We're going," Payal said looking at Ashley, and he reached out and took her hand.

"I'm going," Annabelle called.

They all agreed to go, and the meeting broke up in a considerably better mood than it began. Robert changed into his cycle gear, and was surprised to find Pam waiting for him when he came out of his room.

"I've got something for you," she said, grinning.

It was a tee-shirt, emblazoned with the words 'Cyclists do it in Tandem'.

"Just a thank you for everything you've done for me," she said.

"Have a great weekend, Pam," he said, and kissed her on both cheeks.

"You betcha."

She skipped out ahead of him, and Ashley and Payal waited at the front door, arms around each other.

"Thank you so much," Ashley said, and Payal dazzled him with her smile.

"Ah, it was nothing," he said, smiling. "Didn't want to lose a free weekend away."

Ashley laughed and shook Robert's hand.

"I'm so glad you came here," Ashley said, and Robert tried not to look at Payal, knowing she'd have that sympathetic look in her eyes.

All things considered, me too.

"Doing anything this weekend?" Ashley said.

"I'm going to try and track down some old friends, haven't seen them for years. There's an internet cafe around the corner from me, and even though I'm a technophobe, I'm determined to start learning."

"I'll get you a laptop," Ashley said. "My brother refurbishes them all the time."

They said goodbye and Robert was on his bike in short order, heading home.

"You're very quiet," Annabelle said, holding her left arm out to indicate the turn.

"Sorry. Mulling a few things over."

"Well don't spend— Stop! STOP!"

Robert locked both wheels and skidded the back wheel round, as Annabelle was thrown forward from his handlebars. The van's speed rocked him as it passed, and his shoulder clipped the side, jerking him round, twisting his back. It didn't stop.

"You stupid bastard!" Annabelle screamed, incandescent with rage. "Straight through a red light, what's the matter with you? I hope there's film in those cameras, you idiot!" She flew back to Robert. "Are you okay?"

"Yeah," he said, rubbing his shoulder. "I think I'll soak in the bath when I get home, use some Tiger Balm. Thanks, Annabelle."

That's made my mind up about one thing.

"I've got his number, see if Police Officer Lloyd's got nothing else to do," Annabelle said, fuming.

Robert wasn't far from home and walked the bike the rest of the way, trying to calm his heart. He carried the bike up to his apartment, and parked it in the entrance hall. Annabelle made Tabby dizzy, flying angry circles around him as Robert went to run the bath. His shoulder was stiffening, and he left the taps running to look for the Tiger Balm.

"I'm going to give it up," Robert said, and Annabelle paused in mid-circle, her face stricken. "The bike. It's too dangerous. There's a gym on the Finchley Road, I could get an early train to miss the crowds and— what?"

"I   thought   you   meant...   you   know... trying..."Annabelle said, the relief so evident on her face. Tabby took the opportunity to stagger to the rug and pudge his way back to normality. Robert shrugged.

"There is no try, there is only do. Apparently. I'm going to spend this weekend catching up on a lot of loose ends, and maybe see if I can get my head straight. I want to surprise the team in the Lake District with some vigourous activities, shake them up a bit."

"You've got an evil glint in your eye, Robert Kirk, what are you planning?"

"You'll see."

It was difficult for Annabelle to hide her joy, and she didn't bother trying. After the accident she only just calmed down, and her heart had almost stopped when she thought he was going to give up trying to get his life back again. She sensed changes in him that were making him more positive about everything. How to get Maria back on track, that was the problem.

CHAPTER EIGHTEEN

Robert was woken on Saturday by his phone vibrating furiously on the bedside cabinet. He swore at the pain that shot through his shoulder, but grabbed it, wincing as he lifted it to his ear.

"Hello?... Oh, hi Katie... No, I'm just up, no problem... what, now?... Give me five minutes to shower, and if you could grab some croissants and a cappuccino from the bakery, I'll pay you when you get here... Brilliant, see you."

"That's a hell of a bruise," Annabelle said, frowning. "Have you got any Arnica?"

Robert examined it, craning his neck. It was massive, and ran down his upper arm, front and back. He lifted the shoulder tentatively, rotating it slowly.

"Ow."

"Who's coming round?" Annabelle asked.

"Katie Lloyd," Robert said. "She wants to tell me about some developments in my case."

"I'll bet," Annabelle said, drily. "Make sure you get 'Katie' to check that van out. Pillock."

Robert was showered, shaved and dressed by the time his doorbell rang, and Katie stood there with his croissants and two coffees.

"Thought I'd join you, if that's okay?"

"Of course, come on in."

A wolf-whistle from Annabelle was probably the response Robert would have given if he'd hadn't worried it might be inappropriate, but she did look good.

What is it about cashmere sweaters that makes you want to cuddle up?

The sweater was joined by tight blue jeans, and flat shoes. Her hair was loose, and hung just to her shoulders, and she had a freshness to her that wasn't just soap and perfume.

"What would you like with the croissant?" Robert asked, leading her in. "Jam, marmalade, honey, marmite?"

She made a face at the last suggestion, and he smiled, forgetting his shoulder as he reached out to push the kitchen door open.

"Ow." He flinched with the pain.

"You all right?"

"Yeah. Had an altercation with white van man last night, hit my shoulder on the side of it, when he jumped a red light."

"Tell her to look into it," Annabelle said.

"Where was this?" Katie asked.

"Junction of York Way and Marylebone Road."

"Did you get his number? I can get traffic to check the cameras, they can identify him. What time was this?"

"She's good, you know," Annabelle said, admiringly. "I almost wish she was the one for you. She's married, by the way."

Robert almost dropped the plate he'd just got from the cupboard, but managed to catch it, pretending the shoulder had caused it.

"I did get the number," Robert said. "It was about seven fifteen."

"DR03PLJ" Annabelle recited, and Robert wrote it on a yellow sticky and gave it to Katie.

"I'll get them to look into it," she said, folding it, and putting it in her back pocket.

Robert got out the jams and honey from the fridge, and they sat at the breakfast bar.

"Doctor Sanderson has decided not to pursue you for the damage to his car. I imagine the medical defence union advised him to do it, but you're off the hook, anyway. If it comes up in court, he'll look better if he comes over as a magnanimous person, without a bad bone in his body."

"What will happen?"

"I imagine his lawyers will make out a case for massive work-stress, first offence, totally out of character, full of regret, that kind of thing, and he'll get a fine and three points on his licence." She grinned. "There's a rap version on YouTube of him swearing. You get on and off your bike ten times or so, to the music."

"I'm selling the bike, it's too dangerous on the roads in London."

"That's a wise decision, I've attended a lot of accidents in my time, and far too many involve cyclists."

"What do you have to do, to become a detective?"

They chatted over breakfast, and when she left, Robert followed her down the stairs, admiring the sway of her hips.

"Thanks for all your help," Robert said. "I can't think of anyone I'd rather be arrested by."

"They all say that," she said, smiling. "I'll let you know if the cameras caught the van going through the red."

"Thank you."

On an impulse, Robert leaned forward and kissed her cheek,

"Bye, Katie."

"Bye, Robert. Take care."

He watched her walk away, went back up to his apartment, and spent an hour cleaning the bike, making it look pristine, trying to keep his shoulder mobile.

"I'm going to walk it to the shop on Gower Street, they'll probably take it back," Robert said. "Do you want to come?"

"Absolutely. I want to see you get four thousand for it. Seriously, four thousand?"

"They'll beat me down a bit, but it'll be close to that."

Annabelle shook her head in bewilderment.

He managed to get £3,800, and they credited the card he'd bought it with, so the money went straight into his account. He spent the rest of the morning in an internet cafe, and was surprised how much he found online. The assistant helped him, and he gave the guy a generous tip when he left, clutching a sheaf of papers that had all the information he thought he'd need. He celebrated by eating Mexican and drinking half a jug of margaritas on his own. His shoulder seemed less painful, and he fell asleep in front of the television that evening.

While he slept, Annabelle checked on Maria, and she didn't like what she saw.

"Why does my job have to be so difficult?" she asked herself.

**

His shoulder was even more stiff and painful by Monday, and it seemed every sadist in London was on the underground, and knew it, determined to make him pay, bumping him, pushing him, squeezing him in all the wrong directions. By the time he fought his way from the station at Hampstead he felt wrung out. He saw Maria leaving the station ahead of him, and hung back, watching her pony tail bounce and sway as she crossed the road to the Taxi rank. He waited until she'd gone before he emerged and crossed the road.

Don't fall in love with her, you said.

The atmosphere felt lighter when he stepped inside the clinic, and Payal lifted him with her smile.

"No bike today?"

"I've sold it. Too dangerous to use in London."

"I'm so pleased," she said. "No good being the fittest corpse in the graveyard, is it?"

"Definitely not. Is Pam in yet?"

"I've never seen her so happy. She was hoping you'd be in early, I think she put her back out dancing."

I bet it wasn't dancing...

He found Pam in her room, and she tried to jump out of her chair, her face lighting up as she saw him.

"Ow, ow, ow," she said, falling back into her seat. She looked up at him in pain, but her eyes were the brightest he'd seen since he first met her. "It was worth it, Rob, what a weekend."

"We can swap treatments," he said. "My shoulder's bruised to buggery, could do with some attention."

It turned out Pam had put her pelvis out of line trying to do the splits, dancing.

"I got down there, just couldn't get up, so I pretended to wave like the queen, and they all thought it was part of the act. Carlo knew, he nearly laughed his socks off, but did help me up. I've taken more painkillers than's good for me, but I had the best weekend of my life."

"Seeing him again, then?"

"Tomorrow. We're going to see Song and Dance at the Apollo."

Rob managed a Chicago roll manipulation and Pam's sacro-iliac joint popped nicely back into line, relieving most of her pain immediately.

"Right, get your shirt off." she ordered him, and her hands covered her mouth in shock when she saw the bruising. "Oh my god, what happened?"

He told her.

"I've sold the bike," he said, as she mixed some oils, and they smelled fabulous.

"Good." She looked at the bruising closely, ran a light touch across the area which gave him goose bumps. "I'll do this sitting," she said. "Because it's you, I'm going to rest your arm across my chest, but no squeezing, understand?"

"Spoilsport."

They both smiled, understanding each other implicitly. Pam had the warmest hands Robert had ever had the pleasure of being massaged by, and the thick oils soothed so much of his stiffness and pain, he was almost asleep by the time she finished. She put a warm towel over his shoulder and held it there, standing in front of him.

"I'm sorry about you and Maria," she said very quietly, and he thought she was the only one he'd want to discuss it with."She really liked you, and then had to go back with that arse, Phillip. What's wrong with her?"

"I like this girl, you know," Annabelle said. "She really cares about you, and she's turning into a really good friend, isn't she?"

"Did you know him?" Robert asked Pam.

"I treated him once, and only once, when they were going out together. Desert's disease, he has, wandering palms. Called me a tart because I told him to stop. I couldn't say anything to Maria, she'd have been so upset, and he knew it. He never told Maria he was married, she found out in the end, it broke her heart. He was a complete bastard, but she fell in love with him."

"When did they break up?"

"Three months ago, just after Easter. They'd been together two years – he lied to her, telling her he was always working abroad, when in fact he was with his wife."

"Maybe he's left the wife, now."

"Yeah, right. And maybe the air training institute for little piggies finally got one off the ground."

Robert and Annabelle both laughed.

"Is there nobody else you've met?" Pam asked. "You're so gorgeous, it's a shame for womanhood to waste you."

"There was one I met recently, but she's married, and I'm not capable of being an arse, and wrecking marriages."

Pam kissed him on the cheek. "That's why I love you," she said, matter-of-factly. "You're way better than a husband. Let me help you on with your shirt, and I want to see your naked chest again on Wednesday, all right?"

"Yes, ma'am."

"Maybe it was Pam who lit the candle?" Annabelle said. "She's a terrific person."

His shoulder felt ten times better, and he didn't mind smelling of lavender one bit. Annabelle said it was better than his aftershave, but he noticed people kept away from him on the tube going home, which was an added bonus.

***

The run-up to the Lake District weekend gathered pace. On the Friday morning, Robert decided to catch a cab to work, as he had a small suitcase with four days' clothes, and toiletries to carry. He stood at the roadside and became frustrated as the only taxis going by were already taken.

"Go up to Greenland Road," Annabelle said. "They always cut through there."

She had a pink spangled bag across her shoulder, and Robert swore it had a Mischa Barton label on it. Luckily his suitcase had wheels and he duly trudged up the road, keeping his eyes peeled. A taxi pulled in about forty yards in front of him, and it looked like passengers were getting out, so he hurried to snaffle it. A man got out and pulled out his wallet to pay the driver, and a woman followed. Robert recognised the blonde hair before he recognised Katie, and his heart almost stopped. He was about to turn round, when she saw him, and her face lit up. There was no getting away.

"Robert, how are you?" She turned to the man. "Darling, this is the one I told you about, the one on YouTube."

The sandy hair and the stupid pony tail were instantly recognisable.

"Have we met before?" Robert asked, trying to keep his anger in check as the man turned.

Phillip stared at Robert, and surprise showed on his face, quickly hidden.

"No, I'm sure we haven't," he said brusquely.

"The Prompt Corner Theatre, last week," Robert said. "You must remember, you came in after the show finished."

"No, wasn't me, I've never been there."

"You must have a double," Robert said, forcing a laugh. "Have you finished with the cab? I'm in a real hurry. Bye."

He gave Katie a quick smile and climbed into the back of the taxi, grateful for the training Maria had given him on his first day and gave the clinic address to the driver, as he pulled the door closed. The road behind was clear, and it pulled out immediately. Robert didn't dare turn around to look.

"Did you do that because of what he did to Maria, or what he's doing to Katie?" Annabelle asked. She sat on the upturned seat in front of him, looking shocked.

"I don't know," Robert said miserably, angry with himself for doing it. It had happened so fast, he'd spoken before he could think, driven by sudden anger.

"Sorry, Guv?" the cabbie called.

"Just talking to myself," Robert told him. "Practising my lines."

"Oh. Actor are you?"

"Yeah, got a death scene coming up, gotta get it right."

"You carry on, then," the cabbie said.

Robert stared at Annabelle.

"Shit. What am I going to do?"

"You have to tell her."

"Tell who?" Robert's voiced raised slightly in panic. "Which one?"

"Shit," Annabelle said.

"What are the odds?" Robert asked, shaking his head. "What *are* the odds?"

"Don't ask me, I'm a fairy, not a statistician!"

"Shit. He told Maria things had changed, and she's been taken in by his lies, again."

Neither of them spoke.

"That it?" the cabbie asked.

"Yeah, my character dies after that."

CHAPTER NINETEEN

They left before lunchtime in a 12-seater minibus. Robert had agreed to share the driving, and asked Ashley to get them out of London, offering to drive the second half of the journey. He was still too agitated to think straight, and even with the dash-mounted satnav, he was worried he'd drive into the back of someone in the dense traffic. And that perfume was in the air, confusing him even more.

"You okay?" Pam asked him. "You look pre-occupied."

She'd been texting Carlo for most of the journey, looking contented, humming to herself.

"Yeah, sorry, a lot on my mind. Ignore me, I'm always like this in city traffic."

"There's nothing you can do," Annabelle said. "Who do you want to hurt more, Maria or Katie? Saying anything to either of them will hurt them. He's cheating on both of them, the bastard. Let's face it, the way synchronicity is malfunctioning at the moment, you'll probably find he was driving the white van that tried to kill you."

That almost made him smile.

They stopped at services on the M6 toll road, and Robert took over the driving. He could see Maria and Payal and Brenda every time he looked in the rear-view mirror.

"M6 all the way now," Ashley said. "We've made

good time. If we can get past Manchester before the weekend rush starts, we'll be there before seven."

Robert kept his eyes on the motorway as they passed the familiar signs, making sure he didn't read any of them.

Stop being an idiot, you're coming back here after the weekend.

Conversation in the minibus became more animated, and Robert began to relax more, the further they drove on. He followed the satnav's instructions and just after eight, they pulled up outside the Hotel.

"Dinner's booked for nine," Ashley said, "so you've got time to freshen up and explore a bit, if you want."

Robert helped get the suitcases from the back of the minibus, and looked around. The turn-in was fresh gravel, the flower gardens neat and tidy, and the facade of the front of the hotel was yellow stone, looking old-style, but obviously updated.

"It's just re-opened after a year's refurbishment, apparently," Ashley said. "They say they've completely re-built it. We always come to a different place each year, we were lucky to get the booking."

Robert nodded. There *was* something about it, and the location was superb. He walked with Ashley into reception, a wide, open space with a marbled floor, large oil paintings and very friendly staff.

"Blimey, this is posh," Annabelle said.

When Robert checked in, the girl on the desk handed him a large manilla envelope, along with his key.

"Your activity is all arranged, Mr Kirk, the directions are inside."

"Thank you."

His room was on the first floor, and he helped Brenda and Pam carry their cases up the stairs, as the lift wasn't functional yet. He keyed the electronic lock and went into his room. It was a large open room, double bed, with wardrobe, two easy chairs, a fridge, TV, and French windows opening onto a small balcony. Robert dropped his case onto the luggage stand and checked the ensuite bathroom, saw a wet room shower, toilet and sink, which looked impressive. He went back into his room and unlocked the door, stepping out onto the balcony. The view was spectacular: open lawns leading down to the lakeside, with rolling hills beyond, touched with evening clouds. Each room had its own balcony and as he looked, someone in the room next to him stepped out onto their balcony. He and Maria looked at each other for a moment, and she went back inside. She looked happier than he'd seen her yesterday, but not by much.

"What am I going to do?" he asked Annabelle, ducking back inside his room.

"Absolutely nothing. They used to kill messengers who brought bad news in the old days. She'll hate you even more for telling her, thinking you're trying to get back at her."

"Bloody hell. Poor Katie. Poor Maria, come to that."

"You got them all here, enjoy the weekend. Have a shower and try the local beer."

The shower was hot and the beer was cold, and he fretted until his second pint, when Pam, Brenda and Ian joined him in the bar, and the conversation stopped his mind from wandering. He did a double-take when he realised Ian had cut off the pony tail and had a razor cut number two, all over. Pam ran her hand over his head.

"It's much better, Ian. Makes you look younger, you know," she said.

"When we were here last year, over at Ambleside" Ian began, "I met that..."

"Oh, the artist, the one who did all the landscapes," Pam finished for him.

"Yes." Ian looked a little embarrassed. "She said I'd look better without it, but it was only when we got here I remembered."

"Is she here?" Pam asked, wide-eyed, as she looked round surreptitiously.

"No," Ian laughed, self-consciously. "I just decided when we arrived."

"It suits you," Brenda said and Robert agreed. It did suit him, made him look a different person. "Maybe you should pop over to Ambleside, see if the magic's still there."

"There's magic here, you know," Annabelle said, perched on the Theakstone's Old Peculiar pump. "It's very old, two ley lines meeting right here."

"So people can get laid?" Robert said, before his brain engaged. They all stared at him. "I mean married," he added hastily, pointing at the poster advertising weddings.

"They do that after the wedding," Ian said drily, and Robert almost fell off his barstool at the fact he'd made a joke.

Blimey, cutting off his hair has done something to him. Maybe I should get a haircut.

Ashley and Payal joined them, and they moved away from the bar, taking a table, shifting more chairs around it when Maria and Christina joined them. That perfume reached him, and he felt it really should be banned on the grounds of olfactory terrorism, as it sought to destroy the barriers preventing him from saying something, knowing he couldn't speak up.

But alcohol and good company relaxed them all, and laughter became the order of the evening. Annabelle found some small children and dogs to play with, and Robert watched her zooming up and down the lawns, in and out of the shrubbery.

"What are you looking at?" Payal asked, leaning over towards him, trying to see from his point of view.

"There's a fairy flying around, the dogs are playing with it, can you see it?" he said, smiling. "There's magic here, don't you feel it?"

"What will happen if they catch her?" Payal asked, and he saw that teasing smile again. "You should visit Beatrix Potter's cottage if you want fairies."

"No, that was rabbits," Brenda said. "I'm sure she didn't do fairies."

A good-natured argument on Miss Potter's literary contribution to the world lasted until they were called through for dinner, and Robert was convinced he'd enhanced it by giving them 'Little Peter Rabbit had a fly upon his nose', with all the actions, which provoked a lot of hilarity. Somewhere along the way he'd lost count of the drinks he'd had, and stopped off in the toilet on the way, realising he had a slight list in his gait.

Better start drinking water.

But he wanted his rational, thinking mind dulled, even though he risked saying something he'd regret, if his inhibitions were freed. The fact that he was discussing this with himself was a good sign, but he definitely decided to drink more water. When he reached the dining room, he found the others seated at a round table, and he was placed between Pam and Payal. Luckily, Maria was next to Payal so he wouldn't have to look at her, though he could see her from the corner of his eye, and if he turned to speak to Payal.

The food was really good, and though the sparkling water made him burp, he managed to do it quietly. He was enjoying coffee, sitting back, when he heard the sonic boom.

Nobody'd better be in the lake.

Annabelle halted close to the window, and jerked a thumb over her shoulder. Maria stood outside, in a pool of light from a copper-topped lamp post and he saw the anticipation on her face as she dialled a number and put the phone to her ear.

"It's him," Annabelle called. "She just had a text to call him."

He watched as Maria's face changed from excitement to confusion and then crumpled into tears, her hair falling over her face as she bent forward.

He froze in his seat for a moment and then leaned over to Payal, touching her arm to get her attention. She looked at him smiling and he indicated Maria with his eyes. Payal turned and saw her, and the smile disappeared.

"Oh no," she whispered, and hurried to Maria,

putting an arm round her, drawing her out of view of the table. The coffee soured in his mouth, and the noise from the others was suddenly strident and discordant.

"I'm going to bed," he said, standing up. He waved his arms in front of him as a generalised goodnight. "See you all tomorrow."

"Breakfast's at eight," Ashley said.

"That is cruel and unusual punishment, Ashley. Someone bash on my door if I'm not down by eight-thirty."

They all called their goodnights and he left them to it. In truth, guilt was driving him away. He knew, deep down, that his confrontation with Katie and her husband had provoked the call, and he dreaded being the instrument of more pain for Maria. An absurd thought that he should call Katie to find out, was instantly swamped by common sense, and he was thankful he'd drunk the water.

"He was supposed to come up late, and stay the night with her," Annabelle said. "He's just told her he's reconciled with his wife."

"Bastard," Robert hissed, startling another guest who scuttled out of his way. "Sorry, not you," he called to the startled man. "A different bastard... I mean... sorry."

He thumped his way upstairs and entered his room.

"Don't turn the light on," Annabelle said. "Sshh!"

"What?" he whispered, and then heard the voices. His balcony door was open and Annabelle flew to it, beckoning him. He walked carefully over and recognised Maria's voice. Peering down, he saw her and Payal sitting on a wooden bench to his right. Maria was hunched over and Payal had her arm around her. Their words carried easily up to him.

"— so damn stupid," Maria said tearfully. "He told me they'd separated, the divorce was happening, everything, and I stupidly believed him. Stupid, stupid, stupid."

She wept and Payal smoothed the hair back from her face. "It was all lies, why am I so bloody brainless?" Maria said, gulping through her tears. "I've messed everything up with Rob for a bloody lying, shitting, worthless bastard."

She wept again, clutching at Payal's hand. She cried for some time, and sniffed into a tissue Payal gave her.

"I deserve it," Maria said, vehemently. "Rob was decent and kind, and he didn't push. He made me laugh so often and, god, he *cared* about me. When Phillip came to the theatre he really hurt my arm, and Rob almost broke his finger getting his hand off me. Phillip used that to make me feel sympathy for him, and I was shitty to Robert the next day, I just didn't see straight. God, I hate myself."

"You'd been with Phillip for two years," Payal said soothingly. "It was never going to be easy for you, Maria."

"But I didn't have to hurt someone who'd done nothing but like me, did I?"

"You didn't see straight, you said that."

"He hates me, he's hardly spoken at all."

"Have you spoken to him?"

"No." Maria started crying again, and Robert didn't want to hear any more, it was too painful. He pulled back and closed the French window carefully, then drew the heavy curtains across, and fumbled his way across to the bed and turned the side light on. Annabelle flew to the bedside cabinet, and stood with her hands behind her back, not saying anything. Robert sat on the side of the bed, picked up the hotel notepad and pen and wrote the words he remembered so well.

It's just a bad day, not a bad life.

"Elaine wrote that to me five or six times," Robert said. "I'd arrive at the hospital and she'd be asleep, but she knew I was always coming, hated it if she didn't speak to me, because she didn't wake up before I left again. She'd leave me a note as her way of talking to me. Are they still out there?"

"Yes."

Robert opened his door, and checked nobody was in the corridor. He pushed the note under Maria's door and was back in his room immediately.

"What now?" Annabelle said.

"You're asking me? Raid the mini-bar and get an early morning call."

Annabelle checked on the women in the garden, hoping she'd hear something that would help her bring Maria closer to Robert, but mostly it was Payal consoling her, talking good sense, telling her to wait and see what happened. Maria wanted to go home, but Payal convinced her to stay, which Annabelle was quite relieved about, or she'd have had to rouse Robert, who was snoring under the effects of two miniature scotches. There's always tomorrow, she thought. Loads of time.

CHAPTER TWENTY

The following morning Robert had no idea what to expect, but nothing was said over breakfast. Maria looked pale, but didn't instigate any conversation with him. He realised she wouldn't know who the note was from, and he was happy with that. But anticipation built in him, and he knew he'd have to speak to her. He could always send Annabelle to spy for him.

"So, what have you got planned for us?" Ashley asked.

"You'll see," Robert said. "I want everyone in reception in fifteen minutes, wearing jeans or trousers and comfortable clothing."

They were all on time and he led them to the minibus, ignoring their questions, layering on the mystery. He'd memorised the route and they arrived at the site within half an hour. He pulled up close to the wooded field, behind the two large vans, and turned off the engine.

"This is it, everyone out," he said.

He led them into the field and up to the roped-off area, and they lined up along it, puzzled. It was more of a meadow, reaching back to the trees, with very long grass and clumps of flowers and weeds that grew even taller.

"Okay, here we are."

"What are we doing?" Payal said, and at that

moment eight figures rose up from the grass. They all wore combat overalls, and black plastic face masks and each had a paintball gun across their chests. There was a momentary silence, and then pandemonium erupted as they all talked at once.

"—I'm not handling a gun—"

"—paint will ruin the countryside—"

"—not spiritual—"

"—I'm not shooting someone—"

"—so violent—"

"Ooh, dishy," Pam said. "Can I be captured, please?"

This brought one or two laughs, and Robert was grateful.

"It's just a game, cowboys and Indians for grownups," he said. "The paintballs contain a vegetable dye that dissolves in the rain and has no impact on the plant life, except to provide nutrients. The guns work on compressed air, which is actually cleaner than the air we're breathing right now, so it benefits the environment."

"But, all that violence," Brenda said, wringing her hands.

"It's not right, shooting people," Ian said.

"It's make-believe, nobody dies. Why don't you dowse it?" Robert asked. He caught Annabelle's attention and indicated with his eyes as Ian got his pendulum out. She understood and flew onto the weight, holding on like a child on a swing. Ian moved the pendulum, making it flow in a circle.

"Whee!" Annabelle called and fluttered her wings furiously. The pendulum immediately changed direction and swung back and forth in a straight line. Ian looked up at Robert.

"We should do it," he said.

They were suited and booted in short order, and given the safety briefing.

"All you ladies should wear chest protectors, you can get bruising if you're hit on soft areas from close up," the organiser said. "I was asked to provide a thirty eight double D, who needs...?"

His voice died away as Pam stood up, smiling.

"It's thirty six double F, but it'll do," she said, taking the two plastic cups from him.

"Okay, come and get the paintball guns, masks down at all times from now on, unless you're in the safety area in the woods."

Brenda stepped close to Robert and dropped her voice. "I'm not sure I can do this, Robert. It's so... aggressive."

"It's okay, Bren, you don't have to. Stay right back and defend if you like, you don't have to go after anyone."

Robert asked Annabelle to stay with Brenda, and fetch him if there was a problem. They followed the organisers into the woods for the first game, and gathered round Robert. They all wore yellow facemasks and had yellow armbands to distinguish them from the enemy. Robert had a yellow flag on a long piece of wood, and stuck it in the ground.

"Okay, this is capture the flag. We have to capture their flag, which is over there somewhere, and they'll try and capture ours. Two of you stay here and defend, the rest come with me, spread out. If you're hit, lift your gun above your head and go back to the safe area, inside the netting. Ready?"

They all nodded, though Brenda did so reluctantly. Robert raised an airhorn and gave a loud blast. It was answered by another in the distance.

"Let's go!"

They followed Robert, running for cover.

Annabelle sat in the crook of a tree watching Brenda and Payal guard the flag. Brenda didn't look interested at all, just sat back, cradling the gun, but when the paint balls started flying, she ducked down pretty sharpish. Payal started firing, but after a few seconds a loud splat and a small scream from Payal showed she'd been hit. She got to her feet, holding her paintball gun up and Annabelle saw the yellow paint on her facemask.

Brenda crouched lower, and an opposition player

leaned out from behind a tree sprayed everywhere with paintballs, and dashed to another tree, and did the same.

"Bloody hell," Brenda said, as paintballs burst on the tree in front of her, and one narrowly missed her head. The guy ran for the flag, and Brenda popped up and pulled the trigger of her gun. A stream of paintballs flew through the air and hit him at least six times. He fell over and Brenda rushed over to him.

"I'm so sorry," she said. "Are you all right?"

"Yeah," he laughed. "Good shooting, you've played this before, haven't you?"

Annabelle left Brenda to it, and flew off to check on Robert. The game played furiously back and forth and although the clinic did lose, there was a lot of loud noise back in the safe area when the game ended.

Brenda was cleaning her gun barrel and Robert walked over to her.

"All right, Bren?"

"Wonderful," she said with relish. "I'm visualising all of them as the ones who convinced Jason to go to New Zealand, it's very cathartic."

***

Robert's team were besieging the fort and Robert didn't hear the sonic boom, because of all the noise, but Annabelle shouted in his ear.

"What is it?" he asked, concerned.

"It's Payal."

"Is she hurt?"

"No. You have to come."

Robert ducked back and followed Annabelle back into the woods. Payal was sitting in a hollow underneath a large bush, with her mask pushed up, crying, her hands over her face.

"Let me know if anyone comes," Robert said urgently to Annabelle, and she nodded. He ran to Payal, and crouched down.

"Payal, what is it? Are you hurt?"

"Noooo," she wailed.

Robert put his gun down and lifted his mask, and clasped her to him. She threw her arms around him, and cried into his chest. He held her, stroking her head through the combat hood. Eventually she stopped, and lifted her head from him. Yellow paint was smudged across her face, and he wiped the tears gently from her cheeks.

"What is it?" he asked.

"I'll never get pregnant," she sniffled. "All my sisters and cousins have children, and they keep asking when Ashley and I are starting a family." More tears welled up, and one more decision of Robert's fell into place.

"Payal, I'm going to say something to you, and I mean every single word. You and Ashley are two of the best people I've ever known, and I can't imagine how hard it is for you right now. But you have someone who adores you, who wants to spend the rest of his life with you, no matter what happens. There's nothing more precious than that, believe me, I know. To have someone who wants to spend every minute of every day with you is so rare it's almost unique, and if you have that, you hold onto it with both hands, so tight, that everything else is secondary."

Payal stared at him, and he lost himself in her eyes for a second.

"I don't know if this is going to insult you and Ashley, and I have my reasons for offering, but I'd like to give you the money for the fertility treatment. As a gift, for two people I'm so happy to call friends, and who I've come to like so much that I want to see them happy as well."

Tears welled up in Payal's eyes and Robert couldn't help it, his own eyes watered. She blinked through hers, and reached out to him, wiping his tears away.

"I've sold my bike, got thousands for it," he said, needing to speak, "and I'm earning more than I can spend, thanks to you two. Please let me do this."

She tipped her head slightly, staring into his eyes, and

her hair fell from behind one ear. Without thinking, Robert reached out to retrieve it. Payal pressed her head into his hand and hers came up, cupping his hand in hers, holding it against her. She stared at him, and then released his hand.

"I've never kissed anyone except Ashley," she said, and grabbed his face in both hands and kissed him passionately.

She pulled back and her smile lit up the woods.

"Thank you, Robert," she said.

"For the kiss, or the offer?" he asked, shocked by what she'd done, unable to get his brain into gear.

"Both."

She kissed him again, then sat back and giggled with both hands over her mouth. Every time she looked at him she giggled a bit more, but at last she got control and stopped.

"Thank you. There aren't enough words to tell you how good it makes me feel, but I have to say no."

Robert tried to speak, but she put a finger over his lips.

"It's the most wonderful thing anyone has ever done for us, but it would diminish Ashley, if we accepted. It's an Indian thing, and I love him and I couldn't do that to him, no matter how much I might want to. The man must provide, and Ashley is doing that. We'll be able to afford it next year, and I'll only be twenty seven, then. But thank you, I'll always cherish your gift, even though I turned it down. I..."

She smiled and looked away, then back at him.

"Thank you," she said, and he couldn't think of anything else to say. But he felt good. Really good. Sadness lurked there, way in the background, but he accepted what she said, and understood it.

"Mask on," he managed to say. "We've got a battle to win."

She smiled and fixed his mask first, then her own, and hoisted her paintball gun.

"How do I look?" she asked, but stood and ran before he could answer.

Annabelle hovered in front of him, tipping her head to try and see past the grime on his facemask.

"Could you stop surprising me?" she said. "You're making my mascara run."

"You're not wearing any."

"Doesn't matter. I'll see you later, I've got things to do. Can I trust you not to get into any trouble?"

"Of course not."

Annabelle watched him climb to his feet and jog back towards the sounds of the fight. She shook her head, wondering at his goodness, and it made her more determined than ever to see him happy.

***

The clamour in the minibus going back to the hotel was incredibly upbeat, everyone intent on telling their stories.

"Lunch in ten minutes," Ashley called as they pulled up, to be greeted by a chorus of good-natured complaints. "We all agreed to that last game, it's not my fault we're late."

They tumbled out of the minibus, laughing and joking with each other, and Robert drove it around to the car park. He hurried upstairs, aware of how much his stomach was rumbling. As he reached his room, Maria's door opened, and he got the impression she'd been waiting.

"Robert?" she said, hesitantly. She had his note in her hand, and gestured with it. "Thank you for this."

"You're welcome. Those words have helped me a lot in the past."

She flushed, and he realised she might take it to mean recently.

"I enjoyed the paintball," she said. "Good chance to get rid of gloominess, thank you."

She stepped back into her room, closing her door.

Gloominess?

He said the word in his mind so many times, it became meaningless, but he found himself whistling as he skipped down the stairs to the dining room. He saw Ashley and Payal were sitting next to each other, and the closeness between them was lovely. He sat between Brenda and Christina, directly opposite Maria, and she smiled at him. Briefly, but it was there, and there didn't seem to be any gloominess lurking.

Lunch was as good as the last night's dinner, and they were just finishing their desserts when a middle-aged man approached their table. He was well-dressed and not a little overweight, but looked the genial host he turned out to be. He shook hands with Ashley, and turned to address the table.

"How do you like it?" he asked. "Rooms okay?" A chorus of affirmatives greeted this. "Just re-opened after almost a year," he said. "Knocked down the old block, landscaped the gardens, even changed the name."

"You've done a fabulous job," Christina said.

"Thank you. You all work together, then?"

"Yes," Ashley said. "Natural health centre in London."

"I was treated by an Osteopath several years ago, he was here on his honeymoon," the owner said, putting his hand in his lower back, pretending pain. "Fixed my back up a treat, I gave them a champagne supper on the house."

Oh shit, oh shit, oh shit. Synchronicity is seriously pissed. Shit.

"What... what was the name of the hotel before?" Robert asked, dreading the answer.

"Queen's Arms Hotel, very uninspiring, really."

"That was me," Robert said quietly, more to himself than the owner, but his hearing must have been good.

"I thought you looked familiar," the man said, triumphantly. "This is such a coincidence, let me show you something."

He strode from the room and nobody spoke as they all stared at Robert.

"You're married?" Maria finally asked, and he heard the anger in her voice.

"No, I—"

"Here it is," called the owner as he came back in, flicking through the pages of a book. "I was going

179

through the old guest books this morning, wondering if I should chuck them out. Here we are."

He showed an entry to Robert who didn't look at it. The owner read out what was written there.

"We're coming back every year forever, so please put your back out when we're here. The supper was stupendous. Elaine and Robert Kirk." He closed the book, smiling. "Is your wife with you?"

"No, she... she died five years ago."

There was an appalled silence and Robert couldn't stay there any longer, and he stood up.

"Excuse me."

When he got to his room, his hand trembled so much he could barely swipe the card, but he opened the door, hung out the 'do not disturb' sign, and let out the breath he'd been holding, as he collapsed onto the bed. He didn't know what to do, but he wished Annabelle was with him. He lay there for a long time, and then got up, took a small bottle of water from the fridge and left the room. He walked down to the far end of the corridor, and went down the back stairs that opened directly onto the lawns. A small bridge crossed a stream that led down to the lake and the path meandered into woods after that. He'd just reached the bridge when he heard the voice behind him.

"Robert?" He turned and Maria walked up to him. "Are you okay?" she asked hesitantly. "Is there anything I can do?"

"Walk with me?" he asked, and she nodded.

They walked in silence for a while and he would have liked it if she took his arm, the way she'd done before. They followed the path into the woods, and the sun dappled them as they strolled. The sounds of the Hotel faded behind them, and birdcall and the breeze rustling the leaves replaced it. Another couple coming the other way said hello to them, and he heard Maria reply. He said nothing, uncertain how to begin, but after some time they came to a clearing with three carved benches, made from fallen trunks, and it seemed like a good place to stop.

He sat on the furthest one, so he could see if anyone else approached and she sat beside him.

"Do you want to tell me?" she asked gently. "I have no right to ask that for myself, and I only ask if it might help you."

Robert wanted to take her hand, but didn't. He looked at her and saw the concern in her eyes, and the fact that she was here, at that moment, made him take a chance.

"I hate people feeling sorry for me," he said. "I'm still here, perfectly healthy, functioning, able to be happy or sad, or indifferent to life, able to go on living in any way I choose, and that used to make me feel guilty. It's taken me a very long time, but I've come to learn that grief is a selfish emotion. It's understandable, and we have to grieve our loss, but I was stupid. I clung to my grief and anger. I pushed away the people who loved me, wallowing in my loss, feeling only my own pain. After Elaine died, everyone felt so sorry for me, and what I really needed in the end was a damn good slap, and someone to say it was Elaine who died, not me. I didn't say it to myself for years, and by then grief had become a habit. I didn't think of anything except my loss and my grief. God, I was utterly selfish. Stupid and selfish."

She reached out and touched his arm, he half-smiled.

"If I tell people, they feel sorry for me, and that used to compound it. I left all my friends and family and retreated into seclusion in Cornwall. Elaine would have been so disappointed with me, quite rightly. She died of leukaemia and was pregnant at the time, and not once did she feel sorry for herself. She felt sorry for all those around her, she felt angry because she wanted to stay with me and have the baby and she lost all that, but she never once felt sorry for herself."

He leaned against the back of the seat and his shoulder touched hers, and he liked that.

"Some spark inside me made me come to London and I've started to enjoy life, and think of others for a change. I'm pretty messed up, and I've got a long way to go, but I feel I'm on the right path."

"It's a bad day, not a bad life," Maria said, and he smiled.

"Exactly."

They sat listening to the sounds of the woods around them.

"You shouldn't really take advice from me, with my track record," Maria said, half-smiling. "But have you thought of writing to her?"

"Who?"

"Elaine. The physical act of writing carries an energy all of its own, far more than thinking, or speaking out loud. It externalises what we're feeling inside, and allows us to look at it dispassionately. I should know, someone pushed a note under my door."

Robert thought of the letter Elaine had written to him, and knew he could do the same.

"Thank you," he said. "I'll do that."

They sat for a while longer. "I'm going to walk a bit further," Robert said. "I'll be back later, would you tell the others I just needed a bit of time alone?"

"Of course," Maria said, touching his arm again. "Don't stay out too long, or we'll come looking for you."

"Right."

He watched her walk away, and was glad she hadn't offered to stay with him. He'd crossed the last line, he thought, and wanted some time to mull things over.

He was skimming stones across a lake when Annabelle found him. She watched him for a while, saw him pause as a dragonfly skimmed the surface, and he waited until it had passed before he threw another stone.

"When I was a kid, someone told me dragonflies would sew up your lips, so you had to keep your mouth open when they passed," Robert said, surprising her. "Still do it, even now."

"Dragonflies are fairies in training," Annabelle said. "This is flight school for them."

"I think I prefer that to having my lips sewn up."

"Why are you here on your own?"

"Ah. It might need another complaint to head office, I'm afraid. I spent my honeymoon at this hotel all those years ago, and the owner remembered Elaine and me. Was a bit of a shock when he brought out the guest book she'd written in. I wanted some time on my own."

"You can't get the help these days," Annabelle said, exasperated. "You're not upset, though, how come?"

"Maria walked with me a little, gave me some very good advice. Would you go and check on them all, for me? I don't want them worrying, you can come and get me if they're getting upset."

"Really?"

"Really. I'm enjoying the solitude, it's helping me think."

"Okay. Keep your mouth open, here comes a fairy in training."

Annabelle flew alongside the dragonfly for a short distance and then zipped into the woods. She felt good. Robert was taking the upsets she knew he would have to face and getting over them more quickly. And Maria now knew the truth about the cheating bastard, and clearly understood what a great catch Robert was. Just a little more tinkering for them to fall in love, and her job would be done. Be a shame to move on, she'd really liked this assignment, but with all the cock-ups by head office, she knew she could put in a request for call-back in six months, and it would be granted. It would be lovely to see them happy together.

She flew past Pam, who was carrying a large plastic shopping bag, filled with elderberries. She and Carlo were going to make it, Annabelle thought, and Robert had made that happen. He deserved to be happy, he was a genuine good guy. So few of those around.

"Tina!"

Annabelle stopped to see what Pam wanted with Christina. There'd still been a little tension between them, and she wished she could help them both, but the rules were rules. Christina was walking towards the hotel, but turned at Pam's call.

"I got these for you, Tina," Pam said, hurrying to her. "Sorry we threw your last lot away."

Tina looked in the bag and saw all the elderberries. Pam had scratches up her arms, and looked a little forlorn, Annabelle thought. Christina's face broke into an enormous smile and she hugged Pam, who looked delighted. Unfortunately, the bag was between them and when they broke apart, they both had elderberry stains on their blouses.

"Should get some soda water on that," Annabelle said, watching them laugh about it. "Those stains will never come out, otherwise."

Christina and Pam linked arms and walked towards the hotel. Annabelle saw Ashley with Ian and Brenda, sitting at an outside table with the remains of a cream tea, and heard the animated conversation and laughter.

"So far, so good," Annabelle muttered. "Where's Maria?" She spotted her sitting at the bar, Payal next to her. She saw her raise a shot glass of alcohol. "Uh oh."

Maria had downed it just as she flew in.

"But he's all right?" Payal was saying.

"I think he's fine."

"So why are you drinking like this?" Annabelle asked, frustrated.

"So what's the problem?" Payal asked, and Annabelle held a hand up for a high five from Payal, forgetting herself for a moment.

"Do you suppose he hasn't slept with anyone since his wife died?" Maria said, signalling to the girl behind the bar for a refill.

"I've no idea," Payal said.

"He's a great kisser," Maria said, dreamily.

"Yes," Payal agreed. "I imagine he is," she added very hastily. "But what...?"

The bargirl topped up Maria's glass, and looked at Payal, who held up a hand as a negative.

"What can I do?" Maria asked, holding the glass up. "He's still in love with a wife who died years ago."

She knocked the shot back, signalled for another.

"Well, of course he is," Annabelle said, annoyed. "But he's falling in love with you."

"He must be over her by now," Payal said.

"Would Ashley be over you after five years? I doubt it."

Annabelle and Payal thought about that for a moment, then Payal reached out and took Maria's shot glass that had just been filled, and knocked it back. Unsurprised, Maria waved for two more.

"The problem is, he has an idealised, perfect picture of her in his mind," Maria said.

"Is that so bad?"

"Yes it is. Who could ever measure up to that image? In his memory she doesn't snore, need a bikini wax, or shave her legs, or have bad breath, or lousy periods, or... or..."

"Or fart in bed," the bargirl said, filling two shot glasses.

Maria and Payal looked at the bargirl, who shrugged. Maria nodded, knowingly, and the bargirl turned for another bottle.

"You do all those things?" Payal asked, slightly shocked.

"No, of course not," Maria said. "Well, maybe some of them. The point is, no one can compete with a memory, it's impossible. You can't live up to those expectations, you'd end up both being hurt. It's not worth the risk."

They didn't hear the explosion as Annabelle shot upwards, but a glass crystal from the chandelier above them fell, where she knocked it off, and the bargirl caught it neatly. Maria and Payal look at each other and knocked back the shots. The bargirl poured two more.

"On the house," she said.

They knocked them back.

"What would you do, in my place?" Maria asked Payal, pointing at the glasses. The bargirl refilled them, and waited for the answer. Annabelle zoomed back, kneeling on the bar, hands held in supplication.

"Please Payal, please Payal, pleeeeease!" she begged.

"Honestly?" Payal said, after she'd thought about it for a moment, looking into the distance. "I'd say the risk is worth it. Robert's such a lovely guy, and he's obviously smitten with you. Yes, there might be some tough times, but if you fall in love, you'll always be there to support each other, and there's nothing better than that, is there? If you take the risk and it doesn't work out, the things you'll lose may cause pain and hurt, but they will heal in the end. If you don't take the risk, you'll lose everything."

Payal knocked her drink back.

"You're right," Maria said and threw her drink back.

"Yes!" Annabelle cried, exultant, and another crystal fell from the chandelier, as she exploded upwards. The bargirl caught it and they all looked up at it, then moved further down the bar, away from the chandelier. Annabelle flew above them, sprinkling fairydust all over. "Drinks on the house!"

The bargirl must have been more in touch with the inner world, because she poured more shots.

CHAPTER TWENTY ONE

Robert got back to his room about an hour later, and sat down to write his letter. He knew what he wanted to say, and even though it could never be delivered, he knew it would help him move on. He'd almost finished when the scream startled him so much his hand jerked and he drew a line up the page. It came from Maria's room, and he moved without thinking, as a series of loud gasps came straight after it, someone in terrible pain. He shot off the bed and out through the French window. Hers was open and he didn't think, but leapt across from his balcony to hers. He was in her room in a second, fearing the worst. Small screams came from the bathroom, and he opened the door, rushing inside.

Maria stood naked in her shower and he felt the ice-cold water splash off her onto him. She was covered in goose-bumps and gave another small scream as she saw him, her eyes wide. He spun round, turning his back to her.

"God, I'm so sorry," he blurted. "I heard you scream, I thought you were hurt. I'm so sorry."

He dashed from the bathroom and out into the corridor, and realised he had no door key for his room. Embarrassed, he hurried down the corridor to get another from reception. As he passed Ashley and Payal's room he heard another scream, which made him increase his pace.

187

He got another keycard and went into the bar.

"What can I get you?" the girl behind the bar asked, putting a dish of peanuts and nibbles in front of him.

"A Budvaar and a Tequila chaser," he said.

Something caught his eye on the top shelf with the single malt whiskies, and he realised it was Annabelle, slumped down, snoring. The bargirl was at the end of the bar, opening a chiller cabinet, so Robert picked up a peanut and threw it. It missed her, but hit the bottle she was leaning up against, and she woke up, bleary-eyed.

"I feel terrible," she croaked.

"What have you been doing?" he hissed.

"Celebrating with Payal and Maria," she said, and her speech was a little slurred. "They were here a moment ago..."

"They're both having cold showers," he whispered. "What you could do with, obviously."

"Oh, god," Annabelle said, sitting up, clutching at the bottle for support. She fell forwards and he almost lunged to catch her, but her wings flapped into action and she lurched upright, drifting left and right trying to maintain a horizon. "If I'm not out of the lake in five minutes, send a search party, will you?"

He winced as she bumped into the mirror behind the bar, and was convinced she used a very rude word.

"It's that way," he said, pointing over his shoulder.

"Smartarse," she said and he daren't look as she flew towards the open window, but she must have made it through as he didn't hear a crash or swear-words.

"There you go," the bargirl said, putting his drinks down in front of him, along with the salt and lime slice. "Put it on your room?"

"Yes, please," Robert said, showing his key card.

He licked the salt, knocked the Tequila back in one, and sucked on the slice of lime. Picking up the beer, he wandered out onto the lawn, casually strolling to the bridge over the stream, sipping as he went. He thought he could see something splashing in the shallows of the lake, and kept his eye on it. It was Annabelle, and after a short time she zoomed towards him, flying past, then looping back, obviously air-drying herself, as she was running her hands through her hair as she went. After three or four more passes she landed on the bridge, and clasped herself, shivering. Her hair was a mess, somewhat tangled.

"Bloody Norah, it's cold when the water evaporates."

"I've got a hairdryer in my room," Robert said.

"Nope, I needed to sober up."

"How much did you have?"

"A mouthful of those shots Payal and Maria were drinking," he told her.

"What were you celebrating?"

"Never you mind. I think—" She broke off and stared at him suspiciously. "How do you know they were having cold showers?"

"I heard the screams, Maria's in the room next to mine, remember?"

"Oh, right. Don't drink too much more yourself, Ian's taking you tree-hugging after dinner."

"Seriously?"

"Seriously. He and Brenda want to test the energetics of the area. What?"

"I'm not terribly into that kind of thing, but I'll do it for them. They're good people."

"You didn't believe in fairies until you met me."

"True. Anything's possible, I guess."

"I'm going to warm up."

"Fine, I'll see you later."

Robert took his drink back to his room, and carried on writing to Elaine. It wasn't difficult, and he filled four pages, telling her everything. He thought he'd take the letter with him on Monday and maybe read it to her.

"What are you doing?" Annabelle asked.

She looked a lot better, and had some colour in her cheeks. "I'm writing to Elaine."

"Oh."

"Maria suggested it, and... I'm finding it really useful."

"Good. Did you tell Elaine about me?"

"Of course. I said there's this tiny version of her, constantly nagging me, trying to make me do things I don't want to do. Even if it is for my own good."

Annabelle sniffed, and he saw she looked emotional. "What?"

"I like being a tiny version of her," she said in a rush, then zoomed out of the window.

Robert finished the letter, smiling, and sealed it in an envelope, feeling good about things.

Dinner was good, and he could tell by the little smiles that played around Maria's mouth whenever she looked at him, she wasn't too upset. All the group deliberately avoided the subject of lunch, and he was grateful. By the time Ian led them into the woods, he was feeling quite mellow and chatted with Pam, a little frightened to instigate conversation with Maria.

"I won't be able to hug a tree," Pam said. "Can't get near it."

"Find a small one," Robert said. "Or turn sideways on."

Annabelle seemed in high spirits, which Robert thought quite apt, considering where he'd found her previously.

Ian led them off the path into the woods and they arrived at a small clearing, where the sun still penetrated, and it was pleasantly warm. He asked them to turn off their mobiles, and instructed them how to feel the energy of a tree, how to embrace its soul. Robert went along with it, laying his cheek against a large oak, arms stretching around it. Directly opposite him Maria was doing the same and she looked straight at him. He was uncertain if the tree was pulsating, or whether his pulse suddenly beat stronger but she smiled at him and he couldn't help but smile back. She had those blues jeans on again, the ones that made her legs look so long.

Annabelle flew in circles around them all, sprinkling

fairy dust, and Ian declared the rise in energy was the group growing together, like the trees that surrounded them. Despite himself, Robert conceded there might be some truth in that. It was impossible not to feel good with this bunch of people.

"Okay, now you've all done that, let's try this exercise," Brenda said. She gathered them in the clearing, and opened her bag, handing out a length of dark cloth to each of them.

"This is about sensing more subtle energies, but allowing our own will to direct us. Ian will demonstrate."

Ian tied the cloth around his eyes, lifted his hands to chest level, palms out, and slowly turned in a circle.

"He's sensing for the strongest energy, seeing what draws him," Brenda said in a hushed voice.

Ian took a tentative step forward, then another, tilting his head, as though listening. Then he walked forward slowly and fetched up against a large elm tree.

He seemed a little surprised when he took off the blindfold, but nodded and stroked the tree.

"Very strong emanations," he said. "I thought the oak would be stronger."

Robert thought that might have a lot to do with Annabelle sitting in the elm.

"Okay, everyone try," Brenda said. "I'll keep an eye on you, if you're heading into stinging nettles."

Robert pulled at the blindfold and felt a give in the material. When he put it on, he realised he could see, as though looking through a veil. He shrugged mentally. Karma. But as soon as he held his hand up, he felt the pull. He started in that direction, knowing where it would lead him, and saw Maria slightly to his right, moving in his direction. He took a few paces towards her, and then stopped, uncertain. If she was heading for a tree, it could be embarrassing. Then he saw the small smile on her face and decided to risk it. He stepped closer to her, and she towards him. When their hands were an inch apart, he could hear her breathing, sensed the warmth in her palms. He didn't know how long he stood there, but finally spoke.

"Comé sta tua nonna?" he said very quietly.

"My grandmother is fine," Maria replied.

Their hands touched, and a shiver ran through him. He leaned in and kissed her.

**

Robert woke slowly, dulled by a soft lassitude that affected every part of his body. Sunlight streamed in through the window and he could hear the birds calling. He opened his eyes to see Maria beside him. She lay on her side, facing him. Her hair was loose, swept over her shoulder, and he almost reached out to stroke the soft downiness, but didn't want to wake her. Carefully, he propped himself on his elbow, supporting his head and watched her. Her face was softer without the worry lines in her forehead, and a smile curved one side of her mouth. He would have like to have kissed that corner, to capture the emotion that caused it, but lay waiting, content. She sighed in her sleep, then slowly opened her eyes and looked at him.

"Hi," she said.

"Hi."

He leaned towards her and kissed her gently. She lifted her head and he slid his arm under her and they snuggled up, her arm warm across his chest.

"How did we get here?" Maria asked.

"No idea. Last thing I knew I was blindfolded, thought I was going to be shot. This must be my last request."

"Me too. Let's make it last."

She stroked his chest, twirling her fingers around the hair that grew in the centre.

"Any other last requests?" she said.

"Let me see, now... I'm in bed with a beautiful woman, we're both naked, the day is just starting... there must be something... I think I'll sing."

He pushed her gently and she rolled onto her back and he kissed her on the lips.

"Maria, I just kissed a girl named Maria," he sang quietly, and kissed her on the lips again. He moved his mouth down, following the curve of her neck, kissing her as he went, still singing around the kisses.

"And suddenly that name will never be the same to me."

He kissed the hollow at the base of her throat, her hands came up around his back, gripping into him firmly, as he kissed one nipple and then the other, humming the tune.

"Maria," he sang louder. "Kiss her loud and there's music playing."

Robert blew a raspberry in her tummy button, and felt her shake as she laughed. He moved further down and she gasped.

"Kiss her soft, and it's..."

The rest of the song became indistinct, and drowned out by Maria's moans, as she gripped his hair urgently.

They showered together, and breakfast had finished by the time they got dressed. She'd sneaked back to her room for clean clothes, but still wore the blue jeans, which looked great. Waiting outside his door was a continental breakfast for two, with a rose laid across the tray.

They sat on his bed and ate.

"You could have seriously injured yourself, jumping onto my balcony," Maria said.

"I was so worried, I didn't think. Worth it though, that cold water does make the flesh pucker, doesn't it?" She threw the last of her croissant at him, grinning, and he caught it neatly. "Why did you need the cold shower, anyway?"

"Let's just say Payal and I were in the bar, and wanted to celebrate the fact that you were staying. She thought you might leave, you looked so upset."

"No, it was the shock. I should have told you all before. Stupid of me."

Maria leaned over and kissed him.

"Not stupid. Understandable. Allowable." She kissed him again. "I think I was the most shocked – I'd had all that crap from Phillip, and thought 'oh no, not another married one'.

"I'm sorry."

"Don't be. But don't ever lie to me, okay?"

"Okay."

She smiled and there was a glint in her eye, and she twisted round slightly, placing one hand on her bottom.

"Does my bum look big in this?"

"I don't think so, but the jeans are in the way, show me your bum."

"Oh, very good," she laughed.

She fell on him and kissed him passionately, upending a plate and crushing a Danish pastry against his shirt as he fell backwards on the bed. He cupped her bottom in his hands, squeezing gently.

"Feels good to me."

"Me too," she said, laughing.

They kissed for a while, and she lay with her head on his shoulder, neither of them wanting to move, it seemed.

"Listen, I'm hiring a car and going back to Manchester, later. Can you come with me?"

"I'd love to, but I've got patients tomorrow," she said regretfully. "I think I'm fully booked."

"No problem. I'll be back in London on Tuesday. I know this really great show in a tiny theatre, we could catch supper after."

"I'd like that. I'll do it properly this time."

He changed his shirt and they joined the others for a boat trip around the lake. Pam winked at him and Payal turned her smile up for both of them, and the rest of the morning passed in a blur of laughter and mutual teasing.

"I'd like to propose a toast to Ashley and Payal for arranging this weekend," Robert said over lunch, holding his glass of orange juice up. "It's been the most amazing weekend I've had in years."

Enthusiastic agreement greeted this, and Maria's foot rubbed his ankle as the others joined the toast.

"And I'd like to thank Robert for making it happen," Ashley said, "and especially for the paintball. I've got bruises in places I find it difficult to explain, and even Payal won't rub arnica on them."

They all laughed and Robert looked at Ashley and Payal. She glanced at him at that moment and nodded to him, a tiny almost imperceptible nod, but he saw it, and was glad of it.

"We leave in an hour," Ashley said. "You must vacate your rooms by two."

"Have you got much packing to do?" Maria asked as they headed for the stairs, arms around each other.

"Why? What did you have in mind?" Robert asked coyly.

"Well, I won't see you until Tuesday, I thought we could... play monopoly."

Robert laughed.

"Give me ten minutes to pack. Your place or mine?"

"Mine, there's way too many breadcrumbs in your bed."

He kissed her at her door, and hurried into his room, whistling. Annabelle perched on his minibar, watching him throw his clothes into his case.

"Hi."

"Hi gorgeous," Robert said.

"How are you feeling?"

"I'm okay."

"Only okay?"

"Well, she is amazing. Almost as amazing as you."

"If only you'd listened to me earlier..." Annabelle said, almost blushing.

"I guess I had to find out for myself, didn't I?"

"Yes, you did. Now I have to go."

"You can't leave me, now," Robert said, shocked.

"You don't need me anymore."

"What are you saying? Of course I need you."

"No you don't."

Robert looked at Annabelle, saw the little smile, the emotion she was holding in.

"Yeah, but I like having you around. We can still see each other, can't we?"

"Well there are other losers who need me, you know."

"Lucky guys. What did I do to deserve you?"

"I think you know," Annabelle said quietly. "Love never dies."

"Yeah."

They stared at each other, and he saw Annabelle biting her lip, trying to stop the tears.

"You're ruining my make-up."

"You're not wearing any."

"I'd better go," Annabelle sniffed.

She flew up and planted a big kiss on his cheek and flew back again. Her eyes suddenly widened as she looked over his shoulder, and her hand covered her mouth. Robert twisted to look over his shoulder but saw nothing. When he turned back she was gone.

"That was sneaky," he said.

"I hate goodbyes," her voice came. "Be happy, Robert"

"You too, Annabelle. I love you."

"I love you. Keep away from psychiatrists, won't you?"

"Of course. Bye."

As he sat back against the headboard, a furious hammering on his door startled him and he leapt up. Maria stood there, her eyes blazing. "What is it?" he said, concerned.

"You bastard," she said through gritted teeth, shaking. "You absolute bloody shit. How can I have been so stupid again?"

"What are you talking about?" he said, frightened by her intensity.

"I heard you!" she spat. "You can hear everything on the balcony. You're worse than Phillip and that's saying something. You bastard!"

She turned, and he grabbed her arm.

"Maria wait, I can explain. Please, let me explain."

She tried to release his hand and he realised he was acting and sounding exactly like Phillip.

"I'm sorry," he said, letting go. "I wouldn't do anything to hurt you, you must know that."

"Tell it to Annabelle, the girl you love," she shouted, and whirled from him.

"Annabelle isn't a girl," he said loudly and she stopped, staring back at him. "You know I'm not capable of that kind of thing, you *know* it."

She stared at him, chest heaving.

"Let me explain. I'll come to your room, or you can come to mine, or I'll stand here in the corridor, but I promise you, on Elaine's memory, I only love Annabelle like a sister. I wouldn't do that to anyone, and especially you. Please, Maria, give me three minutes. Aren't we worth that chance? Please?"

She glared at him, arms crossed.

"Three minutes," she said, stalking past him into his room. He closed the door, knowing others in the nearest rooms would have heard. She stood, arms crossed, glowering at him.

"Please, sit down," he said.

He pulled the chair out from the desk, and sat on the bed, away from it. He bent forward and reached into his case, taking out the letter he wrote to Elaine.

"This is the letter I wrote to Elaine, after you suggested it. I want you to take it, and hold it, and when I've finished speaking, I want you to read it."

He held it out to her and after a moment's hesitation she snatched it from him and dropped into the chair, crossing her legs folding her arms, her body language complete denial. Robert took a deep breath.

"Can you hear the lake from here?" he asked, which surprised her. "There are kids playing, you can just hear them if it's very quiet. Listen."

Her head turned towards the window, and then back at him. "So what?" she said, looking even more angry.

"Do you know why Rosie is alive today?" This sudden shift startled her. "Did you ever truly think about how I knew? Everyone was so relieved she was alive, nobody questioned it. We were in a noisy marquee with two hundred other people and the river was further away than the lake here. The Best Man was talking through a microphone, and yet I leapt up, and got her out. You saved her life as much as I did, because you gave her CPR. Do you want to know the truth of how I knew? I have never lied once to you, in all the time I've known you, and I'm not about to start now. I've fallen for you, and I want us to be together, but can you handle the truth?"

She was intrigued, he could see it, but suspicion had crept onto her face.

"I'm going to tell you the truth and it's going to sound fantastic, implausible, impossible, even, but remember that day, the day we saved Rosie, because that's the day I first truly believed in Annabelle, because she told me Rosie had fallen in the river and was drowning."

"What? How? What are you talking about?"

"The first meditation I did at the clinic, do you recall how reluctant I was?"

"Yes... you told Payal you'd rather have chiropractic treatment than meditate, but what—?"

"On that first meditation I met Annabelle, and she's been with me until a few minutes ago, when you overheard me saying goodbye to her." He took out his mobile phone and showed her the call log. "You can see I wasn't using my mobile and I'm happy to come down with you to reception and prove I neither took a call nor made one."

"Well... well... what is she? A spirit?"

"I could lie and tell you yes, and by your reaction I imagine you'd believe me, but I said I'd tell the absolute truth, and here it is: the Annabelle I met in the

198

meditation is, according to the psychologist I consulted, an archetype my mind made up to protect me from the bad memories associated with that day, because it happened to be the day Elaine died. But, as far as I know, and I'm sure you'd realise later, we normally communicate with spirits via the mind. I'm not a medium, I'm not psychic, but if I was talking to a spirit I wouldn't need to speak out loud."

"What is she, then?"

Robert took a deep breath, looked Maria firmly in the eye.

"She's a fairy."

Maria blinked rapidly.

"A fairy?"

"Yes. The shrink said my mind chose the most non-threatening persona I could invent to help me, and if I ignored her she'd go away. I tried, believe me. When I arrived in the clinic on the Monday you heard her talk in Italian, I think she said good morning to you." Maria's mouth dropped. "Annabelle told me, and the shrink sort-of concurred with this, that her job was to find someone I could be happy with, and when she saw you and you heard what she said, she went mental with delight, because you and I were meant for each other."

"What?"

Maria had uncrossed her legs and arms and sat forward, looking at Robert in a mixture of interest and mistrust.

"I tried to ignore her and she forced me to acknowledge her – don't you remember the weird way I was acting?"

"Yes... I do..."

"Now, at that point I still believed she was an invention of my mind, and weird psychic things were going on around me. She spoke to you in the church, asking you to move, remember? And at my flat, she called 'attento' to you, so you'd ask about the candle holder. Either that, or I'm a brilliant ventriloquist who could fill the Apollo for three straight weeks. But when she zoomed up to me and told me Rosie was drowning, I didn't think, I just acted. Annabelle hovered over the river, where Rosie was, and I got to her in time. Just. You know that. From that day on, I had no doubt – Annabelle existed in this world, and she was here to help me. It was her who taught me to ask how your grandmother was, but didn't tell me the significance. She's been working to get you and I together, and she didn't have to work that hard, because you are a beautiful and amazing person, and after we stopped fighting, I came to understand that. You and I fell out again, and yet she made sure I insisted this weekend went ahead. She saved my life when white van man nearly killed me at a junction, and she was wonderful, bossy, pushy and loving. Because you and I are, or were, together, she said it was time to leave, to help others. I was saying goodbye to her and you heard it all. I wasn't on the phone, and I wasn't talking to myself."

Robert leaned forward and took her hands in his. He was sure his own hands trembled a bit and tried to prevent it.

"I want to be with you, Maria, I've fallen hook line and sinker, and I've told you the truth. If you read my letter to Elaine, you'll find everything I've told you, only there's a lot more on my feelings for you. I told her about Annabelle in the same way I've told you. You know I didn't write this in ten seconds, it's not possible. I wrote it yesterday, as soon as I got back. There's a pencil mark through it when the girl in the next room screamed, and I jumped and then sprang to the rescue. Annabelle existed to bring me to you, and I'm so glad she did."

She looked at him and glanced at the letter he'd written where it had fallen on the floor, then smiled. She raised her hand and stroked his face, and Robert breathed an enormous sigh.

CHAPTER TWENTY TWO

Six Months Later

Robert folded his thick jumper and placed it on the sofa. February had been wet and not too cold and they'd had many evenings in front of the log fire, revelling in each other, content to be together, enjoying finding out so many new little things about each other all the time. Eating in the pub, cooking at home, going for long walks on the beach, working together. His cooking had improved dramatically, even though she wanted to take over his kitchen every night. This room was always his favourite; the fireplace, the thick tiled floor, uneven in places, the sofa, the view of the beach. He never could explain his love for dark wood, but the open stairs running up to the bedrooms always made him think of ancient trees, with the wood still being alive, somehow. He'd never felt more content in his life. He wore her present, the 'Make Love Not Tea' Tee Shirt she'd had printed for his birthday, and hummed to himself.

"So there you are," Annabelle's voice said, and he turned to see her cross-legged on the heart carving, which sat on the oak mantelpiece above the fire, along with the wooden cats. "I see from the wax it's been lit many times. Your Heartfire is almost blinding me, could you turn it down a little?"

"That's one thing I can't do," he said, smiling. "I didn't believe a man could find this much happiness twice in a lifetime. Remember that god-awful film with Tom Cruise and Renee whatserface?"

"Zellwegger," Annabelle said.

"Yes, her. That excruciating scene in the lift where she translates the sign language and says it means 'you complete me', and then he says it at the end? I always cringe at that bit, but it's exactly what I feel. It's like we're two parts of a soul, come together after being apart for ages. Every day I have to pinch myself, to make sure I'm not dreaming."

"Whatever would Ian and Brenda think?" she asked, teasing.

"Brenda would approve, not sure about Ian."

"What are you doing back here in Cornwall?"

"We live here, we work here. It's great."

"Aren't you working in London?" she asked, puzzled.

"No, I came down in September and..."

He looked at her, tilted his head, studying her.

"What?"

"You don't know, do you?"

"Know what?"

"Hold on."

Robert went to the window and opened both sides, wide. It was a bright day, but chill air swept in. He opened the door, looked back at Annabelle, then closed the lower half of it.

"What are you doing?" she asked.

"Preparing," he said. "Stay there."

He went to the foot of the stairs and looked up.

"Darling?" he called. "Annabelle's here."

There was a squeal of delight and the sound of feet running in the room above them. Annabelle's eyes were the biggest he'd ever seen, and if he could remember later, he intended to ask her if his eyes were that big, the first time she saw her. A pair of fluffy slippers appeared on the stairs, followed by blue jeans over slim legs, which danced down the stairs. A grey woollen sweater followed and she stopped on the bottom step. She put her hands together and bowed slightly with her head, beaming across her face as she looked at Annabelle.

"Namaste, Annabelle," Payal said. "Welcome."

There was a very loud bang, and Annabelle shot out of the door at impossible speed. Protesting squawks from the usual suspects of seagulls that sat on the sea wall spoke of the near-miss, and there was another explosion as Annabelle shot back in the window, halting in mid-air. Her hair looked like it had been back-combed for a sixties revival, and Robert swore her face was dirt-streaked.

"Wha...? Ha...? How...?"

There was another bang and she shot backwards out of the window. Robert thought some of the slower gulls lost tail feathers as she zoomed past at supersonic speed. He put his arm around Payal's waist, she rested her arm across his shoulders and they waited for Annabelle's return. The boom was just as loud and Annabelle looked even worse this time. A beehive of hair flopped over one side of her head that any bald man would have loved. Soot streaked her face, making her round eyes even more surprised, and her dress had become crumpled so badly a charity shop wouldn't have taken it. Annabelle's face showed her desperation to speak, but she was hyperventilating, her chest rising and falling rapidly.

"Ha...? Wha...?" she said breathlessly, trying to get control of her breathing.

"How did it happen?" Robert asked, and Annabelle shook her hand, motioning him to speak again. "How is it Payal can see you?"

Annabelle nodded vigourously, hands on hips, still attempting to get her breath. Robert and Payal looked at each other for a moment, then back at Annabelle.

"She believes in you," Robert said simply. "Completely and utterly, without any doubt whatsoever."

Annabelle stared at Payal, shocked and Payal smiled, nodding to her. The boom wasn't quite so loud this time, and Robert was glad he'd left both windows open, even though it was getting pretty cold in the room. She'd have smashed the glass if he hadn't.

"I think that should do it," Robert said to Payal, kissing her lightly on the lips. "She should be calm enough this time."

Robert swore there was a screech of brakes as Annabelle flew back in, which was fanciful, but he wouldn't put it beyond the realms of possibility. She moved up and down slightly in the air with each breath in and out, and Robert could see she was regaining control slowly.

"Is it okay to close the door and the windows?" he asked. "Getting a bit cold in here."

Annabelle tossed her head and tried to push her hair back, but her fingers entangled.

"Dammit!" she said loudly, and shook herself. Fairy dust engulfed her, and when it cleared, she was back as she had been when she'd arrived.

"I wish I could do that, you look beautiful," Payal said.

Annabelle smiled at the compliment, and then shook her head, bewildered.

"What happened?" she asked. "How... how did you two end up together?"

They looked at each other and smiled.

"It wasn't easy," Robert said. "And I thought it couldn't happen. Shouldn't happen, even."

"Me too," Payal said. "But it did."

"I think coffee is in order," Robert said as he closed the half-door. "We can sit down and tell you all about it. Didn't you go to the Clinic first?"

Annabelle watched them as they closed the windows, and then went into the kitchen. She saw the easy love that slid between them, the way Payal rested her hand in the small of Robert's back to lean over and get spoons from a drawer, the way Robert moved towards her, to bump his shoulder against hers.

"Of course I did," Annabelle said indignantly and Robert thought she sounded a bit more like herself. "There's a very efficient receptionist on the front desk, and Ashley and Brenda and Ian and Pam and Tina are still there. I thought Payal was at home, and when this new osteopath came out of your room, I whizzed in to check on Maria. She wasn't there, so I naturally assumed you were together, and came straight here. What happened?"

"Maria couldn't believe in you," Robert said. "It's that simple."

"That isn't simple," Annabelle snapped. "The last I knew, was in the Lake District. You and Maria were together, all loved up, and you were happy with Ashley, Payal."

"I *was* happy," Payal said, "and so was Robert, but things changed."

"Well, I see that now, but how?" Annabelle asked in frustration.

"I'll make the coffee, you show Annabelle round," Payal said.

Annabelle followed Robert around the cottage, admiring the polished wood and the beams.

"We've got two bedrooms," he said, climbing the stairs. "Pam and Carlo have been down to stay twice, and Ashley came for a long weekend over Christmas. We had a great time."

"How's that even possible?" Annabelle asked. "I don't understand."

She was almost in tears Robert thought, so he cut short the tour, not bothering with the bathroom. A cat lay on their bed, and he miaowed at Annabelle and stood up to greet her.

"That's Tabby!" she exclaimed and flew around him a few times.

"Yeah, I couldn't bear to leave him, so I stuck up posters, even put a collar on him and attached a note asking his owners to get in touch, but nobody responded. Didn't like the thought of leaving him alone, so I brought him down. He thinks he's died and gone to heaven, everyone in the street fusses him and he loves the other cats around here. Come on, let's go back down, we'll tell you everything."

Payal had the coffee ready on the small table, poured out, and she and Robert sat back in the sofa. She lifted her legs across his lap and kicked her slippers off. Robert plumped up a cushion and placed it at the end of the sofa.

"Sit yourself down," Robert said. "Where do you want us to start?"

"At the beginning, stoopid."

CHAPTER TWENTY THREE

Robert's Story

I fell in love with a smile. The clue to everything a man should know about a woman is in her smile. I know my own was tentative, untrusting, like someone who's afraid their teeth will escape if they show them too much. But Payal's got me, the moment I walked in the clinic on my first day. It was like a searchlight in those movies that catches an aeroplane and it can't escape from the beam, no matter how much it twists and turns. I couldn't have known it at the time, but I didn't want to escape. There was magic in her smile, and I came to understand how much it affected me very quickly. I still don't know how she does it, and I don't want to know, but I wake up every morning and when she smiles at me, nothing bad can touch me throughout the day, nothing. She's like a battery charger, and I'm the battery. Every time she smiles it lifts me, makes my soul happy. This sounds like complete soppy romanticism, doesn't it? Enough to make you put two fingers down your throat, and pretend to be sick, right? But there are no other words I can use to explain how I feel, so you'll just have to put up with them.

When she smiled at anyone else I was jealous, but she kept smiling at me, and I could have got a suntan from it, I really could.

"Okay, I get the picture," Annabelle said. "Get on with what happened."

"If it hadn't been for Payal, we'd never have met," Robert said.

"Really?"

"Really. I was trying to escape the meditation, when she ambushed me in the corridor. It's not fair that one woman has a smile that can lift your soul and eyes that make you dissolve into a column of jelly. I'd got past Brenda and was on my way—"

"Wait, back up a bit. Hadn't you met Maria in between?"

"Oh, yeah, I suppose so."

"Don't give me that, you know damn well you had. You're going to make me seem like an incompetent idiot if you leave her out of your story."

"Oh, okay."

It's fair to say Maria, the taxi-thief and I didn't hit it off straight away. And when she tried to kill me by opening the taxi door on the wrong side of the road, I really shouted at her. Stupid woman, I thought.

"You're leaving something out," Payal said.

"I'm just getting to that," Robert said, miffed. "Who's telling this story?"

"You are, sweetheart," she said, leaning forward and kissing him. Robert hesitated, so she kissed him again.

But there was something about Maria, and I didn't understand what it was until later. It was her perfume. They say that smell is the strongest stimulator of memory, you can smell something like school ink, and the uniqueness of it will transport you back to the schoolhouse in an instant, with a picture of such clarity that you can taste it. But the first time I encountered that perfume, we were fighting for possession of my finger.

"What?"

"Hush, let me tell it."

Maria thought I was a patient, sitting in the staffroom, and tried to get me to leave, bending my finger back. That was when I noticed her perfume, but at the time I was more concerned about my little finger being broken, so didn't pay any attention. Why would I? Anyway, every morning I'd come in, and every morning this woman here would light up the day. I think it's just natural to her, but it affected me enormously. Of course I couldn't, and didn't, say a word, why would I? She was married to Ashley, they were very happy, and I envied them more than anything. Actually, I envied Ashley more than anything. I thought I recognised what Elaine and I had had, and Ashley is such a great guy that I couldn't dislike him one bit. When we went out for a drink and I knocked Maria for six into a puddle—

"What? I didn't know about that."

"It was before you arrived."

I thought the perfume was Maria's because I sensed it in the pub, but when Payal ambushed me in the corridor with Brenda, I realised it was Payal's. On her it smelled so good I wanted to bury my head at the nape of her neck and just stay there. And then, just before the meditation began, I looked at Maria and her hair came undone, and flowed across her shoulders, and it looked great. Wasn't until a while later I understood why I liked it so much, but let's just say, I was attracted to Maria. She's a gorgeous woman, but we'd got off on the wrong foot three times, and I wasn't about to have any more to do with her. Then you came along, and I didn't actually think about any woman, I was so terrified.

"I did a good job of clearing your mind, though,"

"Shut up."

Elaine's letter went straight to my heart, how could it do anything other than that? And the following day you came to the clinic with me. You remember what you said to me as soon as you saw Payal? 'Oh, she is so beautiful, is she available?' and I wished for all the world she was. Did you see the way her hair moves when she turns her head? That's what I recognised in Maria, that flowing of hair. But you saw Payal with Ashley and even you, with all your superpowers, didn't see what was in my heart. I'd have denied it, even if you had seen it, don't blame yourself.

"I wasn't about to, are you going to get to the point?"

Well, head office need to think things through a bit more. Maybe if you'd spoken Hindi, Payal might have heard you. In their defence, there was no way I'd have made a move on Payal, I'm not that sort of person, so perhaps it's just as well. If you'd told me Payal was the one for me, I'd have rejoiced inside, and died inside at the same time, because she couldn't be mine, and totally ignored you, until you went away. I'd have done it, as well. But I was falling in love with her, and it hurt, it truly did. Anyway, you latched on to Maria, and threatened to take all your clothes off—

"What?" Payal said. "You didn't tell me about that."

"Do you want to tell her, dear?" Robert asked Annabelle, who had the good grace to look abashed.

"Robert was being so pig-headed, I had to resort to drastic measures. I told him if he didn't acknowledge me, I'd take all my clothes off and fly around butt naked, let him explain that to the shrink."

"Would you have done it?" Payal asked, smiling.

"No, head office told me he had a puritan streak in him, I knew he'd give in. But it was fun watching his face. If you ever want to get your own way, you should try it."

"Oh, I have done," Payal said with a smile. "It works very well."

"Are you two finished?" Robert asked.

"Yes dear," they said in unison. Annabelle mouthed 'puritan streak' to Payal.

You kept pushing Maria, and now you know why I resisted. If I couldn't have Payal, I'm sure, deep down, I was thinking therefore I didn't want anyone else, and there was no way on earth I would have done anything, and there was no way on earth I was going to tell you that. I did come close a couple of times—

"When?"

"If you'll let me talk, I'll tell you."

"Sorry."

The wedding was the day I finally admitted to myself that I was in love with this wonderful woman. I was no longer *falling* in love, I'd arrived with an almighty thump, and couldn't fall any further. It wasn't the stockings and suspender belt or the—

"WHAT?" demanded Annabelle, and Payal giggled.

"There, it was that giggle, right there. I'll let her tell you about it. Apparently, I have a puritan streak."

You remember I asked you if you saw when my Heartfire ignited? If you'd said it was *before* I danced with Pam, or with Maria, I'd have told you everything, but you were distracted and assumed it was *because* I was dancing with Maria. But I knew, and when I got home that night, all I could smell was Payal's perfume. I went to sleep telling myself not to fall in love with her, even though I knew it was way too late. I tried to tell you after the dream about her perfume, but you thought I was talking about Maria. I was probably glad you misunderstood me, I think if I'd told anyone of my feelings, it would have been too much to take. She couldn't be mine, and that was that, so I tried to get on with life. Maria's a lovely girl and yes, I was attracted to her, so I let you push me. We went for a drink, and we kissed, and I liked her a lot.

Then Alexa came, and we had everyone over to my apartment on that Sunday. You know, if you're looking for something, you think you see it, you make the situation fit, and the small details escape you.

"Are you talking about me, or people in general?" Annabelle asked, bristling.

"People in general, calm down."

211

When Alexa and I were on the train, I mentioned Maria, because she asked me whether there was anyone in my life and I described her, but inadvertently slipped in a tiny detail of Payal's.

"You said she had the most kissable mouth in the world!" Annabelle said excitedly. "Alexa picked you up on it, how could I have missed that?"

Payal looked at Robert, smiling, and he leaned over and kissed the most kissable mouth in the world.

"You also have the most pattable bottom in the world," he said, and kissed her again.

"This is going to take all day, at this rate," Annabelle complained, but she was smiling as she shook her head. Her eyes suddenly widened. "Of course! When Maria came in, Payal was right behind her. Alexa assumed your face lit up because of Maria." She thought about it for a second. "What did Alexa say when you told her about you and Payal?"

"I'll get to that later. But if you'd been there, I'm sure you'd have seen how much my Heartfire surged whenever Payal teased me."

"He's very easy to tease," Payal said to Annabelle, and they mouthed 'puritan streak' to each other.

"Ask her who lit the candle," Robert said to Annabelle, and Payal blushed.

"That was you?" Annabelle said, shocked, and Payal nodded. "But... wha...? hoo...?"

Robert leaned back, holding Payal close protectively, and they braced for the explosion. It didn't come, and they relaxed.

"This is unbelievable," Annabelle said, pacing up and down her cushion. "You were in love with him at that point?"

"Yes."

"But why didn't you...? Why didn't you...? You couldn't, could you?"

"No."

"This is very confusing," Annabelle said.

"Sorry," they both said at the same time, and grinned at each other.

"But why didn't you...?" Annabelle said to Payal.

"Why didn't I what?"

"I don't know, I'm too confused."

"I'll carry on, shall I?" Robert asked. "Payal can tell you her bit later, it should become clearer, but you have no idea how hard I was praying that Payal would light the candle. When it happened and nobody knew who'd done it, I allowed myself to think that maybe she had done it, but I dismissed it as ridiculous."

"Okay, carry on," Annabelle said, flopping down on the cushion.

I'm not sure I should say this, but Maria was always going to be second-best. I don't mean it in a nasty way, because she's lovely, really is, but there wasn't the same spark I felt when I thought about Payal. There was no way I could be with Payal, so I tried to forget my feelings and concentrate on Maria. I seriously thought about leaving the clinic at that point, because it was so hard seeing Payal most days, though I knew it would be even harder if I didn't see her. But when I sat in the cells after my Volvo incident, I had time to think, and I realised how unfair I was being to Maria so I said 'enough, already', and put my feelings for Payal away. Tried to, anyway.

Maria and I got a little more serious, and then we had the bust-up over Katie's husband at the theatre. The next day, when we finally spoke, I realised I did care about Maria, but not that much, and I made serious plans to leave the clinic. But Pam took me dancing, at your suggestion, and I had a great evening. I didn't know Katie was married at the time, and thought I might chat her up, so I shelved the plan and got on with life. When I hit the white van, and found out Katie was married, that decided it – I was going to leave London, and go out to Canada for a while, maybe meet someone there. I've no idea what head office would do, so I didn't mention it to you. Did you ever read Shogun?

"What?" Annabelle said, jolted from the story. "Of course not, I've got better things to do with my life."

Well you're missing a treat. It's an amazing story of a guy in love with another man's wife, and he can't do anything about it. Anyway, there's a section, early on where the wife comes to realise she has feelings for him as well, and wants to do something to express them, but tragedy would follow if she did. So she arranges for him to spend the night with the most beautiful courtesan, as a substitute for her, a way of showing her feelings, but nobody else would know, and they'd be safe. It's one of the best bits of the whole book, because he had no idea she had feelings for him up to that point.

"And are we reaching *our* point any time soon?"

I felt like Mariko, the wife. I wanted to show my feelings without showing them, and I knew she and Ashley wanted to have children and couldn't. I had intended to speak to Ashley about it, a bit worried my feelings would show if I said anything to Payal, and she'd be mortified. I was going to give them the money for fertility treatment as a leaving gift. But then you took me to her in the paintball game when she was upset, and I told her. And when I reached out to push that hair back, she cupped my hand against her head, and my heart nearly burst. For a split-second I almost told Payal what I felt about her, I don't know how I restrained myself.

"I already knew," Payal said, and kissed him.

"You knew?" Annabelle and Robert gasped, together.

"Of course I did, you'd have to be stupid not to know."

"How?" Robert said. "I didn't say anything." He looked at Annabelle, then at Payal. "Did I?"

"You said, and these are your exact words: 'but you have someone who adores you, who wants to spend the rest of his life with you, no matter what happens. There's nothing more precious than that, believe me, I know. To have someone who wants to spend every minute of every day with you is so rare it's almost unique, and if you have that, you hold onto it with both hands, so tight, that everything else is secondary.'" She shrugged, smiling. "I knew you were talking about yourself, any woman would. Why do you think I kissed you? Honestly, men are so thick sometimes."

She kissed him again.

"Why didn't you say anything?"Robert asked.

"What could I say? You were offering Ashley and me the best gift in the world, and you were doing it because you had feelings for me. And I knew I couldn't leave Ashley and deep down, I think I understood you wouldn't want me to. Later, when we found out about Elaine, I felt a little foolish, because I thought you might have been talking about her. But it worked out in the end, didn't it?"

"It did," Robert said, kissing her.

"And I'm still waiting to find out how," Annabelle said crossly. "And why. And where."

When Maria came after me into the woods, she was wonderful. The truth about Elaine had come out, and she really helped me. She suggested I write a letter, you came in when I was doing it, remember? After you'd gone I also wrote a letter to Payal, telling her everything, but I didn't send it, just looked at it now and again. It helped me put my feelings aside, because they'd been written down and existed outside of me, I didn't need to worry about them nearly as much. Then came the tree-hugging.

I so nearly ended up in front of Payal, but those blindfolds were quite flimsy, and I was worried I'd give myself away, and embarrass the hell out of her, so I tore a small hole in mine. The pull towards Payal was almost overwhelming, but I looked, corrected my course and ended up with Maria. We spent the night together, and the next day I saw how happy Ashley and Payal looked, and committed myself to being with Maria. It was the right thing to do. I had to stop thinking about Payal, she was married and happy, and we'd never be together. End of story.

That afternoon, you came to my room to say goodbye. You were pleased as punch, and I felt good. What neither of us knew was that Maria was on her balcony listening to every word I said, and thought I was on the phone to another woman.

Annabelle clasped both her hands over her mouth, and her eyes became round saucers.

After what she'd been through with Phillip, you could understand why she was mad, and she stormed into my room, really angry. I showed her my mobile, so she could see I hadn't just made a call, but she didn't believe me. In the end I told her the truth.

"Mphl, mphl, mphl," Annabelle said through her hands. "What?"

Annabelle took her hands away from her mouth.

"Then what happened?" she said in a very quiet voice.

"She slapped me. Hard. And the most ridiculous thing was, I was glad. Not because she was hurt by what I said, but because she wouldn't believe one word, when so much of what had happened defied explanation. She couldn't believe me, and that meant she couldn't believe in you, so I was glad she and I didn't end up together."

Robert thought Annabelle was about to cry, so he carried on.

I'd hired the car to go down to Manchester, and everyone understood that, so there was no awkwardness, I just kept out of Maria's way. I had a word with Ashley, but he already knew, because Maria had told Payal everything. Can't imagine their journey back to London was very pleasant, but I drove to my parents' house, and went to visit Elaine's grave. I told her everything, and she told me things were going to be all right, like she always did.

I met up with Chris, my best mate, and we got seriously drunk. I laughed so much my ribs were hurting, and I still can't remember how we fell in the canal. The copper who came to arrest us let us go, because he was our mate Billy Sanders kid brother, and I don't think he fancied having us in the back of his patrol car, smelling the way we did. Chris's wife hosed us down before she'd let us in the house, you'd have loved it.

I drove back to London on the Tuesday and Pam told me Maria had left the practice. Left it in the lurch, were her words, and I felt bad, though it wasn't my fault. But it meant I couldn't leave, even though I wanted to, that wouldn't have been fair to Ashley. So Payal continued to lift me with her smile and Katie Lloyd came round to see me, wanting to know the truth. She's a good woman and deserved to know, so I told her. She spent the night, and I slept on the couch. We saw each other a few times as friends, and she told me her husband had gone off with Maria. That kinda made me feel better, because I'm not sure my relationship with Maria would have survived if he'd come calling. And much as I liked Katie, it wouldn't have been fair to hit on her while she was so upset.

Anyway, things carried on for about a month or more and I bumped into an Osteopath I knew, who wanted to come to London to work. Working alongside Payal was so bittersweet, and I knew I couldn't wallow anymore, so I brought him in one day, and he really liked the clinic. It helped me not feel so guilty leaving, but I told Ashley things hadn't worked out for me and let him assume I meant Maria. The week before I left, Carlo phoned and asked me to go for dinner at the restaurant, later. He said she had something important to say, and I assumed he was going to announce their engagement.

"I think you should tell your bit, now," Robert said to Payal.

"Okay."

CHAPTER TWENTY FOUR

Payal's story

The day Rob arrived at the clinic things were chaotic in reception and he had trouble introducing himself. I thought he was quite good-looking. We'd been expecting him, but it was when he silenced the whole room that I first liked him, he just turned round and yelled 'Quiet!' and the whole room went quiet, even old Mrs Wolverton, who never shuts up. Ashley had said we'd be lucky to get him to work at the clinic, but he agreed immediately, and settled in quickly. Maria told me he'd shouted at her when she'd got out of the taxi, and made it sound like it was his fault, but his shorts were a bit shredded, showing more of his leg, which was fun. For some reason I developed a craving for marmite.

"You did not," Robert said, smiling.

"No, but Pam did."

She threw herself at him, and he could have taken advantage of her, but I watched as he joked with her, teased her, and they became friends in a short time. I thought: this is a good guy, I like him. When we went to the pub the first time, he didn't say a lot about himself, but he was a very good listener, which is so rare in a man, isn't it? Maria and he fell out again but I thought she was a bit hard on him. I told her that in the taxi on the way back.

I did use everything I'd got, to make him stay for the meditation – the smile and the big doe eyes work every time. Not because it made up the mystical number, but because there was something about him I liked, and I hoped he'd stay at the clinic long-term. I'd always got a lot from the meditation, and I thought he might, too.

"I got way more than you bargained for," Robert said, and Annabelle poked her tongue out at him.

Then, the wedding... after Rob saved Rosie, and we all rushed down to the river, I saw he was only concerned for her, and was embarrassed by all the attention, didn't want to be the hero. We all looked at him differently after that, but especially Maria. Then we met in the bathroom...

"Who?" Annabelle asked. "You and Maria?"

"No, Robert and I."

I'd been to Ann Summers and bought the sexiest underwear I could find, to turn Ashley on. I was changing out of my sari, and heard him in the shower, so I put it all on, sprayed some perfume, opened the door, posing as sexily as I could in this great underwear, and asked him what he thought. But Robert stood there, wearing just a towel, and I was like a rabbit caught in headlights.

"More like a Playboy Bunny caught in headlights," Robert said, and whistled in appreciation.

We stood there staring at each other, and I didn't know what to say, and eventually he said 'absolutely breathtaking' and you know when stress is really high and it gets you, and you want to do that nervous laugh? That was me. I said we probably shouldn't mention it to Ashley, and he agreed, but asked if it was all right if he dreamed about it now and then. I said that was perfectly acceptable, and then couldn't hold it in any longer. He'd seen virtually everything there was to see of me, and the situation was so absurd, the way we were calmly discussing it, and all I could do was giggle. Robert closed the door for me and I couldn't stop giggling, as I got my clothes on. I giggled every time I thought about it, and when I got downstairs I was still trying to control it.

You have to remember that I'd met Ashley when I was fourteen and we were married at nineteen. I'd never even kissed anyone but Ashley, and I should have been mortified and ashamed by what happened. But it was just so funny, because of Robert's reaction, the way he only looked into my eyes and the way we spoke to each other. I knew then he was a very special person, and I wanted to be around him. And I found I liked that it was him who'd seen me like that.

Then Robert came down and danced with Pam, you saw how great they were, but he wouldn't look at me, and I could see he was self-conscious. That was when I found out how easy he was to tease. But there was something more, some decency inside him, because he didn't leer, or wink, or do anything that most men would have done, and I loved that about him. He was genuinely embarrassed, for me as well as him, but eventually we danced together. I think I giggled again when we were dancing, and he tried not to smile. I couldn't believe the way I was acting, to be honest, but it made me feel so safe, being in his arms. I knew, I just knew, he wouldn't tell anyone else about what happened.

And on the Monday morning I realised what I'd done: I'd fallen in love with him. I sat in reception waiting for him to arrive, with butterflies in my stomach, my heart racing and that dry tightness in my throat. I was so nervous and I wanted to cry. Because I was in love with Robert. Because I loved Ashley, and I was so confused. Then he came in, and all I could do was smile at him. There was no way on God's earth I was going to say anything, no way. But he invited us to his place to meet his sister and everything surged up in me, and I couldn't resist teasing him. It was the only connection we shared, our secret, and I cherished it more than anything.

"I'm so sorry," Robert said, taking her hand and kissing it.

"You should be, making me fall for you."

Maria came to me and told me about kissing Robert at the wedding, and I wasn't jealous, because we'd shared something much more intimate. But she went out with Robert and I was happy for the two good friends I had. But every time Robert came by, the butterflies started, and the day after his sister came, he arrived really early, and helped me carry some things. I touched Ganesha when Robert was standing next to me in Ashley's office, and felt too guilty to ask for anything, but he must have known what was in my heart. I was asking him for guidance when Robert sneaked up on me, with no shoes on his feet. I jumped so high I'm surprised he didn't ask what I was guilty about.

Anyway, Maria told me she was getting more involved, she really liked him and I was relieved, to be honest. I was terrified I'd blurt my feelings out to Robert and he'd run a mile. And anyway, I loved Ashley, I did. Still do, in so many ways.

"Is it true he's been down to visit you?" Annabelle asked.

"Oh yes. He was very happy, and we had a wonderful weekend. He's such a lovely person."

"Then how...?"

It was at the party at Robert's. His sister is just like him, don't you think? She was telling us stories of Robert when he was young and I was suddenly filled with a yearning, a burning wish that I'd been there when he was growing up, to share in everything he'd done. It was ridiculous and such a shock, but I knew I wanted to know everything about him, that's the only way I can describe what went through me. When Alexa told us about the Heartfire candle, I knew I would light it. To be honest, a tiny part of me hoped someone would see me doing it, and I'd have to tell the truth. But only Tabby saw me, and he shrugged. Everyone was milling around for coats and hugging goodbye, and my heart almost stopped when Robert kissed me on both cheeks.

"Alexa was doing it, and I plucked up the courage to copy her," Robert said. "Your face was so warm, and I inhaled that perfume, I'm surprised you didn't notice anything."

"Let me get this straight," Annabelle said. "You two were in love with each other, but neither of you ever said a word, right?"

They nodded.

"Why not, for goodness sake?"

"How could I?" Robert asked. "Payal was happily married, and there's no force on earth that would make me try and break up someone's marriage, no matter what I felt. I didn't know how she felt about me, it would have been madness to do it."

"I felt the same. I loved Ashley, and it would have been utterly selfish of me to do something when I had no idea what Robert thought of me. I knew he liked me, but I never dreamed he was in love with me at that stage."

"But you lit the candle," Annabelle said gently.

"Yes. I wanted to tell him, without telling him, that I loved him. I took a chance, and when nobody challenged me, I decided enough was enough, that I'd live the life I'd been blessed with, and not look for rainbows in a clear sky. And anyway, Maria was falling for him, and as far as I knew, he was falling for her. You don't do that to your friends, do you?"

"Some people might, but you two aren't some people. So...?"

The next day Robert didn't come in to work. There was no reply on his mobile and we all became frantic with worry, which allowed me to let some of my feelings out. My heart was in my throat all morning, expecting a call from the Police to say he'd been injured... or worse. Stupid me only remembered later Alexa had given me her number in case Ashley and I went to Vancouver, and I called her. She called me back and was so calm about it,

I worried a bit less. But only a bit. When she called back and said he was okay, Pam, Maria and I burst into tears, had to have a group hug for ages. I told Ashley it was women's hormones. When Robert phoned and I heard his voice, I think I had a go at him.

"Definitely, and I deserved it. And you teased me about having a shower."

I did, that was more in relief than anything. But it was a wake-up call, in one way. I cared so much about him it was hurting me not being able to express it, so I tried to step back. And Maria was getting very excited about him, she asked me what to do, and I suggested she took him along to the dress-rehearsal of the theatre group. They both looked really happy, and I was happy and sad at the same time. But we all know that fell flat, and Robert got us to the Lake District by a miracle, after none of them wanted to go.

Then this beautiful, wonderful man offered me what I thought I wanted most in the world and I turned him down. I told him some nonsense about diminishing Ashley if we accepted, and he believed me. But the truth was, I'd seen how much Robert wanted me, and all those feelings I'd had came bursting back up, and I couldn't face them. What I wanted most in the world was to be with him, but I couldn't say or do anything.

Then we found out about Elaine. When Robert left the dining room, Pam was on her feet first, wanting to follow him, but Brenda stopped her, saying you have to let people you love go, sometimes. She'd already told me Jason was emigrating and was devastated, but what she said struck a chord with me, and I knew I had to stop. Maria told me everything he'd said to her about Elaine, and we got a little drunk.

"Dear...?"

"Okay, maybe more than a little."

"Annabelle, do you want to say anything at this point? No?" Robert turned to Payal. "I came down to find this woman slumped against a bottle of whisky, snoring. She had to dunk herself in the lake to sober up."

They both looked at Annabelle.

"Oh, all right," she said, grumpily. "Do you remember the chandelier crystal falling the first time?"

"Yes, the girl caught it really neatly."

"That was me, I knocked it off when Maria said Robert wasn't worth the risk."

"Oh."

"It's an energy thing, okay? I have to let it out somehow... a bit like earlier. But when Maria asked you what she should do, I was on my knees in the peanuts, begging you to say the right thing. I knocked the second one off when you told her to take the risk. I didn't know about you two, obviously."

"I wanted to give Rob something back, and thought if he and Maria became an item, he'd be happy. He deserved it."

"But you weren't talking about them, were you?"Annabelle said. "You were talking about you and Rob. Even though you knew *you* wouldn't take the risk?"

"If it had just been me, I would have. But I'd have devastated Ashley, both our families, our friends, and that would have been so selfish. Love is never selfish, is it?"

"No, it isn't," Annabelle said, gently. She shook her head to clear it. "So how the hell have you two ended up together? Somebody tell me, please."

Robert mouthed 'not a good listener' to Payal, and Annabelle stamped her foot.

"I am a good listener, but this is killing me!"

Okay. Well, we had the tree hugging that evening, and you know those blindfolds were very flimsy, so I tore a small hole in mine for the same reasons Robert did. The pull towards him was like a giant magnet, I almost got wrenched off my feet. But I found Ashley and Robert found Maria. I didn't know Robert had cheated, and Maria looked so happy, and I ignored the ache inside me, thinking they were meant for each other.

The next day was great, and just as I began to think I'd done the right thing, all hell broke loose. Maria was inconsolable, and eventually I got the whole story from her. Robert had told her the truth about you and she freaked out. Coming so close on what happened with Phillip, she wouldn't believe a word he said, and was so angry and upset it took me ages to calm her down. She lost it with me when I asked her whatif there was *something* in what he'd said, and wouldn't speak to me again. We got back to London, and I've not seen her since. Eventually, Rob told me she'd gone back to Philip, after his wife dumped him, but Maria didn't answer any of my calls, or texts.

So I carried on as though nothing had happened between Robert and me, because nothing *had* happened. It was so hard, but I was doing the right thing. When Robert said he was leaving, I came so close to begging him to stay, and almost told him everything. The week before he left Pam asked me out to dinner at Carlo's, for a girl's get together. England were playing in the World Cup and Ashley went round to watch it with his brothers on one of those big screen TVs, and I thought it would do me good.

Payal looked at Robert, and they both smiled.

"And?" Annabelle asked.

CHAPTER TWENTY FIVE

<u>Robert and Payal's story – Part 1.</u>

Robert took the tube and arrived at the restaurant just after seven. He was pleased for Pam and Carlo. She'd dragged him out a few times to make up a threesome, and despite being Italian, Carlo didn't seem jealous in the slightest when Pam made Robert dance with her. They had that confidence in each other and he envied them. Payal had smiled at him as he left the clinic, and he'd resisted Ashley's entreaties to watch the football with him. England were bound to lose anyway. Carlo had phoned him before he'd made anything to eat, and he was chuffed to go.

"Robert!" Carlo called. "So glad you could make it, come on through."

The back of the restaurant had a private dining room, with two high-backed booths. One was roped off, so Robert knew they'd be on their own. He saw Pam over the top of the other one, and she beamed at him, waving as she slid out, motioning him in. He kissed her cheek and slid in to the table, noticing it was only set for two. The look of surprise on Payal's face told him she hadn't known either, and they stared at each other. Her perfume flowed over him.

Payal stared at Robert, seeing the same look of surprise on his face that must be plastered across her own. One minute she'd been chatting with Pam about dancing, and the next, he'd arrived, sliding into the seat across the table from her. Butterflies took flight in her stomach, and she could only stare at him, wondering if she was dreaming.

"It's breaking my heart watching you two," Pam said, close to tears by the sound of it, "so I fixed this up, and you can blame me for it. Carlo is taking Payal home at eleven, I've arranged it with Ashley. Robert's leaving next week and you're never going to see each other again. You have four hours to say goodbye to each other, and nobody but your waitress – that's me – is coming in here. You can say anything you like, talk about anything you want, and it will never leave here. Carlo has prepared all the food, there's no menu."

She stepped aside and Carlo poured wine into both glasses, then sparkling water into the second glasses alongside them. He placed focaccia bread pieces with a dish of olive oil between them, and he and Pam left the room.

They stared at each other, and a fat tear rolled from Payal's eye, down her cheek. She was caught in a maelstrom of emotion, and it could have been a tear of happiness. They spoke together.

"I love you," both said.

Robert waited for the building to collapse around them, but it scarcely shivered. Payal waited for the tear to engulf the room and drown them both, but it barely splashed as it struck the table. Robert reached out a tentative hand and it met the one she'd been stretching forward. They gripped each other tightly, comforted by the warmth of their hands, and to still the trembling that affected them both.

"You're so beautiful," he said, and she smiled, watching as his smile shone back at her. "I've been in love with that smile since the day I met you."

"I've been in love with you since the day you caught me in my underwear."

They both laughed, and the spell broke, releasing them. Robert raised her hand and kissed it. Payal pulled his hand to her and did the same. She tipped her cheek to the back of his hand, feeling the warmth of it, pressing it hard before letting it drift back to the table. Robert took his wine glass in his free hand, raising it, and she copied him.

"To Pam and Carlo, who have magic between them and know how to share it."

"To Pam and Carlo."

They sipped the wine, staring at each other over their glasses. Payal put her glass down and stood, leaning across to him. She kissed him on the mouth, and sat back.

"Did you know I'd be here?" Payal asked.

"No. Carlo phoned me when I got home, said he and Pam had something important to tell me. I thought they'd be announcing their engagement."

"Pam told me Carlo was watching the football, and would I like to have a girl's night out."

The magic slowed the clocks, but the minutes crept round anyway. They spoke about their childhoods, their friends, their relatives, the times they shared, but avoided talking of the present or the future. She laughed about his escapades, voicing the opinion he was lucky to be alive. They kissed often, and the food was sensational.

"Tell me about Annabelle," Payal said, as they were part way through their second bottle of wine, so he did, worrying she'd laugh. But she listened intently, holding his hand, and when he finished she kissed him.

"I wish I'd met her," she said, wistfully. "Was she there when I lit the candle?"

Robert's delighted shock made her smile. She told him about the storytelling her mother always wove at bedtime, how she would dream of fantastical places, and fantastic creatures.

"I wanted it to be true," she said, and risked telling him what she'd never told another person. "My life was ordered in so many ways it stifled me, and it was a place I could escape to. I couldn't wish for more love from my parents and family, and they encouraged us all. If we wanted to go to University, they would support us fully. They're very modern, and wanted us to be happy, they said it often. But their love became over-protective, it didn't allow for too much self-expression or creativity if it was seen as a bit 'wild'. All my sisters and brothers and cousins married within our community. Not arranged marriages, exactly, but semi-arranged in some cases; the boys or girls they thought suitable would always be round our house, and that's how I met Ashley. He fancied my sister to start with, but we hit it off, and I fell in love with him at sixteen. I didn't want to go to University, though I had the grades. He's great fun, and we've been so happy."

A silence crept between them, and they felt the same fear. Robert daren't voice the question in his mind and Payal was frightened he might. *What are we going to do?*

"Let's dance," he said, and stood up, holding his hand out to her. Pam must have been watching, because the lights dimmed and the background music swelled slightly. She took his hand and they held each other close. She rested her head on his shoulder and he inhaled her perfume, instinctively knowing this was the last time he would hold her, wanting to imprint it so heavily on his brain that he would recall every detail – the sheer softness of her hair, the warmth of her body, her thigh slipping between his as they rotated slowly, swaying to the music. She knew the same, and tried not to let the tears out, as she wrapped her arms around his neck, listening to his heartbeat, wondering how her own still managed to beat, when it was breaking into pieces. She'd never cared for Take That, but Gary Barlow sang 'Million love songs later' and the lyrics must have been written for Robert and her.

She turned her face to him, and he kissed her. They stopped moving and the kiss went on and on, and neither of them wanted it to finish. She pulled away first, and they could see the tears in each other's eyes.

"I love you," she said. "I always will."

She reached for her handbag and jacket, and walked from the room. He stood, watching her go, seeing the door swing, taking her from his sight, knowing it was over.

Carlo was waiting for her, and opened the rear car door, letting her have the privacy she needed. She stared out at the buildings passing by, praying she and Robert would be together in the next incarnation. She counted herself lucky to have known him, to have held him, and to have shared so much. But that didn't stop her crying.

Robert sat down and poured himself more wine. Pam came into the room and he held his hand out to her. She sat next to him, and snuggled up as he put his arm around her.

"You and Carlo are the best people I've ever known. That meant the world to us, it was the most magical evening I've ever..."

He couldn't finish the sentence. She hugged his arm across her chest, not saying anything. Eventually he took a deep breath and kissed the top of her head.

"How did you know?"

"It's the way you look at each other when you don't know other people can see you. It's always a quick glance, and the corners of your mouth turn up a little, like you've discovered a secret. Payal can't help it, she smiles in a way you never otherwise see."

"God, does Ashley know?"

"Give over, he's a man. Not got the necessary sensitivity. Took me ages to convince Carlo, he thought I was making it up."

"He's a great guy. I thought I was coming here tonight to celebrate your engagement, and I was really chuffed for you both."

"I'm really happy. Who knows where it will go, but I demand you come to the engagement party if it does happen. What will you do?"

"Start my practice in Cornwall again, some of them will be pleased to see me back."

"I'm going to miss you," she sniffed.

"Don't set me off again. You and Carlo will come down and stay with me. My house is on the beach, the seafood is fresh caught every day, and I'm within walking distance of two pubs. What could be better?"

"What happens next?"

He knew what she meant.

"I promised Elaine I'd find someone, and I'm going to do that. I'll probably go out and stay with Alexa in the spring, see what the Canadian women are like."

"Get as far away as possible?"

"Yeah, I guess so."

Carlo stopped two streets before Payal's house, and switched the interior light on, twisting in his seat to her.

"Pam thought you might need this," he said and gave her a makeup bag and a mirror. She looked, saw how badly her mascara had run, and smiled sadly to herself. He turned back in his seat, and she repaired the damage, wishing she could repair the damage to her heart as easily. But she didn't want to. She wanted the reminder of him, even if it was painful. That was better than forgetting him.

"Thanks Carlo," she said, handing him the bag. "Please thank Pam for me."

"I will."

He drove her to her house and she touched his shoulder in thanks as she got out.

"Goodnight Carlo."

"Goodnight Payal. Take care of yourself."

I'll try.

"I'd better get going," Robert said, and Pam stood. He slid out, stood up and hugged her. "Thank you so much, Pam. Look after Payal when I've gone, will you?"

"Of course. Do you want me to call a cab?"

"No, I think I'll walk."

"That'll take you over an hour!"

"Yeah."

England had lost, and he actually felt sorry for the fans who were piling out of the pubs. *What can you do? It's beyond your control.*

***

Robert's handover week to the new Osteopath flew by. Robert tried not to look at Payal and feel his mouth curve, and he managed it occasionally, though she still smiled at him the same way.

Payal wanted his final week to last forever and for it to be over yesterday. Her stomach tightened every time he brought a patient back to reception, and his little smiles to her were wonderful and heart-breaking at the same time. Him leaving was the only way forward for both of them, but inside she cried out for it not to happen. Going to the pub for a last drink would be purgatory, and she briefly considered not going, until Pam caught her eye.

So they managed to sit next to each other in the pub, their thighs touching, crammed round a table, and she nudged him and he nudged her back every so often. Ashley gave Robert a laptop as a leaving present from them all.

"It's got skype pre-loaded, so you can talk to us free of charge," Ashley said. "We're not going to lose touch, you can call whenever you want."

"Will it work on the beach?" Robert asked, trying to stop his stomach swooping at the thought of being able to see Payal after he'd gone. "I'll be in my shorts by the sea with a cold beer, while you're all sweltering in sticky London."

"That's mean!" Pam laughed.

"And you're all welcome to visit me, any time. I've got two bedrooms, I'm on a sandy beach and you know I can't cook, but there are two brilliant pubs within staggering distance."

Brenda gave him a framed photo of a grinning Rosie holding up a sign saying: 'Thank you for my life' which made him a bit choked, and all the clinic staff had signed an enormous good luck card. Payal had written: 'No biking except in the gym, no Volvos except in bare feet, and no bathrooms except in suspenders' with two kisses alongside it and he knew she'd written it after Ashley had signed it. He thanked them all, and put the card back in the envelope, tucking the flap inside. Ashley and Christina went to the bar for more drinks and he felt Payal's fingers touch his thigh. As slowly as he could, he dropped his hand below the table and gripped her hand. She squeezed it so hard he hoped he'd remember the pain, and thought he heard her bite back a sob. She quickly lifted her glass and pretended to choke on a mouthful of wine. This gave him the opportunity to pat her back and then rub it.

"You okay?" he asked.

"No," she gasped.

So he caressed her back and Brenda joined him, patting her, so he had to stop. Choking can produce tears, and Payal recovered, apologising. She thought she'd got away with it, and Brenda's concern helped a lot. Payal risked looking at Robert, and tried to smile, but it was too difficult. But he smiled, and she nodded, understanding.

He hugged everyone goodbye, including Ian and Ashley, and Pam escorted him to the tube station.

"You going to be all right?" she asked."Getting home, I mean?"

"Yeah, I'm not going on the circle line, so I won't go round and round for days, if I fall asleep."

He hugged her tight and she cried a little.

"Keep in touch with me, won't you?" she said.

"Of course I will. You're my bosom friend. The very best."

She laughed and cried at this, and he kissed her on both cheeks.

"Here," she said, holding out a small packet. "Payal asked me to give this to you. You're not to open it until you're in Cornwall, all right?"

"Thank you Pam. Take care of yourself, tell Carlo he has to look after you, or I'll kick his car door in."

"I'll do that."

He kissed her again, and he knew she watched him disappear into the station, but he didn't look back.

Payal rode home with her head on Ashley's shoulder, their hands entwined.

"Going to miss him," Ashley said. "Great guy."

"He is," she agreed. "Shame about him and Maria."

"Very unprofessional, that woman. We should have complained to the acupuncture council. Wonder what she's doing now?"

"She's back with Phillip."

"Did she phone you? I hope you gave her a bollocking."

"No, Robert told me in the Pub. Phillip's wife was the policewoman who arrested him."

"Bloody hell, that's a coincidence, isn't it? Rob's better off without her, that's for sure."

"Yeah."

"That is so sad," Annabelle said, wiping her eyes on a tassel that hung from the cushion. "You both must have been so lonely."

"Yes and no," Payal said. "I had my family and friends, still. I worried about Robert, though. The worst was not having anyone to talk to, about it."

"I had Tabby, he's a great listener" Robert said. "I didn't want to tell anyone about Payal, but I skyped Alexa, and mum and dad regularly, and the new me allowed people in. I'm on the darts team at the Fort

Inn, and I even enrolled on a cooking course at one of Rick Stein's restaurants."

"Did you look for anyone else?"

"No, I couldn't. But I decided I'd go and spend six months in Canada, see who fate brought me."

"I bet your parents were worried, isn't that what Alexa did, and never came back?"

"Actually, they encouraged me. Dad's retiring soon and they're thinking of doing much the same, every year."

"What was in the package Pam gave you? From Payal?"

Robert smiled.

"I wasn't sure it was the right thing to do," Payal said. "I didn't know if the reminder might not help him."

"It was the best present I ever had," Robert said, leaning over to kiss her.

"Can we get on?" Annabelle said. "The end's in sight, isn't it?"

"Yes, it is," Robert said. "I think we should take a walk along the beach, before the sun goes down."

Payal swung her legs off him and stood up. He patted her bottom as she moved away.

"Bring the thick scarf," Robert said. "It's pretty chilly."

She disappeared into the kitchen and Robert looked at Annabelle.

"Have you got anything warmer to put on? The wind off the sea is pretty bracing."

She raised her eyes, and as she stood, she was clad in a long woollen coat, with a muff and hat, all matching, pale blue. She shimmered, and her wings appeared through the coat. Payal returned and handed Robert a thick sheepskin jacket with a high collar. He held her coat for her as she slipped her arms in, they put sturdy boots on, and within a minute they were ready to go.

"Tabby," Robert called from the bottom of the stairs. "Walkies."

He appeared almost instantly and scurried down the stairs to the front door, tail high. Robert opened the door and stood to one side to let Payal and Annabelle through. There were a lot of seagull feathers on the ground by the sea wall, and a cry of alarm went up from those seated in safety on the roof of the house next door, at sight of Annabelle. Tabby hurried across the road, jumped up onto the wall and down onto the hard sand.

"I'll probably have to carry him back, if the breeze gets up," Robert said. "That sand can sting."

"Does he do this every day?"

"When it's not blowing too much, or raining. There's a fish stall along the way, they always save him tidbits."

Payal took Robert's arm and they stepped off the seawall onto the sand.

CHAPTER TWENTY SIX

Robert's story

I packed all my stuff into the hire car two days later. There was surprisingly little, and Tabby seemed to be happy in the cat-basket with the rug folded inside it, though he complained now and then if I had to break hard. I left London late morning, and by early afternoon I'd reached the A303, stopping for lunch at a small cafe. I sat in the back of the car and fed Tabby some bacon, gave him some water, trying to explain where we were going. He wasn't concerned in the least, as far as I could see. Some perverse idiot requested 'By the time I get to Phoenix' on the radio, so I switched it off.

I got a text message from Pam asking me to let her know I'd arrived safely in Cornwall, and replied, saying I was almost there and would text her later. Pulling into the village alone didn't seem like failure, and the stones of the buildings didn't mock me for returning.

I pulled up outside the cottage and turned the engine off, and for an infinitesimally tiny moment Payal was beside me, squeezing my hand so tightly it hurt. And I thought I sensed her perfume. But it was my imagination, trying wish-fulfilment on me, and it wasn't working.

The tenants had left the cottage clean and tidy, and it smelled of wax polish and air freshener. I brought all my clothes in and hung them up, then the wooden cats and the few possessions I owned. Finally the food and milk, and Tabby. I closed the front door firmly, opened a tin of tuna and set it down on the flagstone floor with a small bowl of milk and undid the cat basket. Tabby came out a little tentatively, and I pulled the rug out of the basket and shook it open, laying it on the floor. Tabby looked at the rug, then at me. I texted Pam to say we were safely arrived, signing it off: 'kisses to everyone.'

I sat on the sofa and took out Payal's present, turning it over a few times, and it smelt of her perfume. Tabby ate some of the tuna and started pudging the rug, so I guessed he'd accepted the new situation. I opened the package, undoing the sellotape carefully, not tearing the paper. It contained a small bottle, and I knew it was her perfume. There was a note.

We fell in love and that love was so right, but we couldn't be together.

Like Elaine, I just want you to be happy. I found her letter in your jacket when I was in the loo at your apartment and I agree with her. Take my love and share it with someone. Be happy and I'll be happy. Payal XX **Mērā dila hamēśā tumhārā hai**

"My heart is always yours," Annabelle translated.

"I'd put the internet in for the tenants," Robert said. "Used a translation service to find that out. How she'd hidden the knowledge of the letter, I've no idea, because she didn't mention it at Carlo's."

"I wanted that evening to be about us," she said, hugging his arm with both hands.

I didn't go out to eat, I stayed in, gave Tabby the guided tour, sorted out a dirt box for him, and moved his rug up to the bedroom. I sprayed the pillow next to me with a tiny amount of her perfume, knowing it might have to last me years, and had an early night. Tabby's purring was soporific and I slept better than I thought I would.

The sun went on rising and setting, and I settled into a routine. Alexa was delighted when I skyped, disappointed it hadn't worked out with Maria, but promised to fix me up with amazing women when I came out to Canada. Some of the photos she sent did look damn good. One Friday I realised there was a phase of the moon due, and sat down at seven. I almost heard Brenda's voice and left the cave. I walk along the beach, and head for the rock, feeling the hot sand beneath my feet, the warmth of the sun on my shoulders. There's nobody there, and the beach is deserted. I lie down on the sand, and stare up at the blue sky, remembering the first time I came here. There's a movement in the sand beside me and someone lies down by my side. She takes my hand and her perfume invades my senses.

How's this possible? It's an inner world, my imagination.

It's my imagination, too.

I lift my arm and she slides under it, resting her head on my chest. I kiss the top of her head, and she puts her arm around me.

How are you, Robert?

Would you believe me if I said I was okay?

No. I miss you.

I miss you more.

No you don't.

Yes I do.

Her laugh is what stays with me as I come back. *That was so real.*

"That isn't possible," Annabelle said, shaking her head.

"You said my heart's desire was there if I knew where to look."

"Yes, but it wasn't really Payal, just your mind inventing her."

"But I *was* there," Payal said. "I came out of the cave and saw him lying on the sand, and lay down next to him."

Annabelle stopped in mid-air, looking at them.

"Are you making this up?"

"No," they chorused.

"Bloody hell," she said. "I'll have to tell head office about this."

"Tell them about this, too," Robert said, gesturing.

He loved that look of surprise on her face, the way her jaw dropped, and her wings stopped beating. She only recovered just before she hit the sand. Tabby batted her with a paw playfully and she skittered sideways, then zoomed back to eye level.

"This. Is. Not. Possible.," she said.

"Yeah, not possible," Robert said.

"Absolutely," Payal agreed.

They stood by the rocky outcrop. The sand stretched away in the distance and although the sea wasn't exactly blue, it must have been when clear skies were above it. Annabelle slowly rotated around, her eyes huge disks.

"There's no cave," Robert said. "We figure that's the metaphorical equivalent of the barrier between the conscious and the unconscious minds. Or the inner and outer world, if you like. But there's a legend amongst the local lads of a naked fairy getting an all-over tan this summer. Seen after a few pints of scrumpy, apparently."

Annabelle stared at him.

"That's a joke, Annabelle. But I'll tell you something I'd like an explanation for, if you're speaking to head office. I lived here for five years, and must have walked this beach thousands of times. There've been some winter storms, but this bit is above the tide-line, and the level of it hasn't changed. These rocks weren't here before. They've had archaeologists from Bristol University come and look at them. Fearful excitement all round, because they're igneous, volcanic, and sure as hell don't belong here. They figured locals had put them here, a hoax, like crop circles, and wanted to dig them up. The council were quite happy with that, spoiled the look of the sand, they said. When they did a survey, they said forget it, the rocks go so deep, they're part of the substratum. Or something. Any ideas?"

Annabelle shook her head.

"Do you want to tell her yours?" Robert said to Payal.

"They represent Rob's inner turmoil," she said. "He suppressed all those feelings, and his inner world pushed it into the metaphysical, and it had to have an outlet somewhere. I probably added to it, by coming into his meditation. Now he's actually a happy bunny, he thinks they're slowly sinking back down."

Annabelle turned to study the rocks, then turned in a complete circle, scanning.

"Anybody about?" she asked.

Robert and Maria looked.

"I can't see anyone," Robert said.

"Me neither" Payal added.

"Okay, stand closer to it and don't ever mention this to Head Office."

Robert and Payal stood closer to the rocks and Annabelle flew above it, waving the wand that appeared in her hand. Fairydust settled on the rock and Tabby backed away from it as it began to vibrate. It shimmered, and sank back into the sand, disappearing in seconds.

"The archaeology department are going to love that," Robert said, grinning.

"Payal was right, and it's never going to be needed again. Finish the story."

I carried on with life, and Tabby and I settled down. There was another phase of the moon two weeks later and I decided to come here for the meditation. Brought a blanket to lie on and found my way here again in my mind. Payal came again, and lay down beside me.

I told her we couldn't go on meeting like this, and she giggled.

I wasn't sure I was joking, but it felt so good I just held her tight, and we didn't say anything for a long time, until it started to rain. She asked me if I had a brolly, and I thought it was probably time for her to go back – I thought the rain represented the tears I was holding back.

But she said 'meh', and sat up.

Beside me. On the beach. Right here. She looked at me and smiled, and my Heartfire must have been seen from space. I begged her to tell me we were out of the meditation and she said we'd never been in it. She saw me lying on the blanket and lay down beside me. I asked her to pinch me and she stroked my face, then stood up, holding out her hand. It's just as well she did, because my legs were too weak to function I hugged her and couldn't let go, terrified she'd disappear and I'd wake out of a meditation sent to punish me by being so beautiful I'd never want it to end. I think being soaked to the skin made me believe I *was* in the real world, and I wanted to shout at the top of my voice.

"You did," Payal said. "Don't you remember that guy on the sea wall asking if you were okay?"

I didn't see or hear anything but Payal as we made our way to the cottage. I wouldn't let go of her all the way back. Two large suitcases rested against the front door and I couldn't believe it. I think I started crying then, and Payal had to take the key from me, to get in.

"Yeah, what a wooss," Payal said, kissing him. "Anybody'd think it was a big surprise, me arriving with all my things."

"Darling...?"

"Well okay, two more packing cases arrived at the weekend, but you know what I mean."

We got her cases inside and when Payal kissed me, I finally believed it. Truly believed she was there, in my arms and was staying. I tried to ask her how and she kept kissing me, so I stopped asking. We had a shower together, and then... after... you know... she told me everything.

CHAPTER TWENTY SEVEN

Payal's story

I don't know how I stopped myself from crying when we all left the pub. I knew he wouldn't skype us, but Ashley might, and I could see him that way. The day Robert left London, I couldn't stop thinking about him, I'm sure I cocked everything up in reception. Pam showed me his text and the 'kisses to everyone' made me smile.

But life went on, and the new receptionist settled in really well. She's so much more assertive than me, and picked everything up really quickly. She even instigated some changes in the booking system, which made it more efficient. I sat with her for a week and didn't have to do anything, she was so good. I saw my mum and my sisters more, and I know it's hard to understand, but I stopped monitoring my temperature, for ovulation, you know? I told Ashley we should just leave it to Karma, until we had the fertility treatment and I think he was happier with that. If it was going to happen, it was going to happen.

Then we did the meditation. I didn't really want to, but I'd instigated the whole thing in the beginning, so I couldn't duck out, could I? When Brenda told us to interact with the person on the rock, I didn't believe it. Rob was there, lying down with his eyes closed, and it was so incredible being with him. Until he told me the same happened with him, I thought it was all in my imagination, there could be no other explanation.

Ashley and I got home that evening, and he said he wanted to talk with me. For an awful moment I thought he'd been in the same meditation and seen me with Robert, and I must have looked guilty as hell. Ashley thought I was upset, and poured us both drinks, and we sat in the lounge. When he said he was going to be completely honest, I thought he'd known all along about Robert and me, but—

"Wait!" Robert called, and they both looked at him. "Tabby, here."

Robert opened his coat and gathered Tabby up in it. Annabelle looked at him suspiciously. Robert zipped up the coat, leaving the top open a little.

"Okay," he said, and braced.

"Ashley told me he was gay."

The explosion was the loudest they'd ever heard and a furrow of sand was ploughed as far as they could see, spraying up like the parting of the Red Sea as Annabelle disappeared into the distance. Every seagull in sight headed inland and they heard another boom. Like a racing catamaran, she hit the tops of the waves, bouncing from one to the other, through a hundred yards of curling sea. When she pulled up in front of them, she was drenched, her coat hanging from her, dripping water, she had seaweed in her hair, and she'd lost her hat and muff. A piece of seaweed fell off and Tabby poked his head from Robert's jacket to see if it was safe to come out. She stared at them both for a moment and then shrugged.

"Makes sense when you think about it," Annabelle said, calmly. "The Armani suits, the reluctance to be a father, not wanting to commit. So brave of him to tell you."

She shook herself, the fairydust cascaded and she was dressed in another outfit. Red coat and long flared skirt, both with black brocade trimming around all the edges, and black boots.

"You couldn't leave me with some of that dust, could you?" Payal asked.

"You don't need it, you'd look great in a sack, Payal," Annabelle said. Then her face changed. "So...?"

I was so shocked, I couldn't speak, and he burst into tears. I hugged him and he cried for ages. When he was calmer I took both his hands and told him how much I loved him, and asked him to tell me everything. I'm pretty sure he was surprised how calm I was, and that helped. He'd known for at least three years and hadn't dared say anything. He wanted me to be happy, and carried on because he loved me, trying to fight the feelings he had for other men, thinking once we had a child it would all go away. He was still sexually attracted to me, but found himself attracted to men more and more, and it was tearing him apart. He'd not done anything about it, but the feelings were getting stronger, and he didn't want to hurt me by starting a relationship with anyone, so he had to tell me.

"That must have been so difficult for him," Annabelle said. "Poor Ashley. What made him tell you then?"

When I came out of the meditation, I apparently had the most amazing smile on my face, and it made him feel guilty, knowing sooner or later he'd have to destroy our marriage and me as well. He hated the thought of hurting me, but knew he had to.

And then he said something incredible. He said it was a shame Robert had left because he thought he would have been a perfect partner for me. I was trembling all over and asked why. He said he'd never met anyone as good as Robert, and I deserved to be with someone like that. I stared at him, and he said he was ashamed of himself and for shaming me, and I told him that was complete nonsense and never wanted to hear it again.

I tried to think what to say to a man who was so wonderful that he'd told me the truth about himself, when I'd said nothing about Robert and me. We talked about what we could do. He was terrified of telling his family, completely lost in his emotions, and I was so worried he might do something really silly, that I told him Robert had left because he was in love with me, and didn't want to hurt anyone. Nothing had happened between us, but I'd fallen for Robert as well, and didn't want to do anything because I still loved Ashley. Robert and I did the right thing for what seemed to be the right reasons. Ashley and I stared at each other and I started crying and we cuddled for ages, until I stopped. Ashley smiled at me, and told me how much he loved me and how much he wanted me to be happy. It was what I wanted for him, so I... told him I wouldn't say a word to anyone, but leave him and go off with Robert.

He stared at me and asked why. Because that will give you time, I told him. Time to decide what he wanted to do. If we stayed together it would harm us both, but this way he wouldn't have to worry about hurting me or deceiving me, and we both would have a chance of finding happiness. If I'd stayed and we'd tried to separate, then divorce, both our families would have been incredibly supportive, but every single one of them would have moved heaven and earth to keep us together. It would have been relentless, and we would have hated it, knowing what we knew.

"But... everyone would blame you," Annabelle said, shocked. "They'd all hate you. You'd lose them all."

"Yes. But a wonderful man, who loved me, who told me the truth, deserved that. If Ashley had told his family he was gay and was leaving me because of it, everyone would have despised him, and he would have hated himself for causing so much grief. I seriously think he

246

would have killed himself before doing that. What I was offering was the chance for him to be on his own, without the responsibilities of marriage, and for his family to still love him. I knew that, given time, he could accept his sexuality, and find someone to be happy with. Given enough time, even his family would accept it. Most of them, anyway. It was going to be hard, but I knew what was waiting for me, so it was an easy choice."

"It wasn't easy," Robert said, putting an arm around her and kissing her cheek. "It was the hardest thing you ever did."

"Perhaps it was. But I knew I'd have you beside me at all times, and any hardship can be endured if you're with someone who loves you, who you love absolutely."

Annabelle stared at Payal for a second, then looked at Robert.

"If you ever let this woman go, I will come back and haunt you day and night for the rest of your life."

"Oh, all right then, I'll stay with her," Robert said grumpily, and Payal punched his arm. Tabby complained, so Robert bent forward and let him out. "Do you think I'd ever be that stupid? I've done some pretty silly things in my time, but even I'm not *that* thick."

Ashley and I went to see a solicitor the next day, and started the process of legal separation. We held hands all the time and kissed each other, and I don't think they knew what to make of us. It took them a week to prepare all the papers, and I packed up my things. We daren't have any visitors, because we'd agreed I was just doing a moonlight flit, and leaving Ashley. We were both so happy, it was ridiculous. On the Friday morning, Ashley kissed me goodbye and went off to work. I left a 'note' for him, and caught a taxi to Paddington, terrified I'd bump into someone who knew me. I'm sure the other passengers wondered why I had a silly smile plastered across my face for the whole journey, but I got here, caught a taxi to Rob's, and the neighbour told me he was walking on the beach. There were footsteps in the sand, and I followed them. The rest you know.

"There was one thing I forgot," Robert said. "When we got in the cottage, Payal took a match from the box and lit the candle. And we're living happily ever after."

"Balls to that," Annabelle said. "How has it been with your families? Are you hiding here, or what? Tell me, dammit."

CHAPTER TWENTY EIGHT

Robert and Payal's story: part 2.

Payal kissed him, then sighed. "I have to phone my mum, she needs to hear it from me."

"Stay there, I'll get the phone for you."

"I'm not phoning her naked in bed with you, it wouldn't be right!"

"It's just an ordinary phone, you're not skypeing."

"I'm still not doing it, get me a dressing gown."

Robert put his own on, went into the spare bedroom and got the dressing gown from the back of the door. It was a long fluffy one, and he held it out for her. His breath caught as she stood, turned her back and slipped both arms into it, pulling it closed. She leaned back against him and he circled his arms around her waist, inhaling her, as she rubbed her cheek against his, pulling his arms tight into her.

"Do you want me to leave you with the phone?" he asked her.

"No, just hold my hand. Let's go downstairs, you can make me a cup of tea."

The flagstone floor made her jump and she leaped onto the sofa, showing an awful lot of leg, but Robert didn't complain. "That floor is so cold," she moaned. "We'll have to buy a rug."

"I'll move Tabby's down here. I let him sleep in the bedroom, we were both a bit lonely."

"No, let him stay, we'll buy one together."

"Do you want tea first?"

"No." Payal took a deep breath and it came out shaky. "Let me do this, just sit with me."

Robert handed her the phone.

"Dial 141 unless you want her to have this phone number. Where's your mobile?"

"Ashley put in a new sim card for me and changed the number. I've got everyone's numbers, they haven't got mine. The phone would never stop ringing once the news is out. Ooh, damn, I have to text him first – I promised I'd tell him when I arrived safely and you took me in. I guarantee mum will phone him as soon as she puts the phone down to me."

"I'm sorry."

"Don't say that, ever, because that would mean we're doing something wrong. It couldn't be more right, you know that."

He pulled her to him by the dressing gown and kissed her, feeling her tremble.

"You're right and I love you."

She kissed him hard.

"Sit with me."

She found her mobile in her coat pocket, and texted: Safely here and Robert is wonderful. About to phone mum. Thank you so much, Ash. I love you.

She sent the text and put her mobile down, then turned and put her feet up on the sofa and he sat behind her, at an angle, circling his arms around her as she rested back against his chest. She dialled the number, and he could feel her heartbeat thudding. She tipped her head the way he remembered and slid the phone under the hair, to her ear. She gripped his arm, and he squeezed her gently.

"Hi, mum, it's Payal... I'm fine, how are you?...

250

Mum, I need you to go up to the bedroom and close the door... no, I haven't killed anyone... mum, please... no, I'm not pregnant... please do as I ask you, please..."

Payal sighed out some of the tension, leaning back against him as her mother walked upstairs to her bedroom.

"Mum, try not to be angry with me, and try to understand when I say I have not done this lightly, without thinking ten thousand times of the consequences, but I've left Ashley... Mum?... **Kṛpayā suno, Māṁ. Maiṁgambhīra hūṁ**... **Kṛpayā mata rō**... Mum..."

Payal spoke for some time in Hindi, and Robert held her, stroking her hair now and then when she became tense.

"His name's Robert..." she said, which made him pay attention "...yes, the one who saved Rosie... Mum, he left the clinic because he was in love with me, and he knew it was the right thing to do... no, I chose to go to him, he hadn't contacted me... because I love him, that's why, in a way I can't begin to explain, but I have never felt like this in my life... of course I love Ash, and he's not done anything wrong, but I couldn't stay, we would have ended up hating each other... no... I'll call you tomorrow, don't call my mobile... yes, I promise... bye, mum. **Maiṁtumasē bahuta pyāra karatā hūṁ**."

She clicked the phone off and leaned back against him. Robert squeezed her and nuzzled into her hair.

"Shall I make tea?" he asked.

"No." She twisted round and kissed him. "Make love."

Later, when they were naked in bed and she lay on top of him, he phoned Pam.

"I have to warn her," Robert said. "She'll jump up and down when Ashley tells the clinic staff, and that could cause real problems."

"Put it on speakerphone."

They heard the dial tones and then Pam's voice.

"Hello?"

"Hi Pam, it's Robert."

"Oh hi! How are you? I do miss you, when are you

251

coming up to visit?"

"Might be a problem for a little while. Listen, are you at home?"

"I'm at Carlo's, why? What's the problem?"

"There's something I need to get off my chest."

"Hi Pam," Payal said, grinning.

"Payal?" The shock in Pam's voice made them both smile, and the squeal made them both jump. "Oh my god, oh my god, oh my god!" she shrieked, and Robert swore he could hear the air displacement as she jumped up and down. "Oh my god!"

They heard Carlo's voice asking what was wrong three or four times, while Pam continued to hyperventilate, calling on her deity.

"It's Robert, he's with Payal," she finally managed.

"That's great," Carlo said. "Can I get back to the kitchen now?"

They heard a sloppy kiss.

"Oh my god," Pam said, calmer now. "This is fantastic, I'm so happy for you both."

"Good, because you need to get it out of your system. Ashley's going to come into the clinic soon and tell you all Payal has left him, and I didn't want you to give the game away."

"Oh my goodness, it's just as well you phoned me first, I'd have fainted if he told us."

"Please don't let on you knew," Payal said. "Ashley agrees with us separating, he's very happy with it." There was a momentary silence. "Pam?"

"Is he gay?" Pam asked.

Payal's chin hit Robert's chest, it dropped so far, and they stared at each other in shock.

"Wha...? how...?" Payal managed. "How did you know that?"

"I didn't until you said he was happy losing you. That's not normal, unless he was already unhappy himself, and I seriously don't think there's any woman better than you, he could have fallen for. But a lot of things make sense now, like the way he used to touch you. He'd always caress your hair, brush it back from your face. A straight man would kiss you at that point, but he always smiled and turned away."

"And that makes him gay?" Robert asked, terrified he'd been doing that.

"No, there's loads of other things, he's such a sensitive guy."

"What other things?" Payal said. "Why didn't I see it?"

"You were in love with him, you wouldn't see the way he sometimes looked at other men. I was going to say something to Robert, but didn't think it was fair. Anyway, I thought I was probably wrong, so I didn't say anything. I can't believe you guys are together, it's incredible! Carlo is *so* going to get laid tonight."

"As soon as we're settled, promise me you and Carlo will come down," Payal said. "If it hadn't been for you two, and that evening at the restaurant, we wouldn't be together."

"Tell us when, we'll be there," Pam said, immediately. There was a shout for her in the background. "I gotta go. I love you guys!"

She rang off.

"I think she was pleased," Robert said. Payal laid her head on his shoulder, and he sensed something. "What is it?"

"I'm so in love with you, it frightens me," she said. "I wish everyone's reaction would be like Pam's."

He held her, stroking her hair, smoothing it over her shoulders and down her back.

"Do you think Alexa will like me?" she asked.

"No," he said and she tensed. "She'll adore you. She'll love you as much as I do. Although that might not sound in retrospect quite the way I intended it."

Payal shook with laughter and he gloried in the sensation. "It's so unfair," he said, kissing the top of her head. "As far as your family are concerned you're the bad girl, and as far as mine will be concerned they'll know you as the one who made me fall in love again, and they'll worship you. I'll get the laptop, let's skype Alexa."

"You will not!" she said, scandalised, lifting her head. "We'll get dressed and I'll stay out of sight, biting my nails down to the elbow while you tell her."

He looked into her eyes and then kissed her. "You don't get it, do you? Alexa will make more noise than Pam did, when I tell her. She'll probably be over on the next plane and hug us both to death for at least a week."

They stared at each other.

"And did you know, when you lift your head, your groin pushes into mine?"

"Something told me that, yes."

It took them a while longer to dress, but at last Robert sat on one end of the sofa with his laptop, and Payal on the other end with her legs curled under her.

"You sure she can't see me?" Payal asked, nervous.

"Positive. There's me at the top of the screen, that's what she'll see. Ready?"

"As I'll ever be."

Robert dialled Alexa and waited for the connection.

"Maybe she's out," Payal said.

"No, she isn't," Robert said, reaching over to remove Payal's fingers from her mouth. "She works from home on a Friday."

The ring tones started and were answered almost immediately. Alexa appeared on the screen, a big smile on her face.

Hi, Rob," she said, blowing him a kiss. "Your ears must be burning, we were just talking about you."

"Nothing good, I hope?"

"Of course not. How are you?" She peered closer at the screen. "Have you won the lottery or something? You look so happy."

"No, I just had a great day, that's all. What were you and Carrie saying about me?"

"Meh, trying to work out your perfect woman."

"Really? Did you get anywhere?" Robert's eyes flicked

to Payal, and he tried not to smile.

"It's soooo difficult," she said, rolling her eyes. "Maria seemed so great, I still can't believe she dumped you. There's a girl who works in PR we think you'll love, but Carrie says she's just not got that spark, that inner quality that sets her apart."

"Is that a pre-requisite, then?"

"Sort of." Alexa pulled a face. "They have to have more than just beauty, it's got to be inner confidence, and not arrogance either. Was a shame Payal was married, you know."

Payal stopped biting her fingernails and sat upright, not sure if she heard right.

"Payal?" Robert asked, trying to sound scornful and not laugh at the same time. "Are you kidding?"

"No, she had that quality. She'd have been the perfect woman for you, I reckon."

"Seriously?"

"Absolutely. Apart from the fact she's so drop dead gorgeous *I* fancied her, she's got an inner beauty as well. The way she teased you reminded me of Elaine, and that smile... it would knock any man's socks off. She really liked you, you know."

"You think so?"

Payal reached out with her foot, and dug her toes into his hip, trying not to smile.

"God, yes. When she was asking me about your childhood, her eyes would flick to you, and she had such a mischievous look on her face. I really liked her. Ooh, ooh," Alexa added, pretending excitement, "maybe it was her who lit the candle." She smiled. "She would have been perfect."

Robert looked at Payal and was stunned to see tears gathering in her eyes and an enormous smile. He looked back at Alexa.

"Funny you should say that..." He held out his arm to Payal. "Come here, you."

Payal slid along the sofa, under his arm and rested her head on his shoulder. She saw Alexa's shocked face and waved her fingers.

"Hi, Alexa."

Alexa was speechless for a second, goggling at them, and one hand covered her mouth. Then she took it away.

"You bastard," she said, looking at Rob, trying not to smile and failing, the grin splitting her face. "You pair of bastards. You rotten pair of bastards." Her head turned. "Carrie! Come and see what a rotten bastard I've got for a brother," she shouted. "We can stop looking, he's found someone as big a bastard as him."

She beamed at them both, shaking her head. "You bastards," she said. "How long have you been together?"

"About eight hours," Robert said, and loved the astonishment on her face.

"Seriously?"

"Seriously."

"I thought if I got together with Rob, I'd be able to meet you again," Payal said, smiling mischievously. She tipped her head coyly and Alexa clapped her hands together and laughed out loud.

"We've met our match, Rob," she laughed.

"We told them everything, we must have been skypeing for two hours," Robert said.

"They were so easy to talk to," Payal added. "We're going out in the summer."

"Let's walk back," Robert said. "It's getting cold."

Tabby complained they hadn't been to the fish stall, so they made a small diversion, and collected some bits for him.

"It must have been harder for you," Annabelle said to Payal.

"It was, but the love and acceptance I got from Pam and Alexa and Rob's parents made such a difference. And my mum knew from the start, Ashley told her the day I left that he was gay. He'd always got on so well with her, and swore her to secrecy, made her promise not to say anything until he was ready. I was so happy she knew the truth, didn't have to judge me. Not everyone was so forgiving."

Robert pulled her to him and kissed her cheek.

"So Ashley hasn't come out officially?" Annabelle said.

"Some of them know. His brother blamed me, said it was because I left him, that it happened. Ash doesn't speak to him, now."

"That is very sad," Annabelle said.

"There was always going to be someone who wouldn't accept it, but it's their problem, not ours," Payal said. "I'm with Rob, and I couldn't be happier, and Ash is happy, too."

Robert kissed her again.

"What about you, Annabelle?" he asked.

"Well, head office gave me another assignment, which I've just finished and there'll be more hearings when I tell them about you two."

"You won't get into trouble, will you?" Payal asked.

"Are you kidding? The love you guys are radiating, I'll get a medal," Annabelle said. "I ought to get back and report."

She flew to Payal and kissed her cheek, then to Robert and did the same. She made Tabby turn a few circles for old times' sake, and then flew up to eye level.

"I'm so happy," she said. "Post on Youtube now and then, will you? I can keep up to date that way."

"We'll do that. We're off to Pam and Carlo's wedding in Trieste in May, I'll post all the videos."

"That would be lovely. Look after each other, won't you?" Annabelle said.

"Nothing will give us more pleasure," Robert said, hugging Payal. "You take care, don't fly into anything solid."

"I love you both," Annabelle said. "Bye"

"Bye," Robert and Payal said together and Annabelle faded out. Tabby miaowed.

"Bye, Tabby," Annabelle's voice came.

CHAPTER TWENTY NINE

<u>Four months later</u>

Robert smiled as he recalled the last time he'd been here. "Have you got the passports?" Payal asked.

"Yeah, in my jacket pocket."

They stood in the queue at Gatwick, waiting to drop their bags off. They'd stayed with Pam and Carlo the night before, and both their heads were a little fragile. A passenger services agent came along the line, checking tickets. She scanned theirs in, and looked at her terminal.

"Your ticket's been changed to First Class. Go to the check-in desk over there," she said, pointing.

"Thank you," Robert said.

They wheeled their cases round and Robert smiled at Payal.

"Alexa," he said, and she nodded.

As they neared the desk a sonic boom startled them and Annabelle appeared. She wore a long tartan kilt, and white puffed blouse, with soft leather shoes, like dancing shoes. Her face was a picture of delight and she kissed them both, barely able to contain her excitement.

"Oh it's so good to see you," Annabelle said, and kissed them again.

"How are you?" they both asked.

"Wonderful, and wonderful, and so pleased to see you."

"Come to see us off?" Robert asked.

"No, I'm on assignment, but synchronicity is a wonderful invention, the absolute best. I'm here with my latest challenge." She rotated round and they looked in the same direction. "That one, the one in the grey suit who looks hassled. He's here to meet his boss's daughter, and he's a bit late."

They saw a youngish guy with brown hair, dodging around other passengers, looking quite stressed. He wore a smart grey suit and white shirt.

"Works for a small investment bank, his boss is a pillock," Annabelle said. "He forgot his daughter was arriving, and sent him out here to pick her up."

"Has he met you yet?"

"This is my first day, don't even know his name."

"Shall I go and ask?" Payal said, smiling.

"No, half the fun is finding out from them."

The guy stopped and stared up at the arrivals board, and they watched him. He glanced their way and Robert and Payal both waved to him. He looked over his shoulder to see who they were waving to, and there was nobody behind him. Payal smiled, and he had to smile back. He frowned, and checked the board again.

"Lucky guy," Robert said. "He doesn't know what he's in for. Is he a loser?"

"No," Annabelle said. "He's got a girlfriend already, but she's not the one for him. Going to be a challenge this time. They all are."

"How come you still look the same, apart from the outfit?" Robert asked, ignoring her last comment. "I thought we created you from our imaginations?"

"Ah. Because I got you two 'wrong'," she said, showing inverted commas with her index fingers, "I stay like this until I choose a suitable assignment of my own and make someone happy."

"Great punishment," Payal said. "You look fabulous."

"You know who could use your help?" Robert asked. "Katie Lloyd is really unhappy, and work isn't helping, what with her trying to be a detective, she's really stressed out."

"How do you know that?" Annabelle asked.

"Remember the Volvo? The Register charged me with conduct unbecoming a professional, as it was plastered all over the internet – over a million hits, now. Damned if I got sponsorship from Marmite, though. Anyway, the Register hauled me up after the investigation committee decided there was a case to answer."

"What happened?"

"Not guilty, M'Lud. Unanimous decision by the members of the council. To be honest, they didn't know what hit them. Alexa got John Crowther on it and he called up the girl who'd been knocked off her bike by that quack, as well as Katie, the sergeant at Holborn, the guy who'd actually filmed the whole thing, and destroyed their case. He played the tape in the hearing three times, and asked the Register's counsel to describe which part of preventing a criminal leaving the scene was conduct unbecoming. Katie was brilliant, turned up in full uniform and gave her evidence word perfect. We chatted afterwards, and she came down to stay with us for a weekend. She's so unhappy, could really use your help."

"Okay, you cannot say one word to her, or the deal's off, but I'll register her as my assignment of choice straight after this one. Which is going to be a tough one, Head Office expect me to do better nowadays.

"Can we help?" Payal said.

She looked at Robert and patted her handbag. He looked momentarily surprised and then nodded.

"We don't need it any more, and I'm sure we can get another one from Carrie."

"What are you talking about?" Annabelle said.

Payal unzipped her bag and brought out the carved wooden box that held the Heartfire candle. Annabelle's eyes widened, and she looked around, guilty.

"If he could take it, it might help," she whispered. "But I couldn't know about it."

"Okay."

Robert and Annabelle watched as Payal walked over to the young man and they spoke together. She handed the box to him and strolled back, smiling. The man watched her for a second, then checked the arrivals board again, hurrying away. Payal reached them.

"Done," she said. "I told him it was an Indian tradition to gift something to a stranger when starting a momentous journey."

"Doe eyes help, did they?" Robert asked, putting his arm around her.

"They might have," Payal said, smiling.

"I'd better get after him, see what I'm up against," Annabelle said. "I love you guys."

She kissed them both and they watched her zoom across the concourse.

"Do you think she has a boyfriend?" Payal asked, watching her fly away.

"No idea."

"His name's Alston, and I'm keeping him well away from you two!" came Annabelle's shout and they laughed.

Annabelle perched on the ornate steelwork high in the rafters and watched the two brightest Heartfires disappear into the departures area. She shed a small tear, and was glad nobody could see her. She didn't think it was possible for two people to be any happier but she wished she could be there when Payal discovered her period didn't come in six weeks time, courtesy of the log cabin, the hot tub and the oysters. She sighed heavily.

I've got the best job in the world.

She flew down to see what her new assignment was up to.

Robert and Payal left the first class lounge and headed for their aircraft, their arms around each other. Synchronicity was on overtime that day, because as they headed to the gate, on the other side of the glass wall that divided Arrivals from Departures, Maria was arriving from Italy. They didn't see her as they were laughing and kissing, but she stopped dead, staring in astonishment, watching them pass by. A cart carrying a disabled passenger made her move and when she looked back they were gone.

OUT-TRODUCTION

So that was their story, and I think you'll agree I did pretty well, didn't I? Okay, maybe I wasn't on my *best* form, but Robert told me he'd write to head office for me if I got in trouble, saying he'd had five years of burying his true feelings so deep that nobody, not even him, could see them properly. Hiding what he thought about Payal was a doddle, and as she said, it worked out all right in the end. In fact, both of them said it couldn't have worked any other way, so Head Office were pretty pleased with me.

Lots of you won't believe a word of this, but you can always go to Vancouver and ask them. They decided to move out there after their holiday and even took Tabby with them. I won't tell you whether they were expecting a boy or a girl, but I did hope they might put my name in the lineup somewhere. Oh.

But you don't believe in fairies so that's all right. But if you're reading this, then maybe you do. If you want to find out how I got on with my next assignment – such a dear boy – and then how Katie Lloyd and I solved loads of crimes together, while I was trying to find the right man for her, those stories will be along soon. In the meantime, here's what happened after I left Robert and Payal at the airport.

263

CHAPTER ONE

Matthew cursed for the umpteenth time as he dodged around passengers, knowing he was going to be late, knowing old man Lambert would tear him off a strip if he wasn't there to meet his daughter as she came through.

Promotion at last. Investment Banker to unglorified chauffer in one fell swoop, brilliant.

At least she'd arrived at Gatwick Airport, which was one blessing. Getting the car to Heathrow would have been a nightmare. The biggest car park in the world in the form of the M25 motorway would not be funny at this time of day, but the roads to Gatwick were clear, and he'd made up some time, praying it would be enough. He had no idea which terminal she'd arrive at, and hurried into the South Terminal concourse to check the boards. As he stood, scanning them, he saw she had already arrived in the South Terminal, and was awaiting bags. He breathed a sigh of relief, and looked round to find the arrivals area. A couple stood by the First Class check-in area looking at him, and they both waved. He looked over his shoulder to see who they were waving to, and there was nobody behind him.

Weirdos.

But the girl, a beautiful Indian, smiled directly at

him and he couldn't help it, he smiled back. He frowned, and re-checked Lambert's daughter was definitely coming into the South Terminal, his brain seemed to have been fried by that smile. It *was* the South Terminal, and he waited for the board to tell him if she was in the baggage reclaim or customs hall yet.

He became aware of the Indian woman approaching him, and her smile dazzled him again.

"Hello," she said. "Could I ask you something?"

Her eyes seemed to deepen, and his breath caught.

"Yes, of course," he said.

"I'm just off to Canada, and there's an Indian tradition that we give a gift to a stranger, so the gods will look kindly on our journey. It has to be someone we've never met before, and I like your smile. Would you mind if I gave it to you?"

"Erm... well..."

Her eyes seemed to deepen in colour, and Matthew swayed gently on his feet, mesmerised.

"No, of course... I'd be delighted."

Her smile lit the terminal, and she reached into her handbag, bringing out a wooden box, ornately carved. She handed it to him.

"It's brought me the best thing in my life," she said. "I hope it does the same for you."

"Right... thank you..."

"Hand it on when you no longer need it."

She smiled again and he watched her walk away. His mind cleared of her enchantment and he checked the board again. Damn, she was in customs. He hurried to the monorail service connecting the terminals.

His heart sank as he saw the scrum of people crowding the exit from the customs, and sank even more when he realised he had no way of recognising Lambert's daughter. People were holding up cards with printed names on them, and he wondered if he had time to dash back to WH Smiths for a pad. But if she went by this area while he was gone, he'd never find her, so he stayed where he was, searching his pockets for something to write on. He had nothing. He thought he heard a faint tinkle, like windchimes and turned at the incongruous sound. A woman was flipping her notepad over, scanning the pages, and he sidled up to her.

"I'm really sorry," Matthew said, "but could I trouble you for one sheet of your pad? I'm supposed to be meeting someone, I've no idea what they look like, and I need to write their name down."

"No problem," the woman said, smiling at him. She tore off a page and handed it to him.

"Thank you so much," Matthew said.

He rested the paper on the box he'd been given, and hastily wrote 'Grace Lambert on it as boldly as he could make it. He held it up, very self-conscious, and couldn't understand why men kept reading it.

Duh. Were your parents dumb enough to give you a girl's name?

He stood for ages, and had to keep swapping from arm to arm, as he tired. Every time he thought he'd go and get a coffee another burst of people came out, and the more time went by, the more he became concerned he'd missed her.

If she phones the old man, he'll give her my mobile number, surely.

He watched a younger woman struggle with a trolley piled high with suitcases go by him. She had to lean out to turn the wheels and from the way it stretched her skirt over her thighs he could see she had a great figure. Thick brown hair tied in a plait that hung down her back, high cheekbones and a tan straight out of the Riviera. She wore dark glasses, which Matthew always thought was a bit posy indoors, but she was dressed to kill, that's for sure.

Some lucky guy will be meeting her.

He watched, but nobody claimed her, so she waited at the end of the barriers. He heard the windchimes again, and frowned. There weren't any shops nearby, just the coffee bar behind him and the foreign exchange. He shook the wooden box, wondering what was inside, but it remained silent. *You've probably been given a bomb,* he thought. He flipped open the catch and cautiously opened the lid, keeping his eyes on the passengers emerging from the customs hall.

Inside, a wooden carving nestled on blue velvet, and something about it touched him. A carved heart with a candle holder, shiny wood and he imagined it would be the sort of thing Indian craftsmen would fashion.

A glut of passengers emerged and he closed the box and held his sign up again, wondering what Lambert's daughter looked like.

Let's hope she favours her mother.

A woman came out of customs and staggered towards him. She looked pale and shocked, and he wondered uncharitably if she was a drug mule and a packet had just burst inside her. That was immediately followed with the panicked thought this was Lambert's daughter, and Matthew was about to speak when a guy standing next to him ducked through the metal barrier just as she reached them. Slim guy, stupid pony tail, and the woman clutched at his arm.

"What is it?" the guy asked.

"I've just seen Robert and Payal. Together. Kissing. Together."

"What?"

They moved away, thankfully, as he'd had to hold the sign higher. The woman who'd gone by with all the luggage, walked back down towards him. He tried not to look, but she stood in front of him and looked at his sign.

"It's Graciela Alvarez," she said, "not Grace Lambert."

Her accent was strongly American.

"You're Mr Lambert's daughter?"

"Yes. And you are?"

"God, I'm sorry, I'm Matthew Fraser, I work for your father. He couldn't make it, and asked me to come and meet you. Very much a last minute thing, I'm afraid."

"Sure. Did he send a car?"

"Well, he's at a meeting at Mansion House, needed his chauffer, apparently. But I've got a car waiting, I'll just phone, get it to pick us up. Let me get your trolley."

Matthew scurried round, stuffing the box into his jacket pocket and nearly gave himself a hernia trying to shift her trolley. Once it was in motion it was slightly easier, and he moved it away from the barriers. He got his mobile out and dialled.

"Hi Stuart, we're just on our way. Aye, right enough, see you there." He slipped his phone into his jacket. "It's this way, Miss Alvarez."

She didn't say a word to him, just let him struggle with her trolley, as she walked beside him.

God, I hope we can get it all in.

Matthew thought he'd be lucky if his feet didn't fall off by the time they reached Knightsbridge. He was wedged in the back of Stuart's Mini Countryman, with the full weight of one of her cases across his thighs. The boot was crammed with her luggage and he'd had to sit this way to get it all in. He could barely see over the top of the suitcase, but Stuart kept up a steady stream of conversation, though Lambert's daughter wasn't a great conversationalist, by the sounds of things.

Must take after her father.

"Right," he heard Stuart say. "So your father's English and your mother's Mexican?"

She spoke so quietly he didn't catch her reply.

"Aye, given the chance I think I'd rather live in California than London," Stuart said. "How did they meet?"

Matthew zoned out from it. He felt his personal phone buzzing in his pocket, but couldn't get to it, so he let to go to voicemail. Then he heard the windchimes again. Puzzled, he tried to shake the case that was crushing him, to see if something inside caused it, but there was nothing. The box in his pocket dug into his hip and he tried to pull the jacket up, but it wouldn't budge.

"I think this is it," Stuart said, and the car stopped.

Stuart got out and Matthew heard him open Grace's door. Stuart had been calling her that since Sutton, and she seemed to respond to it. Then his door opened and he and Stuart manhandled the case off his lap, onto the ground. He clambered out, helped upright by Stuart. He was quite relieved to find his feet didn't drop off, though the pins and needles he got made him appreciate what the Little Mermaid must have gone through.

Stuart unloaded the rest of her luggage from the boot, and placed it all on the pavement. They stood outside an imposing Edwardian building, with wide steps leading up to it.

"I'll be off, Matt. You'll be all right for a cab, aye?"

"Yeah, thanks Stu."

They hugged each other.

"Hope you enjoy your visit, Grace," Stuars said. "Try and see Scotland if you can, this is the best time of year for it."

"Thank you."

Stuart leapt back into the car and was gone with a cheery wave. Matthew and Grace looked up at the building.

"Is this it?" Matthew asked, a sudden panic he'd have to carry the luggage somewhere else.

"Sure. My father's apartment is the top two floors," he said. "The keys should be with the concierge. I'll go and see."

Posh word for a doorman.

He stood by her suitcases while she danced up the stairs, and pressed an intercom, talking with someone. She waited and a man came to the door and opened it for her. She spoke briefly with him and then beckoned Matthew.

"Shit," he said, looking at all the luggage.

He took the lightest three for no good reason other than a chance thief wouldn't get far with the heavier cases. He staggered up the steps and nodded to the guy who held the door for him.

"I'll go up," Grace said. "Bring the cases, would you? It's number six."

Jeez, what did your last one die of?

There was a lift, and he loaded the three cases in with her and went back to get the other two. By the time he got them into the building, the lift had returned and he saw she hadn't even bothered to take the first cases out. He wondered if he was exceeding the weight limit when he loaded the others in. But the alarm didn't sound, and when the lift stopped he wedged the biggest suitcase in the door, and lifted two of the smaller ones out. Grace stood with the door to the apartment open, looking impatient, so he walked a little slower, dragging the cases on their wheels. She actually took one of them from him and pulled it inside.

The apartment was impressive. The door entered into a massive sitting room, with luxurious fittings, a high ceiling, and doors leading to an outside balcony. A wide open staircase lead up to the next level, and three other doors lined one wall. Heavy settees and comfortable chairs were arranged in the centre of the room, around a large walnut coffee table with a wall-mounted television vying for attention with the oil paintings that covered the other walls.

So this is where the bank's profits go.

Matthew brought the remainder of her cases in, while she opened the other doors, exploring the apartment. He saw one room was an enormous kitchen, and she checked the fridge. He turned to go.

"Would you find the bathroom and run the tub for me?" she said. "I need to unpack my clothes or they'll crease."

He bit back his reply and went up the stairs. A long landing had four doors and he opened the first, whistling at the size of the room. He wasn't impressed with the bedroom furniture, all the chintzy coverings, it looked more like he imagined a high-class brothel would.

The second door revealed the bathroom. There was

a free-standing bath and a walk-in shower. He put the plug in the bath and was tempted to run only the cold tap, but turned both on. The water pressure was very good, and his suit got splashed. He used one of the fluffy towels to sponge it off.

As he descended the stairs he saw she'd opened two of the cases, and was laying clothes along the back of the settee. She held out her hand with a brief smile, and he took the note before he realised.

"What's this?" he asked.

"Twenty dollars," she said. "Isn't it enough?"

She turned and picked up her purse, opening it.

"I don't want a tip, I did this because your father asked me."

Ordered me, more like, but what the hell?

"I get it, impress the boss. That's a great career move, you think?"

"I did not do it to impress your father, I—"

The door bell interrupted him.

"Would you get that? I need to go to the bathroom."

She turned, and he tossed the twenty dollars onto the table, then strode to the door. A middle-aged woman looked at him, very pleasant, a wide smile on her face.

"I thought I heard noises," she said. "Are you Mr Lambert's son?"

"No chance, I'm just one of his lackeys. I picked up his daughter from the airport."

"That'll be who the flowers are for," she said. "There was a big bouquet delivered earlier, could you come and get it?"

"Why not?" Matthew smiled, cheekily. "I'm doing everything else."

She gave him a sideways glance and he followed her across the hallway. The bouquet was big, and he manoeuvred it out of her apartment carefully. The door to Lambert's apartment had closed and he rang the bell. After a few seconds Grace opened it, the puzzled look on her face clearing as she saw the flowers.

271

"Oh, those are beautiful," she exclaimed. "You shouldn't have, but thank you."

Matthew was so stunned by this he couldn't speak for a moment. She turned with them, heading towards the kitchen. "Wait," he said, but she was already through the door. He started after her but heard the windchimes and they sounded louder, almost urgent.

"What the hell *is* that?" he asked, turning.

He didn't get an answer because Grace burst out of the kitchen, waving the card that must have come with the flowers.

"These are from my father!" she shouted. "How dare you pretend they were—"

"I didn't pretend anything, woman," Matthew retorted, angry. "I was trying to tell you I got them from the neighbour, who the hell d'you think was at the door?"

"You made out you'd got them!"

"I did nothing of the kind, you wouldn't listen!"

The windchimes were becoming really irritating.

"Oh it's my fault is it?" Grace demanded, her eyes flashing daggers.

The windchimes were reaching a crescendo, he knew it must be an alarm clock of hers. Except the sounds were coming from above his head.

"Yes, it bloody is! I'm not some lackey you can—"

"You wanted to suck up to my father, so you volunteered to get—"

"Volunteered? Volunteered? He ordered me to come and get you—"

The enormous bubble of high quality double-backed ceiling paper that had been stretching downwards while they argued split open. At least ten gallons of warm water hit them both, drenching them, killing the argument immediately.

"The bath!"

Matthew raced up the stairs, skidding into the bathroom. When he thought about it later he realised it was a major design fault in an otherwise impressive

272

bathroom. The water from the overflowing bath should have gone down the shower outlet, but the claw feet of the bath were mounted on wood, and had been tiled around, rather than under, allowing water to escape into the ceiling of the room below. He turned off the tap, and jerked the plug from the overflowing bath. He lay one of the towels at the doorway, to stop the carpet soaking it up and splashed his way out.

As he made his way downstairs he saw Grace holding up a dress. He wasn't sure if her face was streaked with bathwater or tears, but he felt he should help. He lifted a sodden jumper from the settee and she snatched it from him.

"Haven't you done enough damage?" she snapped. "Get out, this is all your fault."

"My fault?" Matthew said, his temper flaring again. "Why didn't you turn the bath off?"

"I haven't been in the bathroom, that's why!"

"What are you talking about? You told me to answer the door, said you were going to the bathroom."

"And I went to the bathroom, right in there," she retorted, pointing to one of the doors.

Matthew couldn't believe it.

"Listen woman, in this country, a bathroom means a bathroom, not a bloody toilet."

"Oh that's great," she said, stamping her foot, which was ruined a bit by the squelch it gave. "I'm met at the airport by a congenital idiot, crammed into a pathetic excuse for a car, my clothes are ruined and I get lectured on the English language by some Brit who can't even speak it himself. Call up your gay boyfriend and get out of here!"

"Stuart's my brother, as it happens, and we're not Brits, we're Scottish. We both gave up our afternoons to come and get you, so thanks for nothing."

He stormed to the door, wrenched it open.

"I didn't ask you to!" she shouted.

He turned, angry, and didn't see the neighbour, who'd come out of her apartment.

"Well the next time it had better be worth more than twenty dollars!" Matthew turned and saw the neighbour. "Women!" he added, disgustedly.

He strode to the lift and it opened to his touch. The neighbour looked from him to Grace.

"I think you'll find the going rate is about a hundred pounds, dear," she said to Grace.

The fairy watched from the top of the biggest oil painting as the neighbour closed Grace's door for her.

"Shit," Grace said and fell onto the settee. There was a loud squelch and she jumped back up again. "Double shit."

"Oh dear," the fairy said. "Still, he almost heard me at the end there. That's a good start."

Lightning Source UK Ltd.
Milton Keynes UK
UKOW04f2139141214

243096UK00001B/4/P